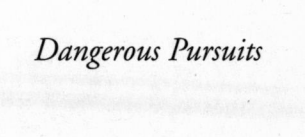

Dangerous Pursuits

Dangerous Pursuits

ALANNA KNIGHT

This edition published in 2006 by
Allison & Busby Limited
13 Charlotte Mews
London W1T 4EJ
www.allisonandbusby.com

Copyright © 2002 by ALANNA KNIGHT

The moral right of the author has been asserted.

First published in 2002 by Constable and Robinson.

A catalogue record for this book is available from
the British Library.

10 9 8 7 6 5 4 3 2 1

ISBN 0 7490 8244 5

Printed and bound in Great Britain by
Bookmarque Ltd, Croydon, Surrey

ALANNA KNIGHT has written more than fifty novels, (including fourteen in the successful Inspector Faro series), four works of non-fiction, numerous short stories and two plays since the publication of her first book in 1969. Born and educated in Tyneside, she now lives in Edinburgh. She is a founding member of the Scottish Association of Writers, Honorary President of the Edinburgh Writers' Club, and Convener of the Scottish Chapter of the Crime Writers' Association.

Find out more about Alanna Knight by visiting her website at *www.alannaknight.com*

Chapter One

It was to be a bad day.

It began with one death, followed by a second, and had I been superstitious and believed that deaths came in threes, time was to show that I had a very lucky escape in not being the third.

Just before breakfast I buried Cat in the back garden. Thane went with me, two mourners at an old animal's funeral.

'An old animal?' friends would certainly ask. Surprised at my sorrow, they would smile pityingly, as if to admit that such feeling was unnecessary and somehow wasteful except for humans taken in their prime, and there were always plenty of them. For elderly pets there was a different kind of grief. And for relatives a special cut-off clause, especially if they had survived long enough into antiquity to qualify for 'having a good innings'.

I had no excuse. I had only known Cat for six months, since I moved into Solomon's Tower that summer of 1895. She presented herself at my door, an ancient moth-eaten mummified feline on unsteady legs, a leftover from the last indulgent cat-owner who had been dead for several years.

With careful nurturing this decrepit hissing creature more dead than alive had been reborn into a purring pussycat by the fire, the companion of my evenings, sitting on my lap as I read; even her shabby fur had been restored to the ghost of its one-time elegance.

And now she was dead. I had found her stiff and cold in her favourite chair when I came down to breakfast. And I had wept. And wept.

It was a long time since I had shed so many tears, believing that I had used up such floods of emotion when my baby had died and my husband Danny had disappeared in Arizona.

Now Cat's death coincided with that bitter anniversary and reopened a wound that bled afresh and would never heal.

The reservoir of tears filled up again. I'd never be able to explain it to my friends and even Jack, sympathetic and offering a comfortable shoulder to cry on, would be somewhat bewildered in his practical no-nonsense policeman's way.

But Thane, the deerhound who had his home somewhere in the vast and secret crags of Arthur's Seat behind the Tower, Thane understood. Waiting for me at the kitchen door, he sniffed at the tiny corpse wrapped in a blanket, raised a paw with an almost human sigh that said everything.

As I said, it was an awful day. In sympathy, the autumn weather wept with me. Day after day, Arthur's Seat was in a capricious mood, majestic and brooding, wreaths of heavy mist slowly descending from its lofty summit to engulf the garden. Then the house would disappear and, shivering, I'd close all the windows and look for further icy draughts to seal.

In earlier days I'd learned to live with all the sudden violent changes of temperament that made up Edinburgh's weather. And still I loved it, with no wish ever to live anywhere else than in Solomon's Tower, this magical ancient place that seemed to have evolved from the extinct volcano that men called Arthur's Seat. A magic that contained a deerhound like Thane who had once saved my life, but preferred to remain invisible to practically everyone else.

Except Jack. Jack at least knew Thane was real. He had systematically searched every square foot of the vast mountain with its craggy rocks and secret caves for traces of this mysterious animal who came and went at will. Or so he said. But he had never found any evidence of where or how Thane lived.

This was a blow to the pride of Detective Sergeant Jack Macmerry who must have an answer to everything, his entire life dedicated to solving mysteries, mostly of a violent nature. I would often find him staring at Thane reproachfully, as if the deerhound should provide some clues to the questions the law officer was dying to ask.

As for me, based on the recent past's bitter experiences, I take nothing for granted, happy to accept Thane as I accept Jack, as a transient part of my existence. Enjoy them both, be grateful and make no demands on a future which might not exist.

This philosophy of course does not please Jack who wishes to put our relationship on to a permanent basis, with a church wedding and mutual assurances of 'till death do us part'.

Sometimes I wonder if this conventional attitude has to do with career prospects and attitudes expected in the Edinburgh City Police for one nursing hopes of rising to the rank of Detective Inspector. Respectability plays a considerable role in decisions by Chief Constables and selection boards. If it were widely known that Jack had a 'widow lady', to put it politely, living in Solomon's Tower, this might prove a fatal handicap to his future promotion prospects.

Perhaps I am being unkind, making excuses for my own reasons for not wishing to marry Jack. I love him, as much as I am capable of loving anyone except Danny McQuinn, for although and officially designated 'widow', in my own mind my husband stubbornly remains 'missing' only. I refuse to consider any finality until proved beyond possible doubt. Until the dream comes no longer where one day I open the door and find him waiting there.

Another factor against marrying Jack is that I have embarked on a career of my own. A lady investigator of discretion, tracking down philandering husbands, thieving servants, missing relatives and wills and even the occasional missing cat or dog.

'Nothing too large or too small. Discretion guaranteed' is how my business card describes my activities, which now provide a modest living, a somewhat irregular income based on word of mouth, the recommendation of satisfied clients.

But try to explain 'career' to Jack and he smiles indulgently, his lecture on the attendant perils of such a dangerous hobby for a woman ready at hand.

'Hobby indeed!'

My indignation is met with a patronising smile. 'Let's face it, Rose. You're an untrained female who had a lucky first break—'

'Lucky, indeed!'

My first investigation into the brutal murder of a Newington maid was very nearly my last. Frequently stressing those almost fatal consequences, Jack pointed out that I should not be carried away by modest success and let it go to my head. The lecture always ends to the effect that in future I must promise to leave the law and solving of criminal activities to the police. A promise I refuse to make.

'If you must do something,' says Jack, that sad shake of his head indicating his better judgement, that the proper place for a woman (and in particular this woman) is in the home, 'you could go back to teaching. Edinburgh's expanding rapidly and in the new areas, like Newington, there will soon be lots of opportunities.'

Defiantly I shake my head and the argument reaches stalemate. Jack finds it difficult to comprehend that a return to school teaching, which occupied me before following Danny McQuinn to America, would be neither adequate recompense nor substitution.

What Jack failed to realise was that crime-solving was in my blood, doubtless inherited from my famous father, Chief Inspector Jeremy Faro of the Edinburgh City Police. From childhood, he had encouraged me to observe, deduce and always ask how and why, without of course realising the significant part it would play in my future. Sometimes I am inclined to think that his influence is why I decline to marry Jack. He reminds me too much of my father – not physically, for Pappa is as unmistakably, dramatically Viking in appearance as Jack is the typical sandy-haired, high-cheekboned Lowland Scot. But in sense of dedication they are identical.

Already Jack's sense of duty rings alarm bells from my childhood, of last-minute cancellations of outings with Pappa.

'The Inspector is out on a case' were words we dreaded from Mrs Brook, as with a sigh she abandoned her kitchen and, putting on her bonnet and cape, prepared to deputise in his absence, a poor substitute as far as sister Emily and I were concerned. That was if stepbrother Vince, already a young medical student, had a more ready and feasible excuse at hand.

And that, I feared, would be the story of my life with Jack, a repetition of days gone by. I knew what to expect, a policeman's daughter who had also once been a policeman's wife.

But Danny was different. I was twelve years old and he – ten years my senior – was Pappa's young constable who had saved my life in a kidnapping attempt by one of Faro's mortal enemies. Hero-worship became love that never wavered for the ambitious detective sergeant who had gone to that land of opportunity, America, to seek his fortune. And, it appeared, to die in Arizona while serving with the Pinkerton Detective Agency.

The habit and love of a lifetime were hard to break. I had – and still – loved Danny, determined to follow him, to the ends of the earth if necessary, to face any hardships, even danger and death. And so it had been. Not something I had strength to face a second time, to make welcome the agonies and uncertainties.

I was not the stuff that martyrs are made of but it seemed that I would have to make up my mind and decide about Jack. And soon. For Fate is not patient, prepared to wait in the wings for mortals to make up their minds.

Other issues are thrown in to aid decisions, where we would hesitate and go on dreaming. In this case Fate equalled Nancy, Mrs Brook's cousin's daughter. Mrs Brook had been housekeeper at our family home in Sheridan Place and on my return to Edinburgh I had used my influence to secure Nancy a situation as a children's nurse in Newington, only to discover that she and Jack had been childhood sweethearts.

Jack assured me that was all they had ever been, but it had become painfully clear to me in the past five months that although such might well be true for him, my powers of observation suggested that Nancy had other ideas.

Nancy was in love with him. When they met by accident here in Solomon's Tower, there were all the recognisable signs, that Nancy loved Jack as I loved Danny McQuinn. She had probably loved him since childhood too and at thirty years old, even for a sweet pretty woman, prospects of marriage were diminishing rapidly.

Jack, manlike, was totally unaware of the effect he had on her and lately, because I wished to loosen the strings of his attachment to me, I had resorted to throwing them together. Although I didn't want to lose Jack completely, since I enjoyed his company and, when I needed a man to love me, I wasn't reluctant to share my bed with him.

Nancy, I was sure, knew nothing of this side of our relationship. I had not considered the possible outcome of my actions, that Jack might tire of trying to talk me into marriage and in despair realise what he was missing in Nancy. Here was a woman who loved him and would be prepared to devote her entire life to his comfort, an excellent wife and mother of his children.

I found lately that Jack talked a lot about Nancy. When I was busy on one of my own investigations and had to decline the offer of an outing, he would say, 'I might take Nancy then, if you don't mind.'

And I was so willing. Watching them go down the road together smiling happily in each other's company, I wondered uneasily what I had set in motion and realised that I must suffer the consequences, for such is the fate of mortals who meddle in other folk's destinies.

Whether by affinity or design, Nancy was fast becoming one of my friends and, getting to know her better, Jack had discovered she had secret longings to be a singer.

The possessor of a naturally good voice, she had immediately joined the parish church choir in Newington and had been auditioned for an amateur group who specialised in the popular Gilbert and Sullivan operas and were at this moment rehearsing *The Pirates of Penzance*.

And there romance had found pretty Nancy. I was in her confidence and wondered how she was faring with the bass who played the Sergeant of Police.

I would swear that she blushed when I asked her in front of Jack: a darting look that spoke louder than any words.

Jack was amused by her conquest, which must have sent her into despair. There's nothing worse than being teased about a man by the very one you secretly long for. She confided in me that Desmond Marks was unhappy with his wife. All was not well at home, according to him, and it was only his love of singing and the escape provided by the Amateur Opera Society and Nancy's friendship and understanding that kept him sane.

'What should I do, Rose?' she asked.

'Have nothing to do with him,' I said firmly.

'How can I when we meet every week?' she protested.

'What I mean is, have nothing to do with him outwith the opera,' I said sternly. 'Don't get involved in his personal problems.'

She sighed. 'But I'm sorry for him, Rose. His wife – she doesn't sound like a very nice person at all.'

I refrained from replying, 'You should hear her side of the story before you pass judgement,' and asked instead, 'Is he very handsome?'

Nancy dimpled. 'Divinely. And such a lovely voice. He really should be on the London stage, a professional singer. But he is too cautious for that. He said he needs his situation in the insurance office and cannot afford to take chances.'

'Any children?'

Nancy shook her head 'Alas, no. There was a little girl but she died of diphtheria.'

'How long ago?'

'Oh, a few years back, but his wife has never got over it.'

I thought about that, a bond of sympathy with Desmond's unhappy wife. Bereaved motherhood was something I understood all to well.

'I gather they are both still fairly young,' I said cautiously.

Nancy frowned, considered me as if I might be a yardstick on which to calculate ages. 'About our age, Rose.'

'Then perhaps there will be more children.'

'No,' said Nancy obstinately. 'They cannot have any more and besides, since the wee girl died – er, well, Desmond's wife has – er, well…' She looked so confused that I helped her out.

'They don't sleep together any more?'

'Oh yes, they share the same bedroom,' she said brightly.

I put a hand on her arm. 'Nancy, I was using the term in

the biblical sense.' And thought: here were confidences indeed from Desmond.

My experience was that unless a married man thought there was something to be gained from it, such as encouragement from a woman being wooed, they were not so forthcoming about their intimate matrimonial troubles.

Nancy meanwhile looked uncomfortable. 'You will keep this to yourself, Rose,' she said sternly. 'I mean that in the best possible way,' she added hastily. 'I know you aren't a gossip but I wouldn't like Desmond to know I talked about him to you and Jack.'

As Jack wasn't present I felt it was an unnecessary warning. I looked at her. Such a sweet trusting girl was Nancy, she deserved happiness and the first step was being wise to the unscrupulous ways of married men.

'Jack would understand, of course,' she said. 'He is such a dear good man. You know that.'

Oh yes, I thought cynically and wondered if she was really as innocent as she pretended to be about our relationship.

'A bidey-in' was the perfect expression to describe him – one of Pappa's favourite expressions, picked up while staying with his favourite auntie in Aberdeenshire. That had not occurred to Nancy. Giving her the benefit of the doubt, perhaps the virgin mind does not dwell upon images of one's friends who are lovers and of what goes on behind closed bedroom doors.

Anyway, to leave the unhappy Desmond for the moment…

I had done my best to persuade Nancy that he was bad news and I hoped most earnestly that she would resolve the problem sensibly, especially as she had just recently left the situation I found for her. A happy ending since her employer in Newington, Mrs Lily Harding, had remarried and gone to live in Glasgow.

A lady of some influence among her first husband's business associates, she had recommended Nancy to the household of General Sir Angus Carthew, who had served the Queen in India and had been decorated for bravery. Just before his retirement and return to Edinburgh, he had married the daughter of a fellow officer who had died fighting the Chitralis in the Himalayas.

The name Sir Angus Carthew was frequently to be encountered in the local press, for he served on many committees and was a patron of the arts and of numerous worthy charitable institutions.

No hints of any bairns forthcoming despite the difference in age and a wife young enough to be her husband's daughter. This was not uncommon however and, perhaps as consolation, the childless couple were at present fostering Sir Angus's nephew and niece.

Their father Gerald Carthew had already made a name for himself as an archaeologist and explorer. On the eve of his departure to lead a scientific expedition into the polar regions, his wife died suddenly, the result of an unexpected complication following a minor operation.

The distraught husband and father was in desperate need of support and, feeling that the most prudent measure to ease his predicament would be to see him off on the work to which his entire life had been dedicated, Sir Angus and Lady Carthew stepped in and gallantly offered to care for the two young children until their father returned and could make the appropriate domestic arrangements. This information about the Carthews' domestic life came not from the newspaper but from Nancy by way of Mrs Laing, the cook-housekeeper.

Mrs Laing was always eager for a gossip since living-in servants were sparse indeed in Carthew House, an unusual and eccentric economy in an affluent family.

Since they returned to Edinburgh, she grumbled, she had fully expected to have the responsibility of engaging a domestic staff.

The children, aged three and five, were in Nancy's own words 'a bit of a handful'. But not even their wayward antics were beyond her patient tolerance and love. Indeed it was that devotion to Mrs Harding's turbulent toddler which had recommended Nancy Brook to the Carthews as a suitable nanny.

For her part Nancy was delighted at the importance of her new situation, especially as the salary offered by the absent father was far in excess of the normal nursemaid's wage, a fact that did not equate with Mrs Laing's hints at their being 'a wee bit grippy wi' their money'.

Nor were Nancy's duties demanding. Her employers were kindly and considerate beyond the norm, providing her with a handsome bedroom and sitting-room.

She was delighted, her hopes set high for an exciting year.

On that score at least she was not to be disappointed, with a sinister turn of events beyond even her wildest imaginings.

Or my own.

Chapter Two

Beyond the garden, the weather was changing, the mist lifting, and I decided that some fresh air would be agreeable. It would be restorative for my depressed state to wander on Arthur's Seat with my sketchbook, particularly as I had a reason.

A promise made to my stepbrother, Dr Vincent Beaumarcher Laurie, junior physician to the Royal family and at present at Balmoral Castle. A water-colour of the Palace of Holyroodhouse, a view looking down from the hill across the gardens and parkland, was his request as a wedding anniversary present for Olivia.

As this was something special and my painting is very much a hit or miss business, best when it is spontaneous, I felt nervous about its success.

'Nonsense,' said Vince. 'Olivia thinks you are a great artist and that you should be doing this sort of thing professionally.'

The anniversary was still a month away but matters had been brought to a climax since, in Olivia's absence, I had been invited to accompany Vince to the Royal lunch in Edinburgh tomorrow.

Princess Beatrice was opening the new Hospital for Sick Children in Sciennes Road. According to the newspapers, it had been built at a cost of £47,000 with 118 beds and extensive outpatients' departments, and designed by architect G Washington Browne, who had already contributed some splendid buildings to the newly developing south side of the city at Newington.

I realised I need entertain only a forlorn hope of having my painting ready for this unexpected meeting with Vince. Or of justifying Olivia's faith in me, I thought, flipping through the pages of my sketchbook of indifferent drawings with growing despair.

'Now or never,' I said to Thane, stretched out with his massive head at my foot. This was his favourite position, which took up most of the floor, but when I was seated he liked to establish what might be termed a toehold of physical contact.

Making certain that my pencils were all sharpened I prepared to leave. On my way through the kitchen, I paused at the larder to inspect the remains of the roast beef, intended for Jack's supper after our concert at the Assembly Rooms that evening. Alas, I had received a message via Lenny, the local 'beat' constable, that Jack was involved in a case.

He was sorry.

How often had I heard those words. I would never manage more than a couple of slices of meat which was already two days old, but it need not go to waste.

From the kitchen window I saw Auld Rory, old soldier and gentleman of the road, as he called himself. Less flatteringly designated an old tramp by Jack, he was wandering past the back garden, his eyes on the ground always searching for any curiosity that might fetch him a few pence.

One stormy evening recently, I had been caught in a downpour without my umbrella hurrying back from Newington. Thane was on the road to greet me as I approached the road leading to the Tower. Briskly he shepherded me somewhat reluctantly towards what looked like a bundle of old clothes by the roadside.

Not a corpse, I prayed, shuddering. Then the clothes stirred, began to cough. Thane ran towards him, barking gently, and turned to me with a look of despair. As if to say, 'Be sensible, Rose, you can't leave the poor old chap lying by the roadside, sorely troubled by a bad cough like that...'

'You invited him in,' said Jack in shocked tones when I told him next day.

'Of course,' I said. 'I wasn't going to pass by on the other side like the man in the parable of the Good Samaritan.'

Jack gave a heavenward glance of despair. 'A tramp, Rose. A stranger who might be anything – anyone – he might have a criminal record, so spare me the biblical quotations. Things and people have changed a lot since they were written. And you are a woman on your own, remember – living in isolation.'

'By my own choice,' I replied.

'Aye, not by mine. There's plenty of new houses half a mile away and you just have to say the word. You could be living among civilised folk…'

He went on in the same vein, his favourite reprise. I listened politely, not wishing to remind him that there had been a particularly brutal murder very recently among those same civilised folk.

A murder that I had solved.

So I let him get it off his chest. The story that always ends with us getting married and settling down in domestic bliss, in a house with pot plants in the windows and lace curtains. One with a nice cosy kitchen and with me doing his washing and ironing, darning his socks, cooking him delicious meals.

And terminally ill with boredom.

Finally I interrupted and said, 'No cause for you to concern yourself. Our old tramp is harmless.'

'And how do you know that?' he demanded.

'Thane liked him.'

'Thane! For heaven's sake. You can hardly rely on a dog.'

'He's not a dog. He's a deerhound.'

Jack wasn't to be put off. 'He's a canine,' he said firmly. 'And animals go by sense of smell. Not to put too fine a point on it, old tramps probably smell great to them.'

I tried to be calm. 'I trust Thane's judgement.'

Jack put back his head, saw the funny side and roared with

laughter. 'Darling Rose, you'll be the death of me, but I love you just the same. Come on now, sit on my knee. Let's be friends again,' he added tenderly.

Such an invitation was irresistible. A few hugs and kisses and there my case rested.

Once again. For the moment.

Jack was convinced that he had won but although I knew I'd never be able to convince him, the reason Thane liked the old man was that he recognised a fellow spirit. Auld Rory had 'nae hame' as he told me.

Like Thane he preferred to sleep under the stars.

A recluse whose home was under hedgerows and in ditches, in earlier times he would have achieved fame as the hermit of Arthur's Seat, his life a gift to the ballad writers.

As he wandered around the Newington area, people who encountered him regularly accepted him as 'the old tramp'. Ladies edging away nervously, often to the other side of the pavement.

Simple but harmless, Rory sang a lot. Mostly it was 'Soldiers of the Queen' and if he had been a man who enjoyed a drink, he would have been accused of 'the drink being on him'.

Of his past history I knew little. In a rare moment of confidence, he said that he was born in India, his father was an Irish soldier from Antrim serving in a Scots regiment, his mother Highland. He had known nothing but army life. So much was evident from the way he walked – or marched – along the road and from the military set of his shoulders.

What he had been like in youth was difficult to consider. And although he was willing to be friendly and courteous too, I was in the role of patient listener. It was difficult to have a conversation with him, as his face was so covered in hair, it was like talking to someone through a thick hedge. He had as much hair on his face as Thane, perhaps another reason why the deerhound found a certain affinity.

He was apt to break off a conversation suddenly and stare into space, cocking an ear unnervingly to listen to the silence – yet another reminder of Thane.

One thing I never doubted: Rory had all his senses but something dire had happened to him during his army life in India.

Once, in a more expansive mood than usual, he sat in my kitchen while the rain poured down the windows and hinted that he had been wounded, tortured by rebel tribesmen and left to die. He had survived by something of a miracle.

'Jesus saved me,' he said simply. He was now a devoted reader of the Gospels, bound to the image of a Christ with whom he shared the fellow feeling of having not even a roof over his head. Living on fresh air and the occasional charity of passers-by, he had no possessions but bible, his clay pipe which I rarely saw lit, and a blanket to keep out the cold.

God would provide, give him his daily bread, he said. More than often I was the provider, I thought, guessing how he would appreciate fresh meat between slices of new bread.

As I put them together I reflected this was the fate of many of my doomed suppers these days. I would willingly have given the old man a bottle of ale purchased on Jack's behalf, except that Rory was strictly teetotal. Long ago in his boyhood he had signed the pledge of temperance and had, in his own words, never seen good reason to break his vows.

Outside Thane ran over to him. There was a lot of head-patting and, on Thane's part, an excess of joyous tail-wagging.

I stood by smiling indulgently with the pleasure of watching a couple of children. Man and dog were friends without a word shared, they knew each other in a bond I could not possibly understand, happy in their existence, fellow creatures living under a firmament of stars.

'Bless ye, lass,' said Rory, taking the package containing his supper, to which I had added a slice of Jack's favourite fruit loaf. 'Aye, ye're a grand wee lass, so ye are.' This I presumed related to my diminutive size rather than my mature thirty years. 'An where's that bonny man o' yours the nicht?'

'On duty, as usual.' I had never tried to explain that Jack wasn't my man in the way respectable folk understood as a lifetime's obligation 'for better for worse, for richer for poorer'. I suspected that an old soldier as worldly-wise and unconventional as Rory wouldn't have cared one way or the other as he opened the package and grinned at me. He doubtless knew the ways of policemen and guessed without being told how this generosity came about.

His glance took in the sketchbook under my arm.

'Ah weil, lass, I'll no' be delayin' ye. God bless.'

As the afternoon light was already waning, I was quite relieved. With the right sympathetic audience, ready and eager to listen, Rory was a natural storyteller. Catch him in the right mood and he would expound at great length on his service in the outposts of the Queen's Empire.

Did I ken that he had once served alongside General Carthew's regiment in the Sudan campaign? He had read about Edinburgh's well-decorated illustrious soldier in the newspapers I got from Jack and handed over to him.

'Did I ever tell ye...?' His stories always began with those words, so that I knew some great tale was about to unfold.

'Did I ever tell ye my laddie was the General's batman?'

I'd heard it before but on one such occasion there was an unexpected embellishment:

'The laddie wasna cut out for soldiering, although he'd been born and reared in the barracks wi' the rest of us. He was a gentle kind o' lad and hadna ony taste for fighting. He wasna a coward though,' he added with a reassuring glance.

'Ye ken I'd seen him separate snarling dogs, and rescue

small bairns who got into danger. He dragged two bairns out of a swollen river too. But he wanted other things from his life, things I didna understand. When his ma died, he was fourteen, our only bairn. Maybe if she'd lived, it would have been different, what happened. She'd have sent him back home, here to her kin. That was aye in her mind, though the dear lass never put it into words, afraid to offend me. So after the funeral, he said he would stay on wi' me.'

He stopped, sighed deeply, his eyes half closed as if seeing it all. 'I never stopped blaming myself, not after all these years, ever since the day they told me that my lad, barely seventeen, had been waylaid and murdered in an ambush.

'They never found his body and he was missing, presumed dead, ye ken. I still canna believe it,' he added with a bewildered shake of his head. 'I was sure then and still am that he's alive – somewhere. Something tells me.'

He had stopped speaking, raising his hand, listening, eyes closed, sniffing the air as if it could tell him where his laddie was now.

Turning, he looked at me. 'I'll find him some day, ye ken. That I will.'

I nodded sympathetically. 'I lost my husband – in Arizona.'

I wondered if I should explain Arizona but he nodded vigorously. 'I ken where that is – in the Wild West,' he added proudly. 'Did the Red Indians get him?'

'All I know is that he was reported missing – most probably killed in a local massacre.'

He was silent then he took my hand and held it tight, his eyes filled with tears. An unexpected gesture, and I looked at him in amazement as a bond was formed between us.

He had loved a son who had vanished, who he refused to believe was dead. I had loved a husband who had disappeared without trace.

After that, he began to arrive at my back door and sit in my kitchen at regular intervals when Jack was absent, as if seeking comfort with another sufferer at the hands of cruel destiny.

The days were closing in. Darkness coming earlier meant long evenings and I looked forward to human companionship with Thane stretched out in front of the fire between us, as I listened to tales of Rory's parents and the Great Famine in Ireland, the massed emigration only equalled in disaster by the Highland Clearances.

I also learned at first hand the reality behind newspaper reports of trouble in India, of the desperate battles, the squandering of men's lives in order to hold on to the outposts of the Empire. Their boast of 'gallant men' defending that Empire masked the truth, of newly raised regiments like the 96th Foot reinforced by a pioneer battalion and a scratch force of Sikhs, more accustomed to handling picks and shovels than rifles, with half-trained tribal levies to support the most dangerous expeditions ever undertaken by the British Army.

The slaughter was glossed over with no list of casualties and only a line or two in the daily papers, which did not dwell on the fierce cruelty inflicted on soldiers or the hardships and tortures that were not for the eyes of polite and gentle readers.

Rory had witnessed the treachery of the Chitralis who, at peace with the regiment, had invited them to a polo match; when the vigilance of the guards was diverted by such an innocent amusement, at a given signal, the match was suddenly ended. Picking up their knives, the tribesmen began a wild dance applauded by the onlookers, delighted by this unexpected entertainment.

Until the tribesmen turned their knives on the polo players and slaughtered every one of them.

Besieged in a mud fort, under attack, the soldiers in Rory's regiment had to eat the horses to survive. It didn't bother Rory, a foot soldier.

'Meat was food. Any kind of meat, ye ken, rats, dogs, anything that was flesh. But an officer might be a wee bittee squeamish about eating his own horse, so they worked out a system that they didna ken whose horse they were eating wi' their soup that night.'

And so another bond was forged between us that day. I had lived in forts with Danny in Arizona besieged by Apaches. I had not questioned what I was eating either. In one such fort I had given birth and subsequently lost our baby son.

Remembrance came back swift and fierce; the bile rose in my throat as Rory talked and darkness steadily enclosed us, the past refusing to be banished in a warm safe kitchen in Edinburgh, with a deerhound lying by the fire.

I wanted to stop him but I could do nothing to stem the tide of reminiscences opening old wounds, all twisting knives in my heart, sharp as any tribesman's treachery.

At last, perhaps aware of my silence, Rory apologised for 'boring me wi' his long stories'.

I assured him I wasn't bored. He looked at me, shook his head, sighed and said, well, he was an early bedder.

As was his habit he left abruptly and I watched him from the door, deciding he must have eyes like a cat as he walked unflinching towards his favourite ditch where an overhang of rock once part of Samson's Ribs hid and sheltered him from the elements.

On the day of my walk to St Anthony's Chapel, aware that the weather was changing rapidly and what the onset of winter might have in store for him, I asked Rory why he didn't go home to the Highland and what had brought him to Edinburgh of all places.

He looked into space for a few moment and I wondered if he had heard me or was a little deaf as I sometimes suspected. Then with a sigh he said, 'I was led here.' And turning his head he looked at me intently. 'God willed that I should come here and find my laddie.'

His late wife's birthplace seemed a forlorn hope in which to find a young soldier who went missing presumed dead long since in India. I didn't conceal my thoughts too well for he shook his head and stood up. Straightening his shoulders he leaned both his hands on the table and stared across at me.

Shaking his head vigorously, he said, 'I ken well that he is here. I've seen him, lassie.'

'You've seen – that's wonderful!' I said, wishing to God that I could see Danny McQuinn wandering around Edinburgh.

His expression was far from joyful. 'Na, na, lassie, nae so wonderful. He was coming out o' one of them posh places in the city. I didna' recognise him at first and he didna' see me.'

'Why didn't you speak to him?' I demanded.

'Na, na. I couldna – seeing what had become o' the lad I loved.' He choked on the words. 'I was glad his ma had gone long since. It would have broken her heart. Like it did mine.'

Overcome by emotion, he dashed a hand across his eyes and walked rapidly to the door. 'I'll bid ye goodnight, lass.'

He went out quickly, avoiding the questions I was dying to ask. Then aware of me watching him, he turned and waved, the package of food still in his hand.

We were to talk again when, unable to resist a mystery, I mentioned the meeting with his son.

'I should have believed them, lassie. My laddie's dead now. Dead for me,' he added firmly.

Events moved tragically fast after than and I never did get the end of the story then.

At least, not from him.

Chapter Three

Thane had watched Rory take his departure, his expression under those magisterial eyebrows very broody, even wistful, as if he would have enjoyed accompanying him.

Inside the Tower, I realised I must make haste. The tilt of the earth in autumn has a dramatic effect on Scotland's landscapes and the best light is toward sunset. Hills like Arthur's Seat are thrown into sharp relief against an often cloudless sky, colours bleached into insignificance under the blast of summer sunshine becoming vividly alive again. Rock fissures take on shadows deep and mysterious, hinting at the presence of lurking caves with ancient secrets long lost to men. The lines of the runrig agricultural system set down by the hill's early inhabitants stand out boldly in the fading light and over all, the breathtaking beauty of deep purples, wine-red heath, trees and bushes dappled gold in sunlight.

It is a magic time when almost anything could happen, an artist's paradise when even an amateur like myself could find inspiration in shapes and shadows.

Conscious of urgency, of the need to get something down on paper for Vince's approval, I followed the path high above the Tower, which soon disappeared among the rocky shapes. As I clambered across, far below me was the road with its magnificent view of Edinburgh's distant spires.

I had walked these tracks so many times in the last six months that I knew every stone, with Thane to lead the way, bounding ahead. Watching him, I wondered how old he was. He looked like a young dog, but his life was still one big unsolved mystery and he didn't help much by preferring to remain out of sight most of the time, shy to the point of invisibility to all but a chosen few.

Myself, Jack and now Auld Rory and Nancy. His

acquaintance, his trust in humans was expanding. As for me, I had not the remotest idea where his lair was or how he managed to keep his coat in that silky condition.

Sometimes it seemed impossible that Thane was a stray dog roaming the hill, a tramp who identified with one of the human species, like Rory. Strays, as I knew, were scruffy and wild: Cat had been a perfect example of an animal who had abandoned the Tower when her old owner Sir Hedley Marsh died and had taken to living rough.

I watched Thane loping joyously ahead. So often when I went out to sketch, he seemed aware of my intentions. He would sit at my side and watch very solemnly as I put pencil to paper. As a reward, I often included him.

My track led across the Haggis Knowe, also known as the Fairies Knowe, with its superb view of the Old Town, Holyrood Palace and St Margaret's Loch.

St Anthony's Chapel came into view steeply some two hundred feet below us. On the path leading up from the road was an ancient well, once famed for its healing powers and allegedly very reliable. Thus on the first Sunday in May, Beltane, the pagan and Christian religions seemed happy to coexist in this area.

The Chapel was built in the fifteenth century, its dedication suggesting that it was once connected to a hospital for those afflicted with 'St Anthony's Fire' as erysipelas was commonly known. Tradition claimed that it was founded to guard the holy well and supported a hermit to tend the altar. His duties included lighting the lamp which shone through the night guiding mariners through the treacherous waters of the River Forth.

All that remains of the ancient chapel is a picturesque ruin. Lit by a magnificent sky of rosy sunset clouds, it was a worthy painting for Olivia – if I could hope to do it justice.

I sat on a boulder overlooking the scene, took out my sketchbook. This time, I wasn't to have Thane's company. Sniffing the air, he barked, a muted 'Woof', and loped away.

Looking round I failed to see anything that could have given him this quiver of excitement. The scent of a deer, perhaps? I didn't have long to wonder as he reappeared.

'Woof!'

'Too late, were you? Pity. Sit down, this won't take long.'

'Woof!' Deeper now, more urgent. He seized the edge of my skirt gently and tugged. The cause of his agitation was invisible but I was familiar with the note of distress in his bark.

'All right, I'll come.'

Gathering my pencils with a sigh I went after him somewhat reluctantly as he darted ahead, loping down through the heather, then turning and rushing firmly back to my side. Making sure that I was doing what he wanted...

I could see nothing amiss. 'What is it – what have you found?'

A dead animal? Hardly. A buried treasure? Surely not. I didn't expect him to understand the human greed for lost gold...

'Woof!'

Once more, he turned to make sure that I was following him before disappearing behind the one remaining chapel wall.

I scrambled down the last few yards and into the ruin.

And there on the ground, her back against the wall, a woman sprawled, apparently asleep.

Asleep or – dead. She looked crumpled enough to be dead.

I shuddered as I approached. Kneeling down, I touched her shoulder gently, praying that she was asleep or had merely fainted. There was no response.

'Hello! Hello, are you all right?'

Even as I said the words the silence mocked me. She was in profile; I turned her face towards me. Eyelids half closed, her face a greyish colour.

As I bent down to loosen the scarf tightly about her neck, there was a faint smell lingering about her. Not perfume nor incense – something indefinable, which I did not recognise until I encountered it unexpectedly much later.

My main concern was for a pulse. There was none.

I sat back on my keels. She was dead. I had seen too many dead by violence to be mistaken.

This poor woman had been strangled with her scarf.

And death had happened very recently.

Which indicated that whoever had done this must still be in the vicinity – perhaps close by!

Trembling I stood up, looked over my shoulder, chillingly aware that with a killer not far off, perhaps watching from behind the boulders, my own life was in imminent danger.

I seemed to be alone. Indeed I seemed to have the whole of Arthur's Seat to myself, towering and majestic in the glowing light. I needed help. I am no hysterical woman to faint at the sight of death. I'd been at the site of an Apache massacre and barely escaped with my life a year ago.

I looked at the dead woman again. This was murder. Of that there was no doubt in my mind. Again I glanced round nervously for someone, a sinister watcher, hidden in the rocks.

I wanted to yell, to shout accusingly, 'Come out, I can see you.' I was aware of Thane standing very close, touching my side, shivering.

He knew danger and death when he saw them.

If only Jack were here, I thought longingly, then suddenly practical, I was searching for a reticule, something that might provide the dead woman with an identity. There was nothing.

If she had died from natural causes, then that was suspicious in itself.

I stared down the hill. The road below was already deep in shadows, the dramatic sunset glow had disappeared from the high rocks behind me, the hill turned cold and forbidding as the twilight of gloaming faded into darkness.

I had the landscape to myself and uneasily I realised that on an autumn day when the weather on Arthur's Seat had been atrocious, there would be few passers-by in carriages or casual strollers out with a dog. But how I would have welcomed the sight of another human being…

I knew what I must do. I must inform the police. I looked again at the woman. She was perhaps thirty-five. The plain face, worries in life indicated by a furrowed brow, was pallid in death. Her dark hair pulled back from a centre parting was gathered into a neat bun from which some of the strands had escaped, perhaps in her struggle with the killer.

Her garments were undisturbed – which hinted at decorum even in death. She had not been the victim of sexual assault or rape.

Glimpses of a starched white petticoat, lace-edged, of a dark blue serge costume, white high-necked cambric blouse, a row of imitation pearl buttons, neatly fastened. Black cotton stockings and boots rather shabby but well-polished.

Not a well-off lady's outdoor garb, especially as there was no sign of a hat anywhere. That omission was odd since most women whatever their station in life wore a hat out of doors. Her clothes were clean, neat and respectable, cared for.

An upstairs servant, or a lower middle-class wife. And there were plenty to choose from to fit her description in the new villa area of Newington.

No gloves and no rings. I lifted her hands carefully,

remembering how Pappa had always stressed the importance of examining hands.

I shuddered as the hands I touched were colder than her face had been. White and dead, but uncalloused with well-kept nails. A seamstress or a shop assistant. She certainly hadn't scrubbed floors for a living.

I was glad of the sketchbook and did a quick drawing, just as she lay, with the chapel wall behind her.

As I finished it, Thane was on the move again, darting down the hill, heading for the road.

'Thane! Come back!' I panicked. I didn't want to be left here alone. Maybe he had seen someone, I thought hopefully as I ran after him and saw the reason for his sudden flight.

Below us the road was not empty after all. Pointing in the direction of the Tower stood a hackney cab. It was stationary but must have been there for some time, or I would have heard the clip-clop of the horse's hooves.

There was no driver in sight – on this unfrequented road with plenty of boulders, that was not an unusual occurrence. Coachmen after putting down a fare often seized the opportunity to stop and, concealed by the bushes, attend to the needs of nature.

'Having a quick one,' as Jack rudely described it.

A deep-throated growl from Thane. A warning 'Woof!'

And there on the road walking in our direction was the best sight in the world for me at that moment.

An Edinburgh policeman on his beat.

'Wait,' I called and leaped down on the last few yards.

But Thane was already there, running round him in circles, barking.

That got the constable's attention. When I reached him he was being confronted by Thane and at a loss as to how to deal with the situation, holding out his hands defensively.

I was surprised and gratified that he hadn't resorted to using his truncheon on the massive deerhound who had appeared from nowhere and was calculated to put the fear of death into even the fearless heart of an officer of the law.

He heard my footsteps, turned and shouted, 'Call off your dog, miss.'

'It's all right. He won't harm you,' I called

As I reached him, Thane came to my side, sat down and looked at the constable with an air of triumph.

'Thank goodness we've found you,' I gasped.

Still keeping a wary eye on Thane, he asked, 'What's the trouble, miss?'

'We've just found a body – a woman, up by the chapel.'

He looked at me impassively, as if I was mad, and asked quietly, 'Is she dead?'

'I'm afraid so.'

He nodded and said, 'Are you sure, miss?'

'Yes, I'm sure. Look, come with me and see for yourself.'

He seemed a little reluctant. Now that I got a closer look, I could see that he was quite young – in fact his face looked too young to have grown the heavy grey and somewhat elderly moustache.

I must be getting old, I thought, when policemen start looking younger.

He must be new to the force, I decided as, with Thane in the lead, we climbed up to the ruined chapel I noticed that he hadn't been issued with the ugly but serviceable uniform boots yet, nor even the more serviceable truncheon.

The dead woman was still there and the young constable didn't say a word. He just stood very still, looking down at her with what I can only describe as considerable distaste and revulsion. Obviously he didn't want to touch her but, aware of my stern gaze and what was expected of him, he knelt at her side, touched her wrist and dropped it hastily.

In the background I sighed. A lily-livered lad who would not go far. Death by strangulation was a fairly clean-cut murder, wait until he came upon the gruesome kind, with lots of blood. He stood up, shaking a little.

'I'm afraid she's dead.'

'I'm afraid she's been murdered,' I added

He looked at me quickly, asked sharply, 'What makes you say that, miss?'

'Look at the scarf around her neck. She's been strangled.'

'The scarf's loose.'

'I did that, trying to find her pulse, hoping I wasn't too late. But someone had tied it tight enough to kill her.'

He gave me a tight-lipped look. 'Well, we'll see when we get her to the mortuary.'

'How are you going to do that?' I asked, remembering the standard police procedure. 'Aren't you supposed to wait and touch nothing until a senior officer arrives?'

He seemed amused and surprised by my knowledge.

'Why would that be, miss?' he asked, humouring me.

I shrugged. 'Clues to her killer – that sort of thing.'

'But we don't know for sure that she's been murdered, do we?'

We stared at one another indecisively and I said, 'Do you want me to stay until you get someone?' I hoped not. It was a bold offer but as soon as I got the words out I was wishing I had not volunteered. By the time he came back, it would be black dark and even with Thane I didn't fancy sitting in the old chapel guarding a corpse.

The constable was impressed by my offer. 'You're not scared, miss?'

'I've seen dead people before.'

'Have you now?' He looked interested, as if he'd like to hear more about that.

I pointed down towards the road. 'I noticed a cab down there.'

He nodded. 'So I saw.'

'You didn't happen to notice a driver?'

He smiled. 'That's all right, miss. I know him. He does a bit of rabbiting. There's a lot of them about when it's getting dusk.'

We walked back down towards the road. When we reached it he saluted me gravely. 'You can be off now, miss. I'll do the necessary. And thanks for your help,' he added politely.

The closed carriage was still unattended. We both stared at it.

'I'll get Charlie to take a message to the station, for the ambulance wagon. No need for you to worry any more about it,' he added smoothly. 'I'm sure there'll be a simple explanation.'

'Simple!' I gasped. 'Is that what you call murder?'

'We don't know that, miss,' he repeated patiently. 'Until we get the body examined. So if you'll excuse me, I'll look for Charlie.'

'You'll need my name as a witness, won't you,' I reminded him as gently as I could.

'Oh yes, of course.' he began searching his pockets. 'Dammit, I had my notebook – I must have dropped it on the way down!' He pointed vaguely towards the chapel. 'You just tell me, miss, and I'll write it down when I get back.'

I tore a sheet out of my sketchbook, wrote it down firmly. He read it carefully and said, 'You live as near as that, miss. Ah well, no need to see you safe home.'

'My dog will do that, constable.'

He gave Thane a thoughtful look. 'We'll be in touch if we need you, miss.'

The usual beat constable, Lenny, knew Jack well and I was

tempted to say, 'Don't bother, my young man is a detective sergeant.'

I don't know why I restrained myself from giving that piece of information, except from a sense of propriety. I didn't think Jack would want my name bandied around the constables, with appropriate nudges and sniggers.

'You're new on this beat, constable. What's your name?'

He seemed taken aback at this request. 'Smith, miss. PC Smith.'

'And your division number?'

'A654.'

'You're new to Edinburgh?'

'Yes,' he said shortly. And anxious to be on his way, saluting me once again, he wished me good evening and disappeared over the edge of the hill, calling, 'Charlie – Charlie, are you there?'

Thane looked all set to follow him and when I called him, he came with me reluctantly, occasionally stopping in his tracks to look back as we made our way back across the hill to the Tower in the darkness.

What was wrong with him? His behaviour was as strange as PC Smith's. Why not use his whistle to attract Charlie, for heaven's sake. What an incompetent, I thought, losing his notebook and being on his beat without his truncheon.

What was the Edinburgh City Police coming to? Pappa would never have tolerated such behaviour. As for Jack, that stickler for efficiency...

I shook my head sadly. Well, we all have to make mistakes and make allowances for beginners.

I'd keep my comments to myself. I didn't want to get the raw young constable into trouble.

Chapter Four

We had almost reached the Tower when I heard the sound of an approaching carriage on the road below. It was too dark to see clearly, and for a moment I thought it must be Charlie driving in the wrong direction.

Then the swinging lantern halted outside the Tower. I ran through the garden and to my delight the door opened and the passenger who descended was Jack, grinning at me.

At the sight of him, Thane loped off up the hill with a look in my direction that said, 'You'll be all right now. You're in safe hands.'

Jack watched him go. 'Walking the dog, were you. Good job I caught you. Well, are you ready to go to the concert?'

I stared at him. 'I thought you were on a case. You sent a message.'

'Inspector Grey let me off. He knows I'm a music lover,' he said mockingly. Telling the cabbie to wait, he followed me indoors.

Closing the door, he kissed me. 'I felt so badly about this, Rose,' he said sounding contrite. 'Duets from the operas with Signor and Madame Rossi. They're not to be missed. According to the reviews, straight from London and New York. Let's go – a bite of supper somewhere first—'

'Jack,' I interrupted. 'There's been a murder.'

He looked astonished. 'A murder? Where?'

'At St Anthony's Chapel. I found – or rather, Thane found a body. A woman – thirtyish. She'd been strangled. I was at my wit's end. I didn't know what to do, but then I saw the beat constable – not Lenny – a new chap. He went back with me. Took over, sent a cabbie back with a message to the station.'

'How long ago was this?' Jack demanded sharply.

'Ten – twenty minutes ago.'

'I'd left by then. They'll send someone but as I'm on the spot I suppose I'd better have a look. And as you found the body, Inspector Grey will want a statement.' Jack sighed deeply. 'Dammit, Rose. There goes our supper and probably our evening out as well. Can't be helped – I'll be as quick as I can. St Anthony's Chapel, you said?'

'Wait. I'm coming with you.'

When he said I should just wait for him, I replied. 'Don't argue, Jack. It's all right. I'm not squeamish about dead bodies.'

As the gig trotted back along the road towards the ruined chapel, I filled in the details about the dead woman, her description and my good fortune in finding PC Smith passing by.

Charlie and the carriage had disappeared, doubtless by now at the station with a message for the inspector.

'So you know PC Smith?' I asked Jack.

'No, but that isn't surprising. A lot of new young bobbies have been recruited recently. They're needed with the outskirts of the city expanding in all directions. Go on…'

At last the dark ruins hovered above us. The cabbie, told to wait, obligingly lent Jack one of his lanterns.

I heard my heart beating fast as we scrambled up the last few yards, Jack running ahead, the light held high.

He shouted, 'Hello there, constable.'

There was no reply, only a chill and eerie wind blowing down from the hill, the darkness unbroken.

'Hello?' Jack called again and turned to me, his angry exclamation indicating that Smith should have been here guarding the body until the ambulance wagon and some senior officers arrived.

So where was he? Jack waved the lantern, shouted again, 'Hello?'

But there was no sign of him.

Worse, the dead woman had vanished.

Jack swore and turned to me.

'Sure this is the right place, Rose?'

I pointed to the base of the wall. 'She was lying right there.'

He went over and knelt down. 'Here?'

'Yes.'

I watched him methodically searching the stones for clues. There were none and he was annoyed with good reason. At last he shook his head and stood up, dusting down the knees of his best trousers.

'What the devil has happened?'

'I'd suggest that as the carriage has gone, your constable got the driver's help and they've taken the body to the mortuary,' I said helpfully. 'He was young and he seemed inexperienced,' I added in the lad's defence, remembering his fumbling attempts at taking a witness statement from me. 'Perhaps he was scared to stay with her alone.'

'Come on, Rose,' Jack said impatiently. 'Even young constables have to learn not to be scared of dead bodies. They'll see plenty of them. I'll have words for Constable Smith when I get back. He should know – for God's sake, it's first rules that you never leave a dead body found in suspicious circumstances until a senior officer – a detective – and a doctor come and have a look at it.'

Raising the lantern again for a closer look at the wall, he added grimly, 'He'll be even more scared of the living than the dead when I'm through with him.' And turning to me: 'This cab you said that was waiting on the road down there…'

'Yes, the cabbie was called Charlie. According to the constable he was out rabbiting.'

'Hmph,' said Jack.

'Since they've all disappeared, I'm sure there's a simple

explanation,' I insisted, 'and your overzealous lad took the law into his own hands.'

'He needn't expect any thanks for that,' said Jack grimly. 'He sounds pretty useless from what you've told me. I doubt whether he'll last long in the force.'

Those were also my thoughts as he went on, 'No doubt the Inspector in charge – probably Grey – will take care of the details. Nothing we can do here, Rose. Better get to the concert.'

'I need to get changed, Jack,' I protested.

He stared at me in amazement. 'You look great.'

'I don't. I have to do my hair. I'm a mess.'

My unruly mop of yellow curls needed constant discipline if it wasn't to end up looking like a haystack. And I was still in my outdoor sketching clothes. That wouldn't do at all. Besides I was looking forward to wearing my new skirt and jacket. In a flattering shade of deep blue, this would be its first outing.

Poor Jack shook his head in bewilderment. 'You look absolutely stunning as you are,' he said, oblivious with manlike indifference to the vanities of womankind.

Half an hour later we were on our way to the concert. But I didn't really enjoy it very much. I kept thinking of that dead woman and working out logical reasons for the thoroughly incompetent PC Smith's behaviour.

Jack didn't stay that night. He decided to go straight back to the station, an attack of conscience, in case Inspector Grey needed information about the dead woman we believed would now be lying in the police mortuary. After seeing me safely back to my front door, he drove off in the hackney cab.

I didn't feel like being on my own and didn't sleep much either. This was the first night for a long while that I had been completely alone in the Tower. When Jack was around my faithful deerhound made himself scarce and this night's sinister events – the walking dead – awakened uneasy memories of Edgar Allan Poe's more lurid *Tales of Mystery and Imagination*.

With Thane sleeping in the kitchen downstairs I would have felt safe. Even Cat's presence had been a comfort. She wasn't in the least like Thane who could tackle anyone, the perfect guard dog, but I still felt reasonably secure with any animal that could make a noise to alert me and possibly frighten off an intruder.

Wide awake I stared out into a dark sky broken by swift-moving clouds, accompanied by an eldritch wind that rattled the windows and sent scurrying leaves pattering like rapid footsteps along the stone paths around the old Tower.

And tomorrow, I remembered, was 31st October – Hallowe'en. That witches' sabbath still made me uneasy, recalling an Orkney childhood with Gran's superstitions and ghost stories, some pretty horrible, especially the dead walking...

Although common sense said that such things belonged to the pages of fairy tales, this would be my first encounter with the most sinister date in the year in Solomon's Tower. I hadn't thought much about it before but now it took on a new significance: I was living on the scene of many strange goings-on through the passing centuries.

Which included, I did not doubt, any number of forgotten grisly rituals and manifestations of a past long lost to history. The upstairs floor showed indications of a place of Christian worship dating to the time of the Knights Templar, but I suspected that the origins of the building went further back to the time of pagan gods on Arthur's Seat.

There were still many unanswered questions, unexplained and tantalising mysteries like the miniature coffins which my father as a schoolboy had discovered, and whose existence had been seized upon by news-hungry journalists as sensational evidence of black magic and witches' covens.

And much nearer home for me, there was Thane.

Where did a mysterious deerhound who came and went with no evident lair fit into a legend that included the deerhounds of King Arthur and his knights? They were said to be sleeping in a chamber deep in the heart of the mountain. A shepherd boy had seen them with his own eyes in my great-grandfather's day but, raising the alert, he had never been able to find the place again.

I had learned to accept Thane. He was real enough and perhaps I didn't want to know the answers in case they included an indignant owner who might appear any day to reclaim him.

Determinedly pushing scary thoughts aside, I let my thoughts drift to the cheerful prospect of seeing Vince tomorrow for this was a big event for me and a big day for Edinburgh's calendar.

At the opening of the new children's hospital, my stepbrother Dr Vince Laurie was to be one of the royal party escorting accompanying Princess Beatrice.

It made Vince feel very important, this medical care of royal personages. He had promised to come and see me before returning to Balmoral. And then just a few days ago I received a letter that I was being invited to accompany him to the royal lunch since Olivia had stayed in London to look after the children and the new baby.

Olivia was a conscientious mother who refused to follow fashion by relying on nannies or to allow anything to interfere with Jason's four-hourly breast-feeding. Right from the start she had declined to hand him over to the care of a wet nurse, which would have left her free to accompany Vince to Balmoral, Windsor, Osborne, or wherever Her Majesty's whim took her.

Vince accepted Olivia's decision, indulging her since they had agreed that Jason would be their last child. Eyebrows might have been raised at this pronouncement against the will of God, but Vince, as a doctor, knew a thing or two which I had found invaluable about birth control. As soon as he realised that Jack and I were more than just friends, he had tactfully sat me down on one of his rare visits to give me the benefit of his advice and instructions. I was not the only beneficiary, I gathered that such knowledge had been useful and was much in demand in royal service, to married and unmarried alike!

I concentrated my thoughts on what to wear tomorrow, going through my limited wardrobe. The most elegant and suitable items were mostly cast-offs from Olivia and my wealthy friend Alice, substantially altered to fit my smaller measurements. This reviewing did not take long but it was exhausting enough to put me to sleep.

Sorely troubled by nightmares I was glad to open my eyes to another dawn, a thankfully greeted grey square in the window. Downstairs I pulled out the tin bath in front of the peat fire and, aided by several kettles of hot water, performed my daily abolutions.

Returning upstairs to the bedroom, I held up the claret silk dress with its ruffles of Chantilly lace. Critically considering my reflection in Olivia's cheval mirror, I saw that I was far from my best. If only I were taller, what a difference that would have made to my morale.

I stood on tiptoe: those two extra inches would have brought me over the threshold of five foot which had always seemed eminently desirable. And if only I had fashionably smooth amenable hair instead of a mop of wild unruly yellow curls. If only—

The sound of a carriage outside announced Jack.

Throwing on a robe, I ran downstairs and knew by one look at his face that all was not well. I could expect bad news.

He kissed me absent-mindedly and said, 'Are you quite certain that the woman you found was dead?'

I looked at him. 'Sure as you are standing there, Jack. A scarf tied tight around her neck, she was strangled – quite dead.'

Jack frowned. 'You said you undid the scarf.'

'I didn't realise then that she was dead – her eyes weren't completely closed. I had to feel for the pulse in her neck to make sure.'

Jack's expression was grim. He shook his head. 'I think you made a mistake, Rose. I hate to question your judgement,' he added quickly, 'but I think she wasn't dead at all. Her eyes were partly open, as you said, because she was merely in shock. She had fainted, had an attack of some kind.' He shrugged. 'Maybe she slipped on the hill, knocked herself out. Who knows? But whatever it was, she recovered, got up and walked away—'

'Jack, that's not possible. I've seen too many dead people to make that kind of mistake,' and taking an unfair advantage, I added, 'I've had more experience than you in that direction, for a start.'

He ignored that. 'Listen to me and try not to get angry. I am as anxious as you are to get the facts right.' He paused and added slowly, 'No dead woman has been brought into the mortuary.'

'Then ask PC Smith, for heaven's sake. He was there.'

'Rose,' Jack said patiently, 'there is no PC Smith.'

'But I gave you his division number – A654.'

He shook his head. 'There is no A654 on the records either.' Tapping his teeth with his forefinger, a familiar gesture when he was worried, he regarded me gravely. 'If she wasn't injured, as I think was the case, the only other explanation is that you were the victim of a practical joke. And you arrived at the wrong moment for whoever it was intended.'

'Jack Macmerry,' I exploded. 'No one in their right senses plays that kind of joke. The constable was really scared. And besides, before I saw him down on the road, I made a drawing of the woman.'

I went to the sideboard. 'Here, see for yourself.'

Jack smiled. 'Damned good drawing, Rose. But she doesn't look dead. Now, honestly, does she?' He handed it back to me. 'And it isn't really evidence of what you're trying to prove.'

'Thane was with me. He knew she was dead. He led me to her. A sleeping woman would have jumped out of her skin when a huge deerhound started sniffing around her.'

Jack sighed. 'Thane! A dog nobody ever sees – but us. He could hardly be called in to give evidence. Try producing him in court as a witness—'

'Then there was the cab driver – Charlie.'

'Did you see him?'

'No, he was down the hill rabbiting. But I heard the constable shouting at him. As I told you, he was going to give him a message to take to the station, ask for the ambulance wagon to be sent.'

'Rose,' said Jack patiently, 'there was no message. No dead person. Look, I'll have to go, I just had to tell you.'

He kissed me. 'I don't want you worrying – put all this out of your mind and enjoy your lunch with Vince. Give him my best.'

Angry, disturbed and confused, I was momentarily speechless at the arrogance of men, at being patronised. I didn't like it, cast in the role of the wee woman, who sees things and has a phantom dog!

He kissed me again, with more feeling this time, aware that

I was unresponsive. 'It will all get sorted out, you'll see.' And at the door: 'I'll be around this evening.'

'Vince will be here,' I said coldly.

'Yes, of course,' he said vaguely, waiting for me to say, please come.

I didn't. My time with Vince was too precious to share, although the two men liked each other and shared a common interest in my future. What they both wanted was to see me married again, settled down in woman's proper role in man's life.

'Have you checked your missing persons list at the station?'

A long suffering sigh. 'Not really.'

'Then please do something for me, Jack.' I tried not to sound exasperated. 'Check who you have on it already and how long they've been missing.'

And taking the sketchbook I tore out the drawing. 'When you have a spare moment, see if there's anyone who could remotely resemble this likeness. And let me have it back when you've finished with it.'

After Jack left, I did as I was told and, thrusting aside all matters relating to the dead woman for the moment, I dressed ready to go into Edinburgh and meet Vince.

Filled with almost unbearable excitement I waited for the carriage coming up the road: an important-looking brougham, with two splendidly groomed horses, a footman and a rather imperious and immaculate coachman in livery that went with the royal coat of arms on the door.

As we trotted past, Auld Rory stood by the roadside clearly impressed. Removing his clay pipe he solemnly saluted, gave me a grin and departing wave. Strains of 'Soldiers of the Queen' followed us as we disappeared down the road and I knew he would be waiting to hear all the details when I got back.

I was put down at the Balmoral Hotel near the railway station where the royal party was staying overnight and luncheon was being provided for specially invited guests.

Bursting with pride I was announced and Vince rushed forward to greet me wearing formal court dress, with a new medal and looking absolutely stunning. 'You're just in time,' he said.

'Will I be all right?' I asked as he looked me over, his expression a mite nervous. 'Is this dressy enough? My wardrobe doesn't rise to much in the way of smart afternoon gowns.' I spread the skirts a little. 'My lifestyle doesn't offer much in the way of occasions like this.'

Vince's smile was a little anxious and I added, 'This is the only one I possess.'

In answer he squeezed my arm reassuringly. 'You'll be fine, the belle of the ball. But don't catch cold…' His gaze took in a preponderance of fur cloaks. I had only a thin matching jacket for my gown. 'Will you be warm enough? It's a raw sort of day.'

As we were ushered towards the dining-room. I felt flushed with excitement, almost indecently warm, and all ready to break out into an unladylike sweat.

'Matters have been delayed,' Vince told me. 'Her Royal Highness has an ear infection. Had it before we left Balmoral. Needed constant medical attention, which is my reason for being with her. It's been troublesome and she slept badly last night. Her Majesty fusses over her, urged her to cancel but she refused to let it interfere with her schedule which must be seen to run smoothly.'

In a worried tone, he added, 'She has a heavy day of engagements ahead.' All this in a stage whisper as we took our places at the end of a long table to await the arrival of the Princess.

Thirty-eight years old, mother of two children, Beatrice, Princess Henry of Battenburg was also known in royal circles as 'Baby'. So her doting mother, the Queen, thought of her. She had never wanted her youngest daughter to marry and as a flagrant reminder of her youth and inexperience (I got all of this from Vince later), she was accompanied to Edinburgh by Her Majesty's favourite lady-in-waiting, Lady Antrim. A rare privilege indeed.

At last the assembled diners stood up to bow or curtsey as the royal party took their places at the centre of the table and Grace was said by the Moderator of the Church of Scotland.

As we waited to be served, I was disappointed to observe that the Princess and her companion were less splendidly attired than I had imagined. Expecting tiaras and elegant day gowns of lace, satin or velvet, instead the Princess looked quite ordinary and subdued in a modest navy blue skirt and a silk blouse with the new balloon-shaped sleeves. Her blue velvet toque had not succumbed to the taste for flowers and feathers and was unadorned, apart from a sparkling brooch, doubtless a precious diamond from her royal mamma's priceless collection.

Lady Antrim was also simply attired in a costume of hunter's green with a matching plain velvet toque.

Grand occasions make me uncomfortable and uncertain about what one should wear, especially as living in Solomon's Tower rarely involved the splendours of dress *à la mode* for ladies of fashion.

I had discarded my thin outdoor jacket and now sat feeling distinctly overdressed in my claret silk gown with its tight sleeves and lace jabot. The jaunty hat heavily overburdened with flowers and fruit grew heavier by the moment and I anticipated the imminent collapse of the miniature garden in the direction of my soup.

Resisting the impulse to push it back from my forehead, I nudged Vince and said reproachfully. 'You should have warned me.'

'About what?'

'About what to wear, of course,' I whispered.

He smiled. 'You look lovely.'

'I don't feel lovely,' I grumbled.

Glancing down the table he whispered, 'I'm sorry, Rose. It's my fault, I didn't know what they would be wearing. At the opening ceremony both the Princess and Lady Antrim were wearing long winter coats and fur hats. Because of this beastly cold day and Her Royal Highness's sore ear, I imagine. Didn't want to take chances. Her Majesty gets over anxious about her wee lamb, you know.'

I looked around the table despairingly at the other ladies from Edinburgh society, modestly clad in unpretentious dark costumes, the occasional pretty lace blouse and jewellery, discreet, unobtrusive but expensive. Pearl necklaces and earrings seemed the only sign of affluence.

Not so the gentlemen, in frock coats with handsome waistcoats, or dress uniforms all bearing orders and decorations.

We were seated at the end of a long table, Vince on my left and on my right, facing him, a high-ranking military man. I soon discovered that they were old acquaintances who had met at 'the Castle', presumably Balmoral. Vince knew the officer well but I was at a disadvantage when we were introduced.

The hum of voices made his name indistinct and I was too shy to ask him to repeat it. I hoped to pick up clues to his identity as Vince asked politely after Lady —. It sounded like Car-something, and was presumably his wife.

'She is fairly well at present but still needs a good deal of rest.'

Vince was sorry to hear that, especially when he was told that she was not yet up to facing large social occasions. I could see my stepbrother doctor's interest was aroused, eager to know more of her condition, doubtless with advice at the ready.

Doing my best to follow the conversation and sustain a smiling look of polite interest, I suddenly realised that the splendid soldier at my side, in dress uniform with medals and decorations, was General Sir Angus Carthew.

Politely declining Vince's well-meaning but ponderous medical advice, he became aware of my presence. Noticed at last, as he turned his head in my direction and gallantly addressed some flattering compliments to Dr Laurie about his pretty young sister.

I responded with as much modesty and grace as I could

muster. As I am acutely sensitive to atmosphere, I realised I must not let this sudden interest go to my head. It was not because of my personal charm, but merely that I presented a means of escape, a desperate manoeuvre on the General's behalf to change the subject of his wife's health to a more cheerful topic.

As we tackled the next course, I observed him closely. So this was Nancy's kindly new employer. He must have been devastatingly handsome in his youth and was wearing well. He could have been any age between forty-five and sixty. And according to the conversation I had overheard, with an invalid wife; a situation which I know from experiences in my professional life often opens up possibilities with tragic consequences.

I put on my best smile for him but after a few perfunctory and polite questions about where I lived and did I like Edinburgh, the standard party conversation between new acquaintances, he lost interest and returned to Vince to talk of golf, polo and the Stock Exchange.

As my participation was no longer expected or desired, I devoted my attention to the enjoyment of a perfectly splendid lunch. Soup, poached salmon and a delectable dessert heavy in chocolate and rich in cream. I made the most of it, savouring every bite.

Conscious of Vince's eagle eye descending upon me as I eagerly accepted a second helping, I didn't care. Unladylike it might be, but there are exceptions. Such occasions were all too rare in my experience and I was not prepared to let this unique opportunity slip past, since my fare in Solomon's Tower tends towards being spartan in the extreme.

All too soon the coffee was served and we all stood for 'the Queen!' as the Princess and her companion retired before proceeding to their next engagement.

The General bowed politely in my direction, shook hands warmly with Vince and said it had been a great pleasure.

Vince excused himself to receive royal instructions and, waiting for him in the foyer, I watched the General walk down the hotel steps.

And then I witnessed a curious and alarming incident.

As the door of his waiting carriage was opened, a rough-looking man approached, apparently a passer-by on the pavement. There was a rapid movement, a scuffle and a fist raised – holding a weapon of some sort.

Stick, pistol? Emerging from the hotel blinking against the bright light, I had only a glimpse of what was happening as the hotel doorman rushed forward. The man was seized firmly while the General leapt into the carriage which sped off in the direction of Waverley Bridge.

The man was released, words muttered, perhaps of apology, and all returned to normal so immediately that I blinked again. Had it been someone who had bumped into him accidentally and had I imagined weapon, raised fist and threatening voice?

'Are we ready now?' Vince had returned. I started to tell him about the altercation but he merely shook his head, displaying little interest beyond asking if anyone had been hurt. Meanwhile, still somewhat distracted, he anxiously considered his gold watch as if it might be unreliable and have gained an hour or two since last being consulted.

Quite unconcerned about the little drama I had witnessed, he nodded absently and said, 'The General is a very fine fellow. You obviously made a very good impression, Rose.'

And that obviously gladdened Vince's heart too, as we stepped into our waiting carriage.

Leaning back with a sigh, he said, 'Her Royal Highness will rest for an hour at least before her next engagement and that will give me time to escort you home and get back.'

Aware of my disappointment, he added, 'Sorry, my dear, but you can see how it is. I have to be in constant attendance just now. She is to make a brief appearance at a meeting of the National Institute for Imbecile Children and the Prevention of Cruelty to Children.'

I wondered if the two were synonymous as he continued, 'I have tinctures to administer if the royal ear becomes too troublesome. They ease the pain.'

Somewhat sulkily, I stared out of the window, feeling sorry for myself. So much for the time I had been promised. ('We will have a whole day together once the lunch is over.')

This was the story of the men in my life. The only difference was that Jack frequently promised a whole evening which all too often didn't happen at all.

It was becoming alarmingly apparent that those closest to me were not mine to command. Vince was enslaved to his royal mistress at Balmoral or wherever her duties took her. And Jack was enslaved to the Edinburgh City Police.

How could a mere woman fight against such odds and what had I to offer, I wondered as the carriage bowled down the Pleasance and Vince asked, 'What have you been doing since I last saw you?'

I looked at the road ahead. Five minutes would see us outside Solomon's Tower and there our ways would part – until the next time it suited and fitted in with Her Majesty's command. With so little time and aware that the story was doomed to failure, I still had to tell him about my sensational discovery of a dead woman at St Anthony's Chapel.

Vince made the right noises and asked, 'What happened then? Who was she?'

'I don't know. When I went back with Jack, she had disappeared.'

Vince looked surprised for a moment, frowned and shook his head. 'I'm sure there'll be a simple explanation, there usually is for most things,' he added soothingly.

As an afterthought, he added the usual stern warning about not getting involved in matters beyond me.

In polite words, to mind my own business, since Vince also turned his face against my adopted profession as a Lady Investigator, thereby gaining Jack's sympathy and ready support.

Whereas Detective Sergeant Jack Macmerry was to be applauded in his fight against crime and could mix with who-the-devil he liked without tarnishing his reputation, a female investigator was in a very unladylike profession, mixing in what was undoubtedly a man's world, just one step above a hospital nurse and open to the direst suspicion and interpretation.

There was more to it than that. In my case there was need for extra caution. Word might get around and damage Dr Vincent Beaumarcher Laurie's credibility and respectability, should such gossip have the misfortune to reach Her Majesty's ears.

A stepsister who rubbed shoulders with the lower classes and who might number prostitutes, pimps, thieves and other low-lifes among her clients. Intolerable – the very idea!

It was all grossly unfair and made me seethe with anger. The campaign for women to be granted the vote had begun in '67 and a suffrage bill came up every year but without success. The Reform Act of '84 gave the vote to more men but no women.

We were not defeated. There were societies growing in every major town across the country. We had faith in the future and determination. The sooner we got the vote and put men in their place, the unhappier they'd be.

Useless to discuss such matters with Vince who, without

the least idea of treading on very dangerous ground, asked after our sister Emily and had I heard from Orkney recently.

That hurt too. 'Just the occasional card or letter.' I refrained from adding that they were vague and perfunctory.

'You should go and see her sometime. It would do you good to get away from Edinburgh for a while. You must miss her and Gran.'

He paused before adding quite casually a suggestion that I was certain occupied a great deal of his thoughts and was doubtless a subject of earnest and frequent discussion between himself and Olivia.

'Have you considered that you could do worse than go back to live in Orkney?'

'I have, Vince dear, especially when I first came here six months ago. But I'm still waiting for that invitation, you know,' I reminded him gently. 'Up to now my hints about longing to see her again have been studiously ignored,' I continued, trying to retain my good humour despite a growing feeling, somewhat spiteful, that Vince would like to have me tucked safely out of the way, back in Orkney, where I would pose less of a threat to his career.

'You shouldn't need an invitation, for heaven's sake,' he said testily. 'She's your only sister and remember, Gran brought you both up in Orkney after our mother died. If I'd been younger I'd have been there too. Stepfather could never have managed.'

Gran, now old and frail, lived with Emmy and her husband and according to those rare communications, needed constant care.

Vince sighed deeply. 'I expect Emily's busy like all of us. I wouldn't make too much of it, Rose. Don't take it to heart. I'm sure she means well. You were very close at one time.'

Realising by my expression that he was on a downward

slope, he said, 'And have you heard from your father?'

'A postcard from London. Imogen is on one of her research trips.'

'They called on Olivia when they were there, did you know?' he said brightly. 'I gather Imogen is very involved with politics these days. Reading between the lines, Olivia said the suffragette movement is high on their list of priorities.'

I warmed to Imogen when Vince's despairing sigh indicated that such women were a bewildering new species.

My own despairing sigh was that I figured nowhere on Pappa's list of priorities these days. They rarely visited Britain and as there was a regular train service between London and Edinburgh, I felt they might have felt inclined to make the extra journey.

When I said as much to Vince he seemed surprised that I should feel bruised by their neglect. And as the carriage approached the Tower and the end of our day was in sight, he said, by way of compensation, no doubt, 'We must have you up to Balmoral one of these days. The Queen is very sympathetic about Olivia and the children being on their own in St James's for long periods when we are in Scotland. She has hinted that they might be invited up for Christmas. Now wouldn't it be splendid if you could come too? I'll see if I can get you included in the invitation. You'd like that.'

I said yes, aware that I didn't sound over-enthusiastic. I didn't want to hold my breath on it or put my heart into a giddy circuit of eager anticipation. Like watching the postman and looking forward eagerly to yet another invitation, only to be blighted once more.

Handing me down from the carriage, Vince hugged and kissed me and said how marvellous it had been to have me with him at the lunch. And for a moment I thought I saw a flicker of the adored stepbrother now lost under the weight of royal approval and command.

'Take care, Rose dear. I'll see you soon.'

'Till then,' I said hopefully. 'You take care too.,' As I stood on the road and waved the carriage out of sight, I felt very out of sorts with my entire family at that moment.

Pappa, Emmy and Vince. I had no real part in any of their lives. And how lonely I would be without Thane now that Cat was gone.

Thank heavens for Jack Macmerry.

As I opened the front door I noticed movement across the road and Auld Rory's head peeped eagerly over the hedgerow.

Guessing that he was wildly curious about that royal carriage, I invited him in for a cup of tea, produced some scones and jam, told him all about the lunch with the Princess and how I had sat next to his old campaigner, General Carthew.

He went suddenly quiet and I found it difficult to read his expression through all that facial hair, a perfect screen for his emotions at the best of times.

'You served with him in India. Did you know his wife?'

'He wasna married then,' he said slowly.

I brought him up to date with her being an invalidish lady who didn't accompany him to social functions and about Gerald Carthew's two children who my friend Nancy was nursemaid to. And wasn't it a small world?

I expected him to say something, but he listened in silence and I was sure he hadn't heard a word or wasn't interested in what I'd been telling him. He pushed aside his cup of tea, bolted down the rest of the scone and, with a brief nod of thanks, he stood up so quickly that the milk jug skidded across the table.

I followed him to the door, concerned about his strange behaviour. I could hear him muttering under his breath as he crossed the road back to his ditch. I waited until he disappeared.

How odd! Was he anti-Royalist, had I bored him with my chatter about royal lunches?

I must confess I was disappointed, having fully expected that mention of the General would bring forth another series of wild adventures in India. Perhaps he was still blaming the General for his son's death. I shrugged and went inside knowing I wouldn't get far trying to work out the machinations of Auld Rory's twisted mind, damaged beyond repair by his experiences defending the outposts of the Empire.

I suspected there were depths even those who got close to him would never understand. He was just a poor old soldier I had taken pity on and I knew I was doing it again, what Jack had warned me about, making too much of people and their reactions.

And obviously if my interpretation of that scuffle outside the hotel was anything to go on, General Carthew was not, as the press would lead us to believe, entirely Edinburgh's most popular hero.

Chapter Six

Nancy looked in on her way to the Pleasance Theatre where *The Pirates of Penzance* were rehearsing for their imminent appearance.

Her generous employers, Sir Angus and Lady Carthew, devotees of Gilbert and Sullivan, happily seemed to regard her minor singing role in the chorus as of equal importance to her duties as nanny. She was very fortunate and she knew it.

We had time for a cup of tea together. She wanted to hear all about the royal lunch. I considered telling her about my discovery of the dead woman at St Anthony's Chapel but decided against it. Nancy would worry such topics like a terrier with a juicy bone, offering many fantastic 'simple' explanations, just as she did for Thane.

She had it all worked out. With a wealthy but neglectful master on the other side of Arthur's Seat, Thane had formed an attachment to me, as animals sometimes do if their owners don't spend enough time with them.

The vanishing corpse would have been similarly explained, so I gave her a full account of my meeting with the General, how I had sat next to him at the luncheon, but I refrained from any mention of the altercation I had witnessed outside the hotel.

Nancy was delighted. Our meeting would make her gossip about the Carthews more meaningful.

'He's such a charmer. So handsome, as well as being the kindest and most generous of men.'

I had to agree.

'Such a pity about his poor wife,' she said

I asked what she was like and Nancy shrugged. 'In the few weeks since I've been with them, I can count the times we have met.'

She paused. 'I had decided she would follow the example of other upper-class parents, or in their case foster-parents, who leave their young as soon as possible to the care of nannies and governesses. But I suppose being childless, having two youngsters around is a bit of a novelty for her.'

'I should imagine that two wee children who have just lost their mamma need all the love and understanding they can get, especially with their father unavoidably absent,' I said, refilling her cup.

'Torquil and Tessa certainly don't go short of that. Their aunt and uncle are devoted to them. According to Mrs Laing they prefer spending as much time as possible with the wee ones on their own.'

She sighed. 'I should be grateful as it certainly gives me much more freedom. Once they are dressed, breakfasted and set up for the day, I don't even have to do any washing for them. The daily laundry maid takes care of that with the rest of the house linen.' She shook her head. 'Sometimes, I have to pinch myself to believe how lucky I have landed.'

I agreed, although I found it difficult to imagine the General and his invalid wife relaxing as the devoted temporary foster-parents of two boisterous young children as Nancy continued: 'Mrs Laing has been with the family for donkey's years – she served the General's parents as a young lass. Although they don't like it known, this is actually his second marriage. He was married the first time when he was very young. To a county woman, a wealthy widow a lot older than himself. Money was involved, of course. Apparently the Carthews were in dire straits, so he did as he was told. There was a young stepson by his wife's first marriage, but Mrs Laing hadn't heard of him until recently.'

She sighed. 'The General is certainly devoted to her ladyship, the ideal husband. Her personal maid left recently and went down to England to look after her elderly mother who was seriously ill. Mrs Laing said that her ladyship was terribly cut-up. And no wonder, normally such ladies have been brought up to be completely useless, can't even do up their own corset, or put up their hair, but Lady Carthew's not like that. And Sir Angus is always willing to play lady's maid, brushing her hair and lacing her up – according to Mrs Laing he makes a great joke of it.'

I wasn't entirely surprised at this information which Nancy found so remarkable. Some men enjoy such tasks. Danny always brushed my hair. He said there was something very alluring and very exciting for a man about a woman's hair.

Nancy laughed. 'I can't imagine the General somehow, especially as maids have to be trained to hairdressing. Coiffures for fashionable ladies are very tricky these days.' She looked at me and smiled. 'A lot would give their fortunes to have your natural curls, Rose. Myself included…'

I grimaced. 'They can be an unruly menace, I assure you. You have no idea how I envy your well-tamed waves.'

She touched her soft brown hair, pleased with the compliment and then, leaning forward, she added confidentially, 'I'll let you into a little secret, Rose. I've suspected since I first saw her ladyship walking in the garden that her magnificent golden hair is – a wig! It's not like yours. There's never a strand out of place.

'And once when Torquil fell and cut his knee, he screamed for his auntie. I ran upstairs after him leaving Tessa in the schoolroom. I knocked on their door, but he wouldn't wait. He struggled away from me and rushed into the bedroom. And I saw the wig stand,' she added triumphantly.

I thought this somewhat naive. Many rich women wore wigs for convenience and they were specially popular among the saloon girls in Arizona who could not afford the luxury of hairdressers, even if they had ever been fortunate enough to find one.

'It is quite likely that Lady Carthew's long illness made her lose her hair.'

'I hadn't thought of that,' said Nancy. 'Poor lady, how awful and her so young. Well, as I was telling you, the General was out of sorts that day. There was a visitor with him and he doesn't like being interrupted. I've never known him be impatient or cross with Torquil before. He demanded to know what all the fuss was about a scratched knee and told the wee lad he must learn to be a brave soldier.

'And all the time he glared at me. I was obviously to blame. I said I was sorry for disturbing him. Although the General hugged Torquil, he had a face like thunder. Told him to be quiet and be a good boy, here was a penny. Auntie would be back shortly and she'd kiss his knee better.

'His visitor was obviously embarrassed, staring out of the window. The General said – rather sharply – I thought, "Just leave the children with us, Nanny. We'll look after them until her ladyship returns".

'Then he gave me one of his lovely smiles and said as Mr Appleton was leaving soon, I could take the rest of the day off. Mr Appleton's the stepson, so Mrs Laing told me, very surprised. Apparently a rare visit.

'When I was leaving I heard their voices in the study. Her ladyship had returned. So I tapped on the door, the General opened it and took Tessa in. And that's why I'm here earlier than usual,' she added happily.

Despite her early arrival Nancy left at the last possible moment for the rehearsal. A few times she asked casually, 'What time does Jack come for supper?' And I guessed this was the reason why she lingered.

She was in luck this time. She had just put on her bonnet

and cape when Jack arrived. There was a great deal of laughter and teasing about Desmond Marks which I watched rather sourly, before Nancy said she really must go or she would be late.

Jack turned to me eagerly to ask how long would supper be?

I did not say that I had been delayed by Nancy's visit and the potatoes were not yet peeled. When I told him half an hour, the gallant Jack smiled delightedly.

'In that case, I'll walk Nancy down the Pleasance. That'll give me an appetite.'

I accepted a goodbye peck on the cheek from both of them and watched as they rushed out of the front gate, still laughing and teasing one another. It wasn't much consolation to realise that this state of affairs was all my own doing either. And when Jack returned in such a good humour, I tormented myself that he was working off a guilty conscience.

I asked if there was any more information about PC Smith and the dead woman. He said there wasn't but reaching in his pocket he took out a piece of paper.

'The missing women you asked about. Four in the Edinburgh area.' He consulted the list. 'A woman of sixty; a fifteen year old; a young married woman, twenty-four, with two children; a thirty-year old schoolteacher.'

I felt I could dismiss the first two. 'Tell me about the last two.' Frowning, he considered the descriptions. 'Mrs Winton, dark brown hair, medium build, average height.'

Apart from the lack of a wedding ring, which wasn't conclusive to a marriage, that sounded promising.

'Her address?' I said, holding out my hand.

'No, Rose, definitely not,' said Jack with a laugh. 'I am not permitted to give out that information. Surely you should know that. This is confidential police business.'

'It is also my professional business,' I responded hotly, but

Jack was unimpressed. He merely shrugged and said, 'Do you want to know what the schoolteacher looked like?" I did. 'She is a spinster, fairish hair, average height.'

It was all terribly vague, these two missing persons who might fit the description of the dead woman.

'Well, will that satisfy you?' Jack asked, folding the paper and returning it to his jacket pocket.

'What do you know about the first two names on the list?'

Jack thought for a moment. 'I suppose there's no harm in telling you that the old lady has wandered away before. Daughter says they had a tiff and she suspects her ma's gone to Aberdeen to her son. As for the young lass, it's the usual story. Run away from home. Living in one of the High Street wynds. Parents insist she's "gone to the bad", though how it could be much worse than her terrible conditions at home, fair beats me.'

I put out my hand. 'Please, Jack. Let me see the list.'

He shook his head. 'No. That's all you're getting, and just to satisfy your curiosity.'

'At least tell me how the last two women disappeared.' He grimaced. 'I suppose so. The married woman walked out and left her husband a couple of weeks ago. Took the children…'

That didn't sound promising. 'Go on.'

'The schoolteacher walked out of a girls' boarding school three weeks ago and hasn't been heard of since.'

Now that was hopeful. I remembered the neat clothes and hair, that aura of respectability.

'You must admit there's nothing there that sounds like your dead woman, Rose. Even if she exists. My theory is still that she'd fallen and fainted, then recovered and is safely back home somewhere now. The sooner you accept that the better.'

I didn't accept it but there was no point in arguing. And that night when Jack was sound asleep and snoring happily, I did something I would never have believed myself capable of.

I went to his jacket hanging over the chair and extracted the list. Tiptoeing downstairs, I turned up the lamp and copied the addresses of the two women most likely to correspond with the one I had found.

Returning to bed, I slipped in beside him and slept soundly until morning without a single pang of conscience.

Jack had that weekend free and he had plans for us to spend it together. He had been behaving very mysteriously, promising a special outing. From that I imagined Sunday dinner at an inn, perhaps across the Forth. If the weather was mild enough he might have in mind a picnic, going across in a ferryboat to the island of Inchcolm, a visit I had also often been promised.

At breakfast he informed me that we were to go down to North Berwick on the train to meet up with his parents staying at a hotel there for a cousin's wedding.

He waited for my reaction, saw my startled expression and said, 'Well, aren't you pleased with my little surprise?'

I wasn't pleased. I was taken aback.

At this stage of our relationship I did not want to meet Jack's parents, who with their friends would immediately presume that we were an engaged couple about to get married.

Jack was an only son. I could not do that to them.

'I'm sorry. I can't,' I shook my head miserably.

He looked woeful. 'Why ever not?'

'You know why not,' I said as gently as I could.

He took my hand across the table. 'Rose, this doesn't commit you to anything. They know about you.'

'Yes, but do they know about us?'

Jack looked confused. 'Only that we are courting. And so they are longing to meet you.'

'Do they know about Danny?'

He shuffled uncomfortably. 'I've never made any secret that you are a widow – of course. A very pretty young widow, Rose.'

I sighed. 'We're not certain sure about that, Jack.' This was the one rock to which I obstinately clung, the one Jack still believed was the sole impediment to our marriage.

'Come now, Rose. It's been a long while since Danny disappeared.'

I stood up, began to clear the breakfast dishes. 'You'd better be off, Jack. You'll miss your train.'

He knew I meant it. 'I'm very disappointed, Rose. And the folks will be too. You'd like them, they're great,' he added pathetically.

'I'm sure they are.'

He looked at me. 'What on earth am I going to tell them?' he said desperately.

I shook my head. 'You'll think of something.'

He kissed me goodbye, clearly as disappointed in me as I was in having that nice surprise I was looking forward to dashed once again. If only he had discussed it with me first, but watching him go I felt angry that he had tried to force me into a position where I would be accepted by his family and all the wrong conclusions drawn.

Sad and somewhat weary, I prepared to face the prospect of a now empty weekend, two days I had set so much store on spending with Jack.

There was no point in feeling sorry for myself. Worse things had happened in my life. So I resolved to set aside my injured feelings and put the information I had copied from Jack's list to good use.

Chapter Seven

As I prepared to put my disappointment to some useful purpose by not hating Jack and instead finding out if the dead woman was one of the two on his missing persons list, the weather smiled on me. The sun shone as if the celestial weatherman had forgotten to consult his calendar, and that this was November, future prospects: ice and snow and skating on Duddingston Loch.

Instead we were presented with trees that were an artist's dream, glowing landscapes and glorious golden days. Mild and windless, warm enough to abandon thoughts of winter coats and consider summer picnics instead.

I thought gloomily about the one picnic I had hoped for – what perfect weather for it – as I looked at the two most probable names on the list I had copied.

Bella Winton, aged twenty-four, last known address 117 Musselburgh Road. I remembered the tall tenements newly built in Newington on what had been the long winding drovers' road south out of Edinburgh towards Dalkeith and Berwick.

That would be my first call.

The second was the schoolteacher Mabel Simms, at St Ann's Boarding School for Girls in Portobello. No picnic, but a glimpse of azure sea and a bracing stroll along the promenade.

Taking out my bicycle I headed to Newington, found the right house with the name Winton on the fourth floor. As I climbed the stone stairs I heard raised voices, a man and woman in the thick of a violent disagreement punctuated by the sound of breaking china. Apprehensively I regarded the name on the door, hoping that I was wrong.

Winton. Furious sounds of violence and crashing within

had me ducking out of sight as the door flew open and a woman emerged still screaming obscenities as she rushed past me down the stairs.

The man, a rough-looking character, unshaven and wild-eyed, dashed after her, adding his derisive comments about wives who were bitches and should never have left their mothers' kennels.

When all was silent again, I emerged from my hiding place to find that the irate couple's neighbour had opened her door. The old woman looked out very cautiously. When she saw me, timidly keeping out of sight, she grinned.

'So that was the Wifie Winton leaving home – once again.' She nodded. 'A good riddance to bad rubbish, ye ken, and maybe a body'll get a bit o' peace – the noise, the fighting half the night has been awful.'

As she spoke she looked me over, obviously intrigued about my business with the Wintons and especially my bicycling outfit, something of a novelty in her experience.

So, raising my important-looking leather case, which actually contained just a few printed business cards, denoting 'Lady Investigator, Discretion Guaranteed,' I muttered something about 'charity organisations'.

'Is that so? We could all do with some o' that,' said the old lady enviously. 'But I doubt ye've wasted yer time, hen. Ye'll get nowt for yer charities from the likes o' the Wintons, or onybody else in this road.'

'Will – er – they be back?' I asked politely, rather hoping that the answer would be negative.

She shook her head. 'No point in yer waiting for that. The wife'll be on the next train back down to England to her bairns – and her auld mother. It happens regularly, every few weeks. Last time it was longer than usual and then her ma sent letters back that she wasn't there. She'd gone away. Well, Winton the silly bugger, got scared and told the polis. There's been no end of a stir I can tell ye…'

I made my escape as quickly as I could.

That was number one off Jack's list.

It was still early so I decided to call on St Ann's Boarding School, a new establishment which had taken over a handsome mansion on the sea front.

Hoping to find out what they knew of Mabel Simms' reasons for disappearing, I wasn't quite sure how to frame my enquiry and as I wandered the corridors unquestioned, I found myself outside the dining-room from the smells of food and the clatter of cutlery within.

A harrassed young woman was shepherding girls into an orderly crocodile and demanding silence. She might have saved her breath. Canute had more luck in commanding the waves to retreat.

As the last of her charges disappeared inside, she turned with a deep sigh and saw me.

'I am looking for Miss Simms,' I told her with a business-like flourish of my leather case.

'She isn't here any more,' was the not unexpected reply.

When I expressed surprise, she said, 'I can give you her home address, if that would help. If you'll just come along to the study.'

I followed, dying to ask about the absconding teacher as she looked in a filing drawer and copied down an address.

'Here you are,' she said brightly. 'That's her sister, Miss Bertha Simms.'

As I turned to leave I asked, 'Were you a friend of hers by any chance?'

She shook her head and looked a mite uncomfortable. 'Not exactly. I was in my first week here when she left. Actually, it was because of my appointment as her assistant. It was thought that she took umbrage and walked out that afternoon at the end of the English lesson. When she didn't come back, Headmistress decided she was in the sulks. She'd been on the staff for years and years, always difficult, but they accepted her tantrums. There were other things.'

She paused, realising she had said too much. 'I mean, this wasn't the first time she'd walked out – but she was good with the girls, who adored her.'

Her wide-eyed look of surprise indicated that this was somehow remarkable. When I said nothing, she continued: 'She was a wee bit unconventional, spoke her mind – no respect for the classical authors we are taught to revere, either. A mimic who had all her pupils in fits of laughter. In her good moods, she made all of us laugh,' she added in tones of envy.

As she was speaking, I felt growing sympathy with the absent teacher. Being unconventional and speaking one's mind were dangerous pursuits and, in the wrong direction, certain ways of making enemies and getting oneself murdered. I liked what I heard of Miss Simms and hoped that she wasn't the dead woman in the ruins of St Anthony's Chapel.

'If you do see her, please tell her we all miss her. I'm sure Headmistress would love to have her back. She was like one of the family here, that's why they insisted the police be told, in case something dreadful had happened to her.'

As she spoke she was eyeing the black leather case. 'Is there something we can do for you?' she asked.

'No. It was Miss Simms I needed to see.' I smiled. 'To do with insurance policies and so forth.'

'Then her sister is the one to see.'

I had a quick look at the address. Right on the other side of the town.

Sighing, I was glad of the warm sunshine and told myself that I would enjoy bicycling across the Meadows and down Lothian road.

Enjoy, was not quite the word I would have used, endured was more appropriate. By the time I had negotiated the Saturday afternoon traffic and had been hooted at by numerous carriages with impatient occupants heading for a local football match, I had decided that I was not and never would be the world's most expert bicyclist. I had a tendency to get my wheels caught up in the tramlines.

Eventually I arrived at the door of a neat terrace house near Haymarket and rang the bell.

There was no reply. I was feeling cross and tired with all my exertions and there was no welcome sight of a tearoom where I might get some refreshment before making my homeward journey.

A young woman pushing a perambulator had arrived at the house next door. She smiled at me politely as I shrugged and said, 'Not at home, I fear?'

'Bertha goes to choir practice on a Saturday. She sings in the local church. Did she not tell you?'

Murmuring something non-committal, I thanked her and wearily made my way through the traffic to the peace and quiet of Solomon's Tower.

I made some tea, and while the kettle was boiling, had a bite to eat and recorded the visits in my case logbook. Then I remembered I hadn't put my bicycle away. I was wheeling it into the barn when I saw Nancy hurrying up the road, heading from the direction of Newington Station and carrying several parcels.

She was somewhat breathless as she indicated them. 'I had to go into Edinburgh and collect some clothes for the children.' Seizing my arm, she gasped, 'I had to see you so I got off the train. The chance you might be at home—'

'Come inside,' I interrupted.

She regarded the bicycle anxiously. 'I'm so glad I caught you, Rose. Are you in a desperate hurry?'

'Not at all. I've been out. I'm just back.'

She followed me into the Tower. The tea was still hot and I put some scones on a plate. Eating one gratefully, she watched me and at last she said, 'Rose, I just had to see you. Desmond's wife has left him. He told me at our rehearsal last night. He's absolutely devastated.'

Considering Desmond and his wife's cat-and-dog existence as related to Nancy, I suspected this was an exaggeration and that he might be secretly relieved at this solution.

'When did this happen?'

'A few days ago.'

'And he didn't tell you until yesterday?'

She spread her hands wide. 'The poor fellow didn't know she had run away. She told him she was going to visit her sister in Leith, but when he went to collect her last night, he found Nellie packing a bag. She was very surprised to see him, since Nora had never been to see her, nor was she expecting a visit.'

She sighed. 'What really worried him was that Nellie said Nora knew she wouldn't be at home, that she was going to Aberdeen for a friend's wedding. What was more, she couldn't have forgotten, since they had talked of nothing else for weeks. She had even borrowed one of Nora's hats.'

'So where had she gone?' I asked, although the pattern emerging was beginning to sound a little familiar and I would have placed a bet that a letter from Nora telling him that she had met another man would be the next thing Desmond would hear. Nancy said, 'He hasn't the slightest idea where she is. He's worried sick. He said he'd give her until this weekend and if she didn't come back, then he'd notify the police.'

And add another name to Jack's list, I thought grimly.

She paused and looked at me. 'When he asked if I could do anything to help, I said I knew someone who could.'

I stared at her.

'Yes, Rose. I knew you were the very person. So I told him I had a friend who was good at tracking down missing persons, that she did it professionally.' She chuckled proudly. 'That put him in a real state. He thought I was advising a spirit medium. And I had to tell him it was the living you were in contact with, not the dead. He said he'd pay anything you care to ask for. He just had to find Nora. Not that he wanted her back, but he had to be sure that she was safe and well and that nothing had happened to her.'

I asked the question I had been dying to put to her. 'Is there someone else?'

She blushed. 'You know how he feels about me, Rose—'

'I don't mean you, Nancy. I mean, does he have any reason to believe that the breakdown of their marriage might have been because Nora had met someone?'

Nancy shook her head, saying firmly, 'Never. He was quite sure about that.'

I was thinking he wouldn't be the first husband to live in a fool's paradise and believe that his wife would never look at another man, when she said, 'Will you take it on? Please, Rose, say yes. He's in a very bad way. And with *Pirates* he needs all his energy and concentration. It is such a demanding role.' She took my hand. 'Please, Rose. As a favour to me,' she added desperately.

When I said yes – with considerable reluctance, I had to admit – Nancy laughed. 'I was so sure you would agree that I said I'd bring you down to meet him after the rehearsal tomorrow evening.'

My eyebrows rose a little at that. If this got around, the Sunday Observance Society would be out in force.

Nancy saw my expression.

'Some of the cast object to working on a Sunday, but then with our less fortunate folk (as most of them are) working all week, Sunday's their only free day for rehearsal. You don't mind, do you, Rose?'

When I said I didn't, she added anxiously, 'You will be understanding, won't you, please? He's such a dear friend.'

I promised understanding and Nancy's sigh was that of a job well done. Outside it would soon be dark, the hill radiant in the last rays of the setting sun.

'I must be getting back,' she said.

'There's a short cut from my back garden across the lower reaches of the hill, which probably leads directly into a lane at the back of Carthew House. Shall we try it?'

As we set off and I insisted on carrying some of her parcels, I told her how I on one walk had observed the roof of the old mansion amid vast gardens. It was built at the time of the Jacobite Rising, and Prince Charles Edward Stuart – Bonnie Prince Charlie to those who loved and loyally followed him – had stayed there before the Battle of Prestonpans.

Nancy was fascinated by this piece of romance. As we walked Thane loped down the hill to join us. Nancy was one of his favourite humans, one he could trust now that she had almost given up offering useful suggestions as to where he lived and was beginning to accept him with a certain amount of resignation as 'Rose's dog'.

As we climbed, we were rewarded by fine views of the East Lothian coastline stretching towards Musselburgh and the Firth of Forth with its tiny islands like humpbacked whales.

Thane raced ahead. Nancy was delighted with this new discovery of a short cut to the Tower. 'It will only take ten minutes and means that I'll be able to use it instead of the long way round. How clever of you, Rose, you must know this area very well.'

'I have had a lot of time to explore with Thane, and many years ago Pappa and Emily and I must have walked every inch of Arthur's Seat,' I added wistfully as, to tell truth, I recalled only one happy occasion when we had a whole day's family picnic.

At last we glimpsed the imposing mansion far below us, much modified by the passing decades; pepperpot turrets and gardens were visible through the trees, still clad in the golden glory of autumn.

'I'm so lucky,' Nancy sighed. 'A lovely house and such lovely people. Thanks to the short cut, I'll be in time to give Mrs Laing a hand with their supper. She does appreciate that.' And with a shake of her head, 'I do agree with her, it would be an improvement if they employed a table maid, at least. With all their money, surely they could afford that.'

As parting drew near, Nancy was back with her favourite topic. Jack. Where was he?

I told her that he had gone to visit his parents and left it at that. I wasn't prepared to turn the knife. I waved her goodbye and walked slowly homeward to the Tower.

Let Nancy keep her dreams. I wasn't going to be the one to destroy them, for Jack it seemed had been replaced. Momentarily he had taken second place in importance in her life.

Chapter Eight

Next morning, before the bells started ringing, I decided to go to church. Taking out my map, I knew that I must use my bicycle, although such activities were much frowned upon on the sabbath. But that prospect did not deter me. By the nature of my present life and chosen profession, I was long past obeying conventions.

Regretting I had not asked Miss Simms' neighbour which church she attended, I dismissed those unlikely to have females in the choir. I had noticed that the parish Church of Scotland was down the road from where she lived so I would chance that being where Bertha Simms sang in the choir.

I wasn't a churchgoer but that did not deter me either as I parked my bicycle in the kirkyard and hurried in during the first hymn. The church was only ten years old. I liked the feeling of tranquillity and took the opportunity to pray for Danny that he was still alive and would be brought safe home to me. Had it been a Catholic church then I would have lit a candle for him.

From my pew near the choir I observed that five of the songsters were women and decided that Mabel Simms' sister was most likely one of the two youngest. The service ended, and shaking hands with the minister outside the church, I asked where I could find Miss Simms.

He pointed me in the right direction and I approached the one that I had marked down as most likely.

She smiled. 'No, that's Bertha over there.'

Bertha was in animated conversation with a young couple. Tall and slim, in her early twenties, when she moved away towards the path through the kirkyard I saw that she was lame with one leg shorter than the other.

I caught up with her outside the gate and introduced myself

by saying I had just visited St Ann's and had been told that Mabel had left. I didn't want to tell a direct lie. Perhaps the chastening effect of having just emerged from church brought a reluctance to immediately break one of the Ten Commandments – subject of the morning sermon – so I decided to remain as vague as possible.

Bertha nodded sadly. She accepted my statement without question, much to my relief. 'I'm sorry, I don't know where Mabel is.' She regarded me curiously. 'I haven't seen you in church before. Are you new to this area?'

When I told her that I lived in Newington, she looked puzzled but hid her curiosity under a bright smile.

'That is a long way to come. Look, I live just across the road – might I offer you a cup of tea and some refreshment before you go all that way back again.'

I indicated the bicycle by the wall.

'How clever of you. I would love to have one of those,' she added wistfully and I could understand her reasons which doubtless included concealment of her lameness.

She repeated her invitation, which I accepted gratefully. Being invited into the house was an unexpected outcome, better than I had dared hope for.

The interior was neat and well-cared for, revealing something of the owner's character with pretty cushions and an embroidered tablecloth, and over all a refreshing smell of furniture polish. As Bertha bustled about the kitchen, I decided to gently confess the truth that I was in the business of tracking down missing persons.

Thankfully Bertha did not seem shocked in the least, merely nodding in agreement. 'Headmistress is a dear caring soul, she has been good to both of us knowing we had no parents, but she does get quite carried away at times.'

She hesitated, staring out of the window and then said, 'I

don't believe Mabel is in any sort of danger. You see, she is very independent, always has been, likes to take off on her own and not tell anyone.'

She shrugged, turned to me again. 'But as it is longer than usual this time, I suppose the school were right to get anxious.'

'She didn't come home before she left?'

'Oh, yes. But I was out unfortunately. I do some dressmaking for a lady near by. I saw that she had packed a bag but she hadn't left a message – which was odd. That was what concerned me.'

Pausing, she smiled wanly. 'We have had to get used to it. It is all part of her nature. She writes poetry, you know, and she needs to be alone. And it is difficult living in the school to get a moment to herself. Mabel is a free spirit…'

As I listened I thought this was strange behaviour even for a free spirit.

'We inherited this house from an old auntie who left a legacy to pay for our fees at St Ann's. It's a fair distance from the school, that's why Mabel lives in. I can't do very much because of my leg, but I take in sewing and Mabel's salary is a great help. We don't lack anything.'

The promised cup of tea had been extended to lunch and as we supped Bertha's excellent vegetable broth and ate our bread and cheese I sat facing the sideboard. There were several photographs of the two sisters but in childhood only. None had any resemblance to the dead woman.

Bertha followed my gaze and smiled when I said, 'You were pretty little girls. What does Mabel look like now?'

Giving the photograph a tender glance, she said, 'She is still fair, pretty wavy hair. But not like that thin little girl any longer. She's rather plump now although, because she's tall, she carries it well.'

I felt a sudden sense of relief. The missing persons'

descriptions seemed to rule Mabel out as the woman I had found. But there was something else worrying me about that free spirit and I asked, 'Tell me, is Mabel in the best of health?'

The teacup clattered on to the saucer.

Bertha panicked. 'Why shouldn't she be? Why do you ask that?'

'It is merely a standard question when someone goes missing,' I replied.

'If I tell you, promise you won't breathe a word – will you?'

I promised and she continued, 'Ever since childhood, Mabel has taken fits – epilepsy. They were bad when she was young but for years now they have been very rare. So rare in fact that we tend to forget all about them. Headmistress knows, of course, but she loves Mabel and is very sympathetic, knows how to deal wiith any attacks. Naturally, she is very discreet. Wouldn't do for any of her girls to see her.' She sighed. 'Two years now, since the last one. We all hoped she had outgrown it.'

I took my departure, promising to keep on with my investigation and let her know any results immediately. If only Mabel had been dark and thin and slight then someone who was subject to epileptic fits could well have accounted for the 'dead' woman I had found and for Jack's explanation regarding her subsequent disappearance.

The visit had been disappointing in its results but I was glad that the tragedy I had encountered had not overtaken Bertha Simms and her missing sister.

Nancy arrived at six thirty, having already given the children their supper and prepared them for bed.

'I left them in their nightgowns,' she added with a happy sigh, 'sitting up in bed like a couple of wee angels waiting for their aunt and uncle to come and read them a story.' She sighed and repeated once again, 'I am so lucky. I must be one of the few nannies in Newington, in Edinburgh even – or anywhere else in the whole country for that matter – to be free of duties from early evening until next morning.'

I suspected that if Lady Carthew returned to health and was able to accept social invitations, such as visits to the theatre and supper with friends, or failing that, if she was removed by some more permanent and melancholy event before Gerald Carthew's return, then Nancy's lifestyle would also be transformed to one considerably lacking such enviable freedom.

As we walked towards the theatre, the subject immediately turned to Desmond. Nancy was plainly most anxious that I should like Desmond.

Our timing was very good. We had just entered by the stage door to the last strains of 'A policeman's life is not a happy one'.

'That's Desmond singing,' she said proudly.

I had to agree that he had a most agreeable voice, well above the amateur range. He didn't see us at first, in earnest conversation with a younger man, also one of the cast in constable's uniform.

We hovered near but failed to attract his attention.

Nancy sighed. 'We'll wait in here, Rose.' She led the way into a side room temporarily empty but used for refreshment, as evidenced by the imposing presence of a huge tea urn and a large plate of highly suspect rock-cakes.

'I'll tell Desmond and then I'll leave you together. I'm sure he'll want to talk to you alone and I have to see the wardrobe girl about alterations to my costume.'

When Desmond walked in through the door in costume, straight off stage, it gave me a considerable jolt. At first glance he looked exactly like PC Smith; cape, helmet, moustache and all.

His smiling greeting, his handshake, hardly registered as I was shocked into realisation that I now had the explanation of my encounter with the bogus PC Smith. And the reason for the cabbie's non-appearance.

The 'constable' had murdered him too.

My thoughts were so confused and terrifying that I had great difficulty in acknowledging Desmond's polite platitudes. As he smiled engagingly, awaiting my answer to some point he had just made, I struggled to regain my composure and bleat out a response which I hoped was adequate.

I must have succeeded in being convincing since he nodded enthusiastically. Desperately I tried to concentrate.

He had stagey good looks and was not at all the type of man I would ever find irresistible, but I could well imagine the young women in the chorus swooning over him, hanging upon his every smile.

My mind still with 'PC Smith', I asked him about uniforms. Had any gone missing?

He was clearly thrown by this sudden interruption and change of subject. Staring at me, he said he hadn't the foggiest idea. 'They aren't under lock and key, of course, if that's what you mean. So I suppose it could happen,' he added with a puzzled frown.

Aha, that was significant. Very, I thought. Only half listening to his concern about the missing Nora – he was eager and more than willing to spread their whole dreary domestic life in its entirety before me – I soon gathered that theirs was not a happy marriage and, as Nancy had reported, had not been so for a long time. Nora's 'wee holiday' with her sister was her idea to ease the strain.

He wished he could get a divorce, but Nora was a Roman Catholic, so both their lives were to be ruined by staying together, he groaned.

I took all the details, was promised a photograph, sister Nellie's address and so forth.

Preparing to leave, he stood up, regarded me solemnly and said, 'There is one thing more you might as well know, Mrs McQuinn. If I were free I would ask your friend Nancy to be my wife. I love her,' he added simply.

Unwillingly impressed by his apparent sincerity and honesty, I still had a lot to mull over.

Nancy came back into the room and shyly touched his arm.

As I left, my thoughts returned again and again to the bogus constable and the discovery I had made. The convenience of police uniforms in the unlocked costume cupboard.

By the time I reached the road to the Tower I had some theories which I was bending into shape. Perhaps PC Smith had not murdered the cabbie. One murder victim is more than enough for the amateur killer to deal with. More likely he had hired a driverless carriage, lured the woman to St Anthony's Chapel on some pretext or another, or even kllled her first and then put her body in the carriage.

I dismounted and stared at the scene above me. A stiffish climb to the ruined chapel, but not for a strong young man. A man like the one I had just been talking to. I remembered his athletic build, his broad strong shoulders.

And now for the first time, I realised my own peril that night in discovering his victim before he had finally quit the scene.

I had spoken to him but he could have disguised his voice. I might know his face again, despite it being partly concealed by the police helmet of course, and that fake moustache.

But I was a witness, I knew enough to identify him. And had it not been for Thane, I would doubtless have met a similar fate that night!

I remembered Nancy saying that when she had described me to him as someone who could help, she had been amused since his first thought was that I was a spirit medium.

He had panicked. Why?

Was it a guilty conscience – because he already knew that Nora was dead?

Had I found the killer? Was Desmond Marks, an accomplished actor, made up as a constable with a false moustache? He could have deceived his victim about the uniform too, by saying he had just left a rehearsal and hadn't had time to change.

I thought of my closed avenues of investigation. Of the two most probable missing women on Jack's list, one very much alive and the other whose description as 'plump' did not fit either.

Unlike the dead woman.

I had been off on the wrong track.

Now a new and dangerous path presented itself: the strong possibility that the woman I had found was in fact Desmond's missing wife Nora.

Chapter Nine

I did not sleep much that night, going over the details of that very illuminating visit to the *Pirates of Penzance* rehearsal, the accessibility of constables' uniforms and the significance of Desmond Marks' missing wife.

Early next morning I had a visit from Nancy. I was somewhat surprised to see her before breakfast, and she was not alone. She was accompanied by the Carthew children, Torquil and Tessa.

'I brought them by your short cut, Rose. They were so thrilled at climbing the hill, weren't you, children?'

Shy nods were the replies as she continued, 'Isn't it marvellous? Now that we know the way, we'll be able to come often.'

I said, 'Oh yes,' hoping I sounded as if I shared her enthusiasm and that I might not have reason to regret giving her such easy access to the Tower.

She took me aside and whispered, 'I have to talk to you. about last night – Desmond, you know,' she added in a sepulchral whisper, as if I might have forgotten that little drama.

The children were holding hands, standing close together, round-eyed, two delightful curly-haired angels from a storybook picture, staring in amazement at tapestried stone walls as if they had found themselves in a setting out of Grimms' Fairy Tales.

Nancy regarded them fondly. 'Now, children, you sit down at Mrs McQuinn's table here with your picture books. I brought them specially,' she said removing them from her basket. 'Tessa, you show Torquil how to do letters. You're already so good at that.'

The children did as they were bid, looking round shyly for

my approval, which turned to polite thanks when I produced a couple of biscuits.

As soon as they were settled, Nancy motioned me towards the window. 'I do hope we aren't intruding, but I am so concerned about Nora's disappearance. I simply couldn't wait until this evening, not another minute! I felt I'd never get through the day – and then I had the perfect excuse to see you – taking the children out on a new walk they had never done before…'

Pausing for breath, she regarded me intently. 'Well, did you get all the details from Desmond?'

When I said yes, he'd been very helpful, she sighed. 'I'm dying to know what you think of him. Isn't he nice?'

I said yes again, hoping I sounded enthusiastic enough. She seemed pleased and the thought occurred to me that she was relieved that I had not fallen madly in love with him.

'I enjoyed his singing very much. You were right about his voice. The police constables' uniforms look very authentic.' I paused and added, 'Do any of the costumes ever disappear?'

She frowned. 'I don't think so. Why do you ask?'

I attempted a hearty laugh that fell flat. 'As a crime investigator I immediately realised how a bogus policeman could have a jolly time fooling the public.'

'What a dreadful idea!' Nancy sounded shocked. 'I'm sure none of our people would ever think of such a thing.'

'When I mentioned it to Mr Marks—'

'Desmond, please, Rose.'

'He told me they weren't kept under lock and key. And I thought, how convenient. Anyone associated with the Opera Society could borrow one – say, for a fancy dress party – and replace it without its absence ever being noticed.'

My rather lame statement had shocked Nancy who regarded me wide-eyed. 'But that would be against the law,

Rose. surely you don't approve of such behaviour.'

I realised I was getting myself into a tight corner. I had not told her about the body at St Anthony's Chapel and I certainly wasn't prepared to go into that now – or ever. If I did, I could be sure that Nancy would provide the simple explanation, possibly the one Jack was so keen on having me accept.

'So none of the costumes ever disappear?'

'Stolen, you mean,' she laughed. 'Never, that I have ever heard. Why should anyone want to steal them?'

I tried another tack. 'Do any of the cast ever take them home for cleaning or alterations?'

'Sometimes wives or sisters are willing to help out. I do myself from time to time. The cast are all shapes and sizes and we can't afford to keep buying new costumes.'

I thought about that. 'Like Desmond. He's very tall and broad. I suppose he has problems getting a uniform to fit him.'

She smiled tenderly. 'He does indeed.'

'I don't suppose his wife was very willing with the sewing machine either.'

And then I had a piece of luck that almost sealed up my case against Desmond.

Nancy said, 'Oh, she often helps out. She's an excellent seamstress, that was her training and the company paid her a small fee for her services. Before her marriage she worked as mantle maker with one of the big Edinburgh shops – Jenners, I think it was.'

I had a fleeting memory of the dead woman's hands. Most certainly they would have fitted such a profession.

'Desmond's rather clumsy, such a big man,' she added tenderly, 'his cape got badly torn on a nail. There were doubts whether it could be repaired, but he said that Nora could work wonders with needle and thread—'

'When was that?'

She frowned. 'About a week ago.' She seemed surprised at my interest in what was a very humdrum event. 'Desmond brought it back; luckily she had mended it before she went to Leith.'

'Before she disappeared?'

'I expect so.' She laughed. 'She would hardly have wanted to take it with her.' Pausing she gave me a puzzled look. 'I don't see what a costume repair could have to do with Nora's disappearance. Or do you think that was what they quarrelled about and why she packed her bag and left?'

Without waiting for a reply, which I would have found extremely difficult, she added loyally, 'I mean, isn't it often the little things that spark off rows between husbands and wives? My parents were like that,' she added ruefully. 'Always bickering about nothing.'

'Danny and I didn't bicker,' I said.

'But you were lucky always to be so happy.'

'We were grateful to be alive to survive each day in the kind of hardships we faced in Arizona,' I said, mentally adding another clue to the case against Desmond Marks, wife-murderer elect.

In my mind a picture was forming. A borrowed uniform cape, easy to carry away, the helmet too, a little powder on his already luxuriant moustache…

I remembered also the significance of those boots as PC Smith raced ahead, boots too soft and elegant to be those issued with a constable's uniform. Now I tried to bring to mind anything else about Desmond's feet when he walked off stage. I wished I had taken more notice.

'Have you ever met Nora?' I asked. 'What was she like?'

Nancy shrugged. 'We only met a couple of times when she came to discuss costumes. Desmond normally took them home to her.'

And with a blush, 'That was before – before he confided in me. I didn't take much notice of her to be honest. She was – well, mousey. I don't want to sound unkind but she was not the kind of woman any of us could imagine a man like Desmond finding attractive.'

'I have a theory about that, Nancy. Have you ever noticed how handsome males take plain mates in the animal world? And I've observed it is often the same with humans – what I call the "Peacock Syndrone". It applies particularly to men who are handsome and vain.'

Nancy frowned impatiently at this suggestion applied to her nice kind Desmond. 'You asked—'

We were interrupted by the children. Bored with inactivity, they had begun leaping up and down off the chairs, playing horses. Torquil had climbed on to the back of the sofa and was stranded there.

'Children, children! Behave – at once!' And as silence descended once more, Nancy said, 'You asked me what Nora looked like. No shape, thin, straight straggly hair, sallow complexion – and spectacles.'

She thought about that. 'She did not even have a striking personality to make up for her lack of good looks. Nothing about her was in the least memorable…'

All of which fitted ominously with the appearance of the murdered woman, I thought in dismay.

Nancy left soon after to return to Carthew House, gathering up her small charges, who seemed eager to stay, by promising them – and me – that they would come back again very soon.

I walked as far as the lane with her and as they waved goodbye, Thane appeared over the hill and joined me on the way back to the Tower. He liked Nancy but apparently had canine reservations about small children.

He followed me into the kitchen and stretched out in front of the fire. I talked to him as I always did, trying out my theories, not that I expected answers but encouraged since he managed to look intelligent and interested, sighing occasionally, as if he sympathised and understood every word.

I had made soup from a ham bone which he received delightedly and I settled down, logbook in hand, to record these latest events in my investigation.

This excellent habit, never to rely solely on memory, had been instilled in me by observing Pappa who noted down all his cases day by day. Now as a professional investigator I realised its importance, an invaluable aid, especially as Pappa had also maintained that keeping a logbook often became a means of helping him solve clues. He was a great believer in the action of writing bringing significant facts previously overlooked to the forefront of his mind.

Absorbed in my task, I reluctantly went to answer a tap on the front door.

Desmond Marks was on the doorstep, hat in hand.

Chapter Ten

Surprised at this mid-morning visitor, since I presumed insurance men like Desmond Marks would be going about their business, I invited him into the kitchen.

Thane immediately lumbered up from his place by the fire to inspect this stranger in his realm, whereupon Desmond staggered back in alarm as the huge deerhound lurched in his direction.

'Thane! Come here! He really is harmless,' I said apologetically.

Desmond had gone quite white. He was trembling, arousing a darker more sinister recollection of a bogus constable similarly affected on the road to St Anthony's Chapel.

Aware of my concern as I seized Thane, he said, 'Sorry, I'm sure you're right but I dislike large dogs. I had some nasty childhood experiences when we lived in the country.'

At this poor excuse Thane gave me a despairing look and subsided once more beside my chair, while Desmond continued to stare at him apprehensively.

I said, 'I'll put him outside if you wish—'

'No, please don't. I'll take your word for his good nature,' he added with a wan smile.

I invited him to take a seat at the table, which he did as far away from Thane as possible. Trying to ignore the deerhound's presence, he said, 'You were so kind at rehearsal, offering to try to find Nora for me.'

He sighed deeply. 'I really am exceedingly worried about her. I hardly sleep at night going over where she might be, what might have happened to her. My work is suffering and that is why I am here.'

He waited politely. When sympathy wasn't forthcoming, he

continued, 'I told my employer I was out on a claim – he doesn't know about Nora. I am keeping that to myself at present. I hate telling lies, you know.' He paused to give me an engaging smile. 'But this is so important, the sooner you can get started to look for her, the better.'

I listened politely, rather coldly deciding that his eagerness to have my assistance, to get me on his side, as it were, was also calculated to be proof of his innocence. I wasn't taken in, fully aware that it is not unknown for murderers to behave in such a way to throw the police off the scent. In many cases this often includes a ghoulish return to the scene of the crime.

From his pocket Desmond took out a photograph and slid it across the table. 'You will need this. Taken at our wedding, ten years ago,' he added with a sigh, a sad smile. 'I hope most earnestly it helps in your investigation. But I would like it back. It is rather precious.'

Promising to give it my best possible care and responsibility, I studied the piece of card carefully, politely taking the interest expected of me.

A conventional studio sepia photograph beloved by bride and groom and their relaives, dedicated to a lifetime on the sideboard. A handsome plush armchair and potted plant, the inevitable furnishings. Nora was seated with her skirts elegantly spread, richly corseted, wearing a tiny flower-bedecked hat and veil. Her head was coyly inclined towards Desmond who stood alongside, one hand on her shoulder denoting present hopes and future ownership, proud but unsmiling.

Quite frankly the photograph told me nothing, except that with the passing of a decade, a plain woman like Nora could have also been the dead woman.

'Have you any ideas how I should proceed, Mr Marks?'

'Please call me Desmond.' The smile again, followed by a

forlorn shrug. 'Anything – anything you can think of that will help you find her,' he added desperately.

I waited for suggestions. 'Where would you like me to start?'

He frowned, biting at the moustache. 'I thought by visiting her sister Nellie in Leith, if that isn't too much trouble.'

I gestured trouble aside and he went on, 'As I told you, she was about to leave that day when I called to collect Nora. Our meeting was very brief. She did not encourage me to talk to her about Nora or even invite me in. Her excuse was that she had a train to catch. But for all I knew she might have been lying and Nora listening, sitting by her fireside.'

Pausing, he let that sink in. 'Quite frankly, as you will find out immediately you speak to her, Mrs McQuinn, she doesn't hold me in any high regard. I'm afraid if Nora confided secret plans in her sister, as I strongly suspect, then she would be the last person to reveal them to me.'

He regarded me hopefully. 'But if she knew that you were investigating – officially – then she would feel obliged to tell you anything she knew. Especially if she felt there was a possibility that I might be shown up as the guilty party,' he added ruefully.

'Guilty? In what way?' I asked carefully.

He shrugged. 'Oh, you know, the usual thing, a cruel unfaithful husband. And that would please Nellie. She'd like that very much, having me exposed as a bounder,' he added heatedly. 'All her warnings to Nora not to marry me, that I wasn't good enough for her, brought home to roost.'

He laughed bitterly and I decided not only was he a good singer but a good actor too.

I thought for a moment. 'Mr Marks,' and ignoring the invitation to first names, 'I have to ask you this. It might be painful but it is essential that you give me a truthful answer.

You realise that I must be in full possession of all the facts before I begin the case. It will also save a lot of time – and money,' I added, the latter not yet having been discused.

'Money is no object, Mrs McQuinn. I don't care how much it costs, I have to know the truth. All my plans for the future depend on it.'

I presumed those plans included Nancy as he added, 'Please go ahead. I am in your hands. I am sure you must realise that I am absolutely desperate, so ask what you will and I will do my best to provide the answer.'

Choosing my words, I said, 'Can you think of any possible reason, of any occurrence during the last few days or weeks, one significant conversation or action, which might suggest why your wife has left you?'

He sighed, shook his head and was silent for a few moments apparently thinking deeply before replying. 'She has often hinted in the past when we had sharp words, not to expect to find her when I returned from work. That she was ready to pack a bag and leave me.'

He shrugged. 'I didn't take it all that seriously, angry wives are liable to utter such threats in the heat of the moment. And there were plenty of moments, I assure you. Nora had a wicked temper and would flare up at the least opposition to any of her wishes. But to be practical, where would she go?'

He spread his hands wide. 'There were few options open to her. She has no family apart from her elder sister, no income of her own. Nothing to support her except a husband – myself.'

'Did she have any employment before you were married?' I asked although Nancy had already provided the answer.

'She worked as a dressmaker, poorly paid, long hours. When we married she had no more than fifty pounds which she had saved over the years. She was so proud of what seemed like a vast fortune. But it disappeared long ago on furnishing our first house.'

'You think she might have had some such situation in mind again that she wished to conceal from you. Some means of making a living and regaining her independence.'

He looked at me in bewilderment. Then he laughed. 'I'm sure that idea never entered her mind, Mrs McQuinn. Whatever our disagreements, although I say so myself, I have provided her with a very nice home. She would hardly sacrifice our standard of living to return to her dreary pre-marriage existence. I can assure you, nothing is lacking in our home in the way of comfort.'

Except a loving husband, I thought as I said. 'So you do not regard taking employment as a possibility and you think that her sister may know her present whereabaouts and be keeping it secret. You suggested that she might have been concealing her when you called.'

He nodded grimly. 'Those were my suspicions – my instincts – exactly.'

'So there is a possibility that she might still be there, regarding her sister's home as a refuge.'

He shook his head. 'No. That is quite impossible,' he said briefly. 'Such would have been only a very temporary arrangement. It is a tiny house, not at all what Nora is accustomed to. There are very few luxuries. Nellie's husband Ben is a dock labourer. A rough sort of chap, not like us, if you know what I mean.' He paused, inviting comment. There was none.

'He drinks a lot and I can't see him willingly taking in another mouth to feed now their two girls are married and away. He was thankful to be rid of them, according to Nora. No, Ben would be the last person to take Nora to live with them. I cannot imagine that he cares in the least what happens to her nor feels the slightest obligation for her welfare.'

I was silent, aware that I'd learn a lot about Desmond from a talk with Nellie's husband.

As he was watching me making notes, I read over the salient points and said, 'There is one more question I must ask you, Mr Marks, perhaps one that hasn't occurred to you yet.'

'And what is that?'

'Have you any reason to suspect that your wife was being unfaithful, that there was perhaps – another man – in her life?'

In reply Desmond put both hands on his knees, slapped them soundly and, throwing back his head, roared with laughter. It shocked me, such merriment seemed inappropriate and somehow quite indecent.

Shaking his head, gasping for breath, he leaned forward confidentially. 'Mrs McQuinn, that is the one thing I can assure you is not, and never has been in question. Nora might have had her reasons to feel angry with me—' He cocked a flirtatious eyebrow at me. 'My behaviour has not always been out of the top drawer, if you get my meaning...'

I got his meaning quite clearly and it was at that moment that I decided I neither liked nor trusted him.

He was just too handsome, not that I would dislike a man for his good looks. Danny McQuinn was handsome but in a completely different way. Danny had the born in the bone, generations-old breeding of the Celtic race, back to the ancient tribal kings of Ireland. Far from the superficial glossy stage-managed exterior of the man sitting in my kitchen, boastful and bragging, so sure of himself, certain in his belief that no woman could resist him.

And that was further confirmed when he added, 'I could swear on a stack of bibles that my wife never so much as looked at another man.'

There seemed little more to be said beyond advising him to notify the police. This, I told him, was the usual procedure when someone has been missing for several days and concern is experienced about their whereabouts.

He agreed eagerly. 'I have already done so. I called in at the Central Office on my way here.'

His behaviour was keen enough to convince me that if he had killed Nora, then he had hidden her body very cleverly.

I thought about that. There were hundreds of caves and fissures on the vast expanse of Arthur's Seat large enough to conceal a body. And many within easy access of the ruined chapel, no great burden for a big, strong man like Desmond to transport.

And a very good reason I hadn't thought of before, for her being murdered there.

As he prepared to leave I decided he was probably telling the truth in one respect at least: that Nora had never looked at another man, although soon disillusioned by her handsome husband, whose goodness was all in the wrapping, as the saying goes.

Seeing him to the door, I said I would take on the case by visiting Nellie in the first instance.

He had her address all ready on a slip of paper but I suspected Desmond knew even then that it would be a waste of time. He was totally in command of the situation, merely adding to proof of his innocence, by sending me off on a wild goose chase.

I was going to need a lot more than what I would hear of Desmond's character from a sister-in-law who disliked and despised him. Much of what I expected to hear would be written off as useless, biased and circumstantial evidence that Desmond Marks might have murdered his wife.

Thane went with us to the door, his closeness to Desmond's

heels eyed with trembling uncertainty despite my reassurances. Desmond's exit was very badly timed.

Jack was walking up the garden path. Almost the very last person I expected or wanted to see at that moment.

Chapter Eleven

I introduced Desmond to Jack. As they shook hands I added, 'Mr Marks is a friend of Nancy's from the Opera Society.'

Jack inclined his head politely, looked Desmond over with that shrewd all-encompassing policeman's regard. I felt that he was not impressed by what he saw, and that the mention of Nancy did not endear him to Marks either.

As Thane lunged forward to give Jack the usual tail-wagging boisterous welcome, goodbyes were said, hastier than strictly polite on Desmond's part.

Jack followed me into the kitchen.

'And what was all that about?' he demanded genially.

'Just another client,' I said, sounding casual and determined to be mysterious.

Jack looked at me. 'I thought it was just distressed ladies that interested you.'

I smiled enigmatically. 'A good-looking man makes a pleasant change.'

With every intention of leaving the matter there but hoping that he might press for more details – be a mite jealous, for heaven's sake – I was disappointed when he seemed to have lost interest. With a somewhat perfunctory kiss he deposited a large brown paper parcel on the table.

'A present for you. From Ma.'

I unwrapped, carefully cradled in layers of newspaper, two pots of home-made jam, raspberry and strawberry.

'From our garden,' said Jack proudly.

Unearthing an apple tart on a plate and a large meat pie, I was touched by this lavish gift. 'How very kind of her, Jack.'

'Brought them all the way from Peebles. She was really disappointed when you couldn't manage the wedding,' he added reproachfully. 'They'd both been looking forward to meeting you.'

Suitably contrite but still firm in resolve not to be blackmailed, I promised a letter of thanks.

As I tucked the parcel's contents on to my usually forlorn pantry shelves, Jack was watching me. 'Ma's cooking is out of this world. Just wait till you taste it,' he added knowing my weakness for a good meal.

'A piece of pie for you, perhaps?'

'Not after that wedding feast – and a huge breakfast before I left. Honestly, I couldn't take another bite.'

And the way he was looking at me as I closed the cupboard door hinted that he had other things than food on his mind. He put his arms around me, stroked my hair and whispered, 'Well, what have you been doing while I was away? Enjoying yourself, I suppose.'

I shrugged. 'Seeing folks. Went to the rehearsal of *Pirates* with Nancy.'

'And…?'

'And what?'

'Aren't you going to tell me about your new client?'

'His wife is missing. He's just notified your people but he wants me to try to find her.'

'When did you meet him?'

'Yesterday. He looked in after their rehearsal.'

'On a Sunday. It must be urgent!'

'What difference does the day make? Do the police stay in bed all day on Sunday or go to church and just let criminals get on with it?'

But Jack wasn't going to let the subject rest there. His unwillingness to forgo facts revealed all the dexterity of a highly trained terrier with a particularly succulent bone.

In this case, the bone was called Rose McQuinn. I sighed.

He would have to know the whole story sooner or later, so I told him all that had happened since the *Pirates* rehearsal with Nancy. About the coincidence of the constables' costumes and Nora's disappearance.

At the end I made the mistake of adding, 'I think you're well ahead of me now, Jack. You will undoubtedly have already worked out the answer to this particular mystery.'

He stared at me, unable to resist the challenge. 'Will I now?' he asked cautiously.

'The facts all add up to the woman I found in St Anthony's Chapel.' I paused to give him a look of triumph. 'It's so obvious. I am almost certain that she is Marks' missing wife.'

From all the clues I had given, I expected him to applaud, to agree enthusiastically and offer congratulations. Instead, he merely froze and said dismissively. 'Don't be ridiculous, Rose. where do you get such ideas from?'

It was my turn to stare at him indignantly. 'What do you mean – such ideas?

'I mean, pure coincidence and circumstantial evidence, that's what.' And with a deep sigh. 'For heaven's sake, Rose, let's face facts... There never was a body—'

So we were back there again! 'Calling me a liar, are you?' I interrupted coldly.

'No, I'm just advising you not to be carried away by a natural mistake.'

'A natural mistake – is that what you call a dead body'

'Stop it!' Jack thumped his fist on the table. 'Stop it – and listen to me. We went back together. There was no body, dead or alive. I've told you what happened. The woman fell and fainted, got up and walked back down the hill.'

'All in my over-eager imagination, is that it?' I demanded coldly.

'Not quite. That's more than my life's worth.' He grinned.

'Come on, Rose, let's be realistic. Let's say that this new lady investigator business has gone to your head – just a little. Admit it, you had one rather spectacular success and now you're so keen for clients, so anxious to be a successful detective, just like your father, that you are in serious danger of inventing crimes to solve.'

That was it. That was all I could take. I flounced from the table, called him a lot of names. Very crude and unladylike they came forth from my lips, giving him the full benefit of my low-class life in America and worthy of the saloon girls in Arizona.

And I had the last word, the trump card I'd saved. 'Incidentally, Thane didn't like Mr Marks either. And I trust his instincts.'

'Thane!' He laughed. 'May I remind you once again that Thane is a dog, for God's sake. What does he know about human crimes, about murderers? Give me a break, Rose—'

And I did just that. I showed him the door, banged it loudly after him. From the window with Thane at my side, I watched him walk away. I was certain of one thing though. I hadn't seen the last of Jack Macmerry.

Or so I thought. I told myself he would be back.

Meanwhile I had work to do. I had a crime to investigate and at first light tomorrow I'd be on my bicycle heading for Leith to interview Desmond Marks' sister-in-law.

I have to confess that I love the challenge of a new investigation. It brings me closer to Pappa and I understand why solving crime was his *raison d'etre*, that blood rush of excitement at what he called his first clue – the prospect of following that single thread through the labyrinth.

And it's in my blood too. I can't help what I inherited and Jack Macmerry can go hang! He can't talk me out of that!

What makes me mad and determined to make a success of this new career is the knowledge that had I been a lad instead of a lass, not one solitary eyebrow would have been raised. The very opposite in fact. As Chief Inspector Jeremy Faro's son, I would have been encouraged to follow in his illustrious footsteps by joining the Edinburgh City Police and climbing the same promotional ladder, aware from my earliest days that this was expected of me and that I must not disappoint him.

But I had the misfortune to be born a girl. I wondered if this strange heredity is what binds me just a little to Jack and to Auld Rory. Both have thrived on danger and danger doesn't bother me. It merely puts me on my mettle, part of the chase, part of my being too, since I've experienced more peril during those years in America's Wild West than most middle-class Edinburgh ladies ever had nightmares about, or could even imagine, let alone endure, in several lifetimes.

It is so unfair. Since my return home, I have seen more and more clearly that experience has set me apart from a conventional life. Settling down to the kind of marriage that Jack has in mind would be impossible.

Such were my angry thoughts as I rushed out to the barn and took out my bicycle, the signal for Thane to leave me and trot off back up the hill.

I rode down through Edinburgh on to Leith Walk. With some difficulty, at last in a dark gloomy and depressed area of warehouses and coal staithes, I found the address that Desmond had given me.

The streets were long and narrow, grey and faceless tenements five storeys high. Even the sea, visible beyond the harbour seemed like it was a very poor relation of the Firth of Forth visible from the top of Arthur's Seat.

Parking my bicycle in the lobby, I climbed several flights of stone stairs to the fifth floor, accompanied by smells of cooking and less pleasant smells of tomcats and urine.

Knocking on the door, I prepared myself for difficulties in persuading Mrs Nellie Edgley who I was, and why I was there. But she merely nodded and invited me into the kitchen, as grey and colourless as the building itself.

A well-scrubbed wooden table before the black-leaded kitchen range, a rag mat and two wooden chairs with cushions made from thinly diguised cast-off clothing. Bare walls apart from a sentimental print popular in my childhood – bringing back memories of the one in Sheridan Place – of a little girl hugging a big dog. All colours faded to indefinite grey-blues, it hung above a box-bed recess at the far end of the room, a cheery prospect for the occupants' awakening. In many Edinburgh houses of a like nature, parents and young children occupied the same bed in the one and only room.

A lace curtain at the window concealed the view across the cobbled street into a similar high window of a depressingly similar tenement whose privacy was also protected from prying eyes, should such curiosity be imaginable or desirable.

A few coals from a dismal fire threw out smoke and did little to warm the chilly room. It smelt strongly of poverty which has a definite smell uniquely its own. In the closes of Edinburgh's High Street and here in Leith, even Nellie Edgley's attempts at neatness and cleanliness were rendered futile.

The miasma was there, indestructible and forever, the lingering ghost of a battle constantly waged, and no amount of scrubbing and pails of hot water carried up five flights of stone stairs would ever disperse it.

Taking the uncomfortable chair opposite her and trying not to shiver at the intense cold, I could have written the story of her relationship with Nora Marks before she uttered her first words.

She was pathetically eager to share her reminiscences regarding her sister, while I searched the pale drawn face, heavily lined by years of toil and hardship, for any likeness to the dead woman I had found in St Anthony's Chapel.

One thing became immediately obvious, that Nellie's curiosity equalled that to be expected of an acquaintance, a neighbour, rather than the deep concern and anxiety for a sister's disappearance. Here was no indication of any great bond, so much became immediately evident.

'There's twelve years between us, ye ken,' she explained. 'I was taken from the school and working in one o' the big houses by the time she was born.'

Her lips tightened in bitterness as she said that on her rare days off she was not allowed to go out and enjoy herself. Oh no, she was expected to look after her small sister. And I could hear through her voice a whole lifetime's resentment for the spoilt and indulged late arrival.

Worse was to come. When their parents both died of consumption within a year, Nellie had another role ready made, that of mother to Nora. She wasn't sorry when at eighteen Nora went off and married Desmond Marks.

'Not that it made any difference, never made her think of all we'd done for her, bringing her up over the years. She put on airs, aye, that she did. Too good for the like of Ben and me. As for her man, well, he was a right snob. Thought himself gentry 'cos he didna work wi' his hands...'

As she paused for breath, I felt that this tirade of resentment might drown the reason for my visit, so I put in hastily, 'Was there anywhere else she might have gone? Friends her husband didn't know about?'

The answers were negative. Nellie hadn't the slightest idea and I realised that her sister was a stranger to her and had probably been so from the day she was born. And most important for my investigation, her sister would be the last person Nora would ever confide in.

That set me thinking. If she had her own reasons for leaving Desmond then she had taken a fair chance that he wouldn't get any information out of Nellie. And if he had killed her then his action of coming in search of her might be to divert suspicion by craftily suggesting innocent anxiety.

She followed me to the door and said, 'Mind how you go, lass. There's a march on at the docks.'

'What kind of march?'

She gave me a pitying look. 'A protest march, what else. The men want more money from the brewery, though God knows they'll only spend it on drink. My man Ben's one of them. He's gentle as a lamb and on his own wouldna say boo to a goose. He's let the bosses trample all over him all these years. Just yelled at me about it all.'

She sighed. 'Men are like that. On their own they're harmless, scared of the bosses. But get them in a mob, and someone to lead and tell them what to do, get their anger running high…' She shook her head. 'Then it's a different story. Once their blood is up, they can be right dangerous bullies. So watch your step, keep out of their way. And if you see them coming, look sharp.'

I assured her I had every intention of doing so and getting out of the area as soon as I could.

I had no reason or desire to linger and hoped that riding home through the fresh air would get rid of the smell of dirt and poverty that clung to my clothes and hair.

Chapter Twelve

I walked back down the stone stairs and took my bicycle from the lobby, feeling that the visit to Nellie Edgley had been a complete waste of time. From what she had told me, although it would be considered purely circumstantial in a court of law, it wouldn't take much persuasion for me to believe that Desmond had murdered his 'missing' wife.

The one thing I lacked was motive. Maybe he did want to marry Nancy, but that could have been a screen for my benefit and I wasn't prepared to believe that he was or ever had been passionately in love with anyone but his own image in the mirror.

As for Nancy, she was a nice girl, nice being the exact word to describe her. Pretty, respectable, but without any out-standing traits of personality, or seductive qualitites which made her more desirable to the average male than hundreds of other pretty, respectable Edinburgh lasses. Not by any stretch of imagination could I see her arousing sufficient lust in any man to make him decide to get rid of his wife. Especially Desmond who was in the insurance business and struck me as a cautious man who would not take chances unless he could bet they would turn out to be certainties.

And I still could not find a place in my theory to explain why he should trouble to disguise himself – for his wife's benefit – as a constable. Wouldn't she be immediately curious, not to say even suspicious, and ask why he had borrowed a uniform from the props of the Opera Society and powdered his moustache? The only rather lame explanation he could have offered was that he had come direct from rehearsal and hadn't time to change. Change, in this case, meaning only the removal of cape and helmet.

Supposing Nora had accepted that, what possible

explanation had he given to lure her out to Arthur's Seat, drag her unwillingly up the steep slope to the ruined chapel and then murder her by tightening the scarf about her neck?

Interrupted by a woman with a deerhound, presumably he had panicked and put her body into the hired carriage, intending to dispose of it. And that remained the vital question. Where was her body now?

'Let the punishment fit the crime' belonged to *Mikado* not *Pirates* and the killer's action didn't suit this particular crime.

It didn't strike me as feasible from what Nancy had told me of their life together that, if Desmond and Nora were on such bad terms, she would have gone with him willingly. All that dressing up would have raised questions in the mildest, most unimaginative of women – which by all accounts, Nora was not.

Why go to all that trouble? Childless, they lived alone, there were no relatives likely to interrupt at an inconvenient moment. So why not kill her in the privacy of their own kitchen or bedroom, the usual settings for most domestic murders?

Desmond might be a good actor, but he didn't strike me as capable of planning the perfect murder. I would have still opted for that fit of violence and the subsequent burying of her body under the floorboards or in the garden.

Such were my thoughts as I wheeled my bicycle out of the close. With a moment to look back and consider my surroundings, I realised that I had not been in Leith for more than ten years, my last visit during Pappa's dramatic 'Murder by Appointment' investigation, when I was abducted by Irish Fenians and held in a warehouse near the harbour.

As I rode down the road, I recognised the scene of my rescue, not far distant from where the Edgleys lived. I thought of Imogen Crowe who had intervened and protected me, how she had put her own life in jeopardy on my account.

And Pappa had rewarded her for saving his daughter by helping her escape back to Ireland instead of going to prison. An act of treason to the State he had served so loyally, thereby almost certainly hastening the end of his career in the Edinburgh City Police and any hopes he might have entertained of promotion to the rank of Chief Superintendent.

Standing opposite the warehouse, remembering those dark scary hours brought back the longing I had to see him again. Was he happy as he wandered about Europe with Imogen? He set foot in England, and visited London according to Vince, but never returned to Edinburgh. That hurt too.

The sky, heavy and dark with rainclouds, unleashed its burden. As I looked round for shelter, I saw that a number of people were rushing to and fro. But not for the same reason.

The sound of galloping horses, men shouting and police whistles, still out of sight round the corner but drawing steadily nearer. Suddenly the tramping mob erupted, just ahead, marching in my path, protestors with banners. Flourishing them angrily, they chanted slogans, demanding more work and more wages. Bread for their starving children.

A straggler hurtled towards me eyeing the bicycle and I decided it would be prudent to vanish from the scene as soon as possible.

Quickly riding out of sight of the protestors, I rode towards the shelter of a doorway. In my anxiety, my front wheel came into violent collision with the curb.

Then I realised I wasn't alone. A young man was also hiding, his face partly concealed by a muffler. His clothes were rough and shabby and I wondered why he wasn't out there with his comrades.

I must have looked scared for he touched his lips and said, 'Shh, miss. It's myself the bastards are after.'

Deciding I'd better be off elsewhere, I made a move into the open. He grabbed me, an arm around my neck and said, 'Not so fast, miss. You'll do fine as a hostage,' he added grimly. 'The bastards won't shoot me when I have a young lady as a shield – you're my insurance.'

I was terrified. I knew he meant business and as he spoke I thought I recognised the voice. I had heard it somewhere before and recently.

I had to think quickly. I knew the drill. I moaned, went limp against him. The vapours were expected of well-brought-up young women in such a dangerous situation. Unfortunately for him, I wasn't one. I had learned the rules of unarmed combat in saloons in the Wild West.

Cursing, he held on to me, trying to hold me upright. I jerked upright and kicked out very forcefully at his groin with my upraised knee. Taken completely by surprise, he let go of me. I heard him groan and curse as I leapt out of the doorway and seized my bicycle where it had fallen. I thought he was rushing after me. My calls for help would have been lost, gone unnoiced and unheard amid the noisy shouting.

The marchers were close at hand, passing by.

The man staggered forward to join the leaders, obviously with the intention of losing himself in their midst.

'There he is! There he is!' The shouting came from behind me.

A whistle, a warning shot and a mounted policeman galloped forward. A pistol shot – the man threw up his arms and was hidden from view. The policeman dismounted, his truncheon raised.

It wasn't necessary. The man lay sprawled on the road like a broken doll, his blood already spreading, staining the cobbles.

Personal terror turned to horror as I retreated once again into the sheltering doorway. For all his treatment of me, the man had been deliberately murdered and I wanted justice. I wanted to know what he had done to deserve such a fate without proper trial.

The marchers had halted at the sight of blood streaming from the inert figure. They watched in silence as the policeman approached cautiously and lifted the man's head.

'He's dead.'

At those words the protestors who had begun so boldly, now in the face of sudden death, panicked. Another warning shot fired above their heads, just to let them know that the law meant business. They got the point and began to disperse, the less bold having already discreetly vanished when the first shot was fired. The second shot convinced even the hardier souls and they too melted away.

From the ranks of police and horses, two men in plain clothes emerged.

Detective Sergeant Jack Macmerry and Inspector Grey.

'Just as well, sir,' I heard Jack say to the occupant of a carriage who had joined them.

'He's dead, sir, won't give you any more trouble.' This from the inspector.

The man who stepped out of the carriage was General Carthew and, as if for the first time, I recognised the significance of the huge black words painted across the sides of the warehouse: 'Carthews Brewery'. Of course, that was where his grandfather had made enough money to buy a fine mansion on the far side of Arthur's Seat.

Suddenly Jack spotted me, said something and rushed to my side.

'Rose, what the devil are you doing here, for God's sake?'

'Not for God's sake, Jack,' I said. 'For a client's sake. I'm on a case.'

'What kind of a case would that be?' he demanded suspiciously.

'A missing wife.'

'You chose a funny time,' he said.

'I'm not exactly laughing, Jack Macmerry. I've just seen a man die, shot in cold blood.'

'What do you mean, shot in cold blood? Don't be ridiculous. It was an accident.'

'No, it wasn't. I was a witness. I saw it all.'

Jack sighed deeply. 'Rose, the man was a criminal, a wanted troublemaker.' He took my arm gently. 'Not very pleasant, but don't let it upset you, dear. Things like this happen all the time.'

'Do they indeed?'

'They do indeed, believe me. So don't try to teach the police their business,' he said shortly.

As we argued, Jack was wheeling my bicycle. It was making a funny noise too, as if in protest, and I saw that the front wheel had buckled when it fell.

I began to explain why it had happened and he said, 'It's all right, I'll have it fixed, good as new.' And glancing over his shoulder, 'We'll get you a lift back into Edinburgh.'

'I don't want—'

But Jack had me very firmly by the arm and was leading me over to where Inspector Grey was leaning into the carriage in earnest conversation with the General. As we approached I was conscious of their curious eyes as Jack held me firmly like a prisoner in custody.

Before I could protest, he said, 'Sir, I wonder if would give this lady safe conduct back to Princes Street?'

The General gave me his most charming smile. 'It would be my pleasure – Mrs McQuinn.'

Jack's eyebrows rose at that as the General went on, 'I have already had the pleasure of Mrs McQuinn's company. At HRH Princess Beatrice's recent luncheon. Mrs McQuinn was accompanying her brother...'

Jack was impressed, but still held on to my arm as if I might refuse and make a fool of him in front of authority.

The coachman opened the carriage door, the General bowed, held out a hand. In all truth I was relieved by this unexpected turn of events. It was raining heavily now. I was cold and shaken too.

'Thank you,' I said to the General and over my shoulder to Jack, 'My bicycle?'

'I'll see it safely delivered back to you,' he muttered, saluting the General smartly.

My last sight was of Jack rejoining Inspector Grey. Heads close together, they were directing a group of constables.

Presumably the disposal of the dead man's body where it lay in a pool of blood in the middle of a main road was the matter under urgent discussion.

Chapter Thirteen

The General and I sped away from Leith and the scene of the protestors' march as if nothing so horrific as a young man's brutal death had happened a few minutes earlier.

As I thought darkly about how it would never be reported as deliberate murder in the name of the law, at my side the General talked amiably, as if he had already forgotten or dismissed what we had witnessed. And one in which he was concerned.

He won't give you any more trouble, sir.

I wouldn't forget those words.

The General was asking where I lived, I told him and he tapped his stick on the roof, redirecting the coachman to Solomon's Tower. He seemed to know the directions, nodding as I explained, and insisted that it was not at all out of his way.

'We must see you safely home, Mrs McQuinn. Dr Laurie, who is my good friend, would wish it.'

Turning, he smiled at me. 'I met your father, Inspector Faro, once. A brilliant detective, the best of his generation.'

Pausing, he shook his head. 'Most unfortunate that he – er, associated with known terrorists. I am afraid he is persona non grata in Scotland these days. I gather that Her Majesty was most displeased.'

I felt suddenly ill. Was this the real reason that I heard so little from Pappa? Her Majesty's displeasure would be an added reason for Vince's infrequent visits. Now I imagined them tempered with caution too.

As for Pappa, were his letters to Britain censored? For that was the indication I gathered from the General's solemn words.

I stared at him. As if he had not shattered my world with this revelation, he was talking about the amount of wildlife on Arthur's Seat and how it had diminished in recent days.

No chance any more of a good day's deer shooting...

I thought of Thane. 'Did you hunt with deerhounds?' I put in quickly.

He looked at me and laughed. 'There haven't been deer hunted on the hill in my lifetime, Mrs McQuinn. I know I must seem a little old to you, but deerhounds had their heyday here before my grandfather was born.'

He paused to look out of the window. We were nearing the Tower and Auld Rory, his curiosity aroused, had come out of his ditch and was staring in at us. Unlit pipe clenched between his teeth as always, he had seen the fine carriage with me inside. I guessed I wouldn't be long indoors before he appeared, eager and curious.

The carriage stopped. 'Did you know him – that man?' I asked the General, my thoughts returning to the shocking scene we had left at Leith.

The General turned sharply from the window and demanded, 'Why should I know him? Why do you ask such a strange question?' he added with a nervous laugh.

And following his gaze I realised he had been watching Rory, who was still standing at attention, smartly saluting.

'I mean – the man who was shot back there – did you know him?' I repeated.

The General drew a deep breath, managed a benign smile, a bewildered shake of his head. 'My apologies, my dear. What were you asking?'

But I wasn't to be fobbed off. I repeated. 'That young man – with the strikers – did you know him?'

The question, so unexpected and out of context with polite conversation, took him by surprise. He looked hurt and offended.

'A well-known troublemaker, Mrs McQuinn. Irish, of course,' he said sternly.

I smiled sweetly. 'My late husband was Irish – and a detective sergeant in the Edinburgh Police.'

'Is that so? Well, I never. Lady Carthew is part Irish,' he said consolingly. 'So they're not all bad people, I assure you.' His tone was unruffled, his smile charming. Whatever had upset him, his composure restored, he handed me down from the carriage, bowed gallantly over my hand and wished me well.

'I shouldn't waste too much sympathy on the unfortunate incident we witnessed back there.' He paused and added gently, 'We are doing our loyal duty, you know, Mrs McQuinn. If you have doubts, remember your father would understand. He was instrumental in saving Her Majesty's life several times, particularly from the Fenians.'

Remembering our earlier conversation, he allowed that to sink in. 'Do please give him my warmest regards when you hear from him.' Perhaps my face told him the rest and he added, 'I take it you do still hear from him.'

'Not very often. I'm afraid we are not great letter writers as a family.'

The General smiled bleakly. 'That is a pity. But I shouldn't bank on an early visit. He has declared his allegiance and as far as Scotland is concerned,' he reminded me gently, 'it would be inadvisable for him to set foot in Edinburgh. Especially with Miss Crowe who would immediately be thrown into prison. There is still a warrant for her arrest, you know. And a substantial reward.'

'The man back there,' I insisted. 'Was he a Fenian too?'

The General eyes swivelled back down the road. 'I – I'm afraid I have not the slightest idea.' And regaining his normal charm, he said smoothly. 'The rioters' ringleaders will be apprehended and punished.'

And I wondered again about that momentary loss of composure. Of course he would be well informed and maybe he already knew the identity of the young man who had died, in what was made to look like an unfortunate accident. Perhaps he had been a Fenian, one of a group of terrorists who had threatened the Throne and had been infiltrated into the dock workers to cause more trouble and disruption. But he was dead and as my good Catholic Danny would have said, 'May he rest in peace and rise in glory.'

Amen to that.

As soon as I closed the door, I expected a visit from Rory, certain that he would be overwhelmed with more than his usual curiosity especially when he recognised my companion in the carriage as General Carthew, under whom he had seerved in India. And with the additional personal link of the young son he had lost, killed while he was the General's batman.

But Rory didn't put in an appearance after all.

Darkness came early and R L Stevenon's *Strange Case of Dr Jekyll and Mr Hyde* was not the most comfortable companion. Not for a reader sitting alone in an ancient Tower who had just witnessed a young man shot dead. Deliberate murder, however the law chose to label it.

My unease was increased with a storm of horrendous proportions brewing up and rattling the windows. Already there was enough wind blowing to penetrate stone crevices and give wavering life to tapestries of Trojan wars lost long ago.

I have a fairly robust nervous constitution but even with the lamp turned up, the words swam as pictures of the day intruded, coming between me and the text, so that I was reading each paragraph twice over and not understanding a word.

I took up Jane Austen's *Emma* as a cheerful alternative but after ten minutes I had completely lost Emma and her trials and tribulations which seemed more trivial than ever and utterly remote from the world I had left in America and returned to in Edinburgh.

Disappointed, I laid the book aside. Tonight there was to be no escape provided by fiction; tonight harsh reality refused to be banished.

I sighed. Even Thane had deserted me and as I looked around the vast room, the shadows on its stone walls grew darker, deeper and more menacing, the swaying tapestries, full of gore and dying heroes, more depressing than ever.

The events of the day, the strikers' protest march and the man who had died, had succeeded in scaring me badly, whatever I might pretend. So I decided to call it a day and go up to bed, resolving to make an early start in the morning, to sensibly consider the next move in my investigation of Desmond's missing wife.

Perhaps – a sudden wild idea – I'd take Thane and see if he could sniff out the place near the ruined chapel where the body might have been hidden. Why hadn't I thought of that before? I felt quite elated at my own cleverness.

I yawned. I'd go to bed, sleep soundly on that resolution.

But first of all, I'd lock the back door securely.

I went to the dresser to take the key from its usual cup hook.

It wasn't there.

I suddenly went cold. Where had it gone? Frantically I searched my pockets. Had I taken it with me when I dashed out that morning so angry with Jack? Had I slipped it into my skirt pocket and had it fallen out as I bicycled?

No. That wouldn't do. I never took the back door key with me since I didn't lock either door during the day. As for carrying the front door key, it was hundreds of years old, a sturdy piece of iron four inches long that conjured up thoughts of a dungeon full of dangerous criminals in the Bastille.

I stood by the table, trying to work out calmly and logically what had happened. Jack said I was careless about keys, relying on the Tower's isolation, and only at night when I was sleeping alone and Thane wasn't downstairs in the kitchen did I make certain the back door was locked. His mighty presence was enough to deter the Devil himself. There was also a latch on the door convenient for Thane who was adept at using his nose to lift it and letting himself in and out when required.

Trying not to panic, I turned out my pockets once again. Went to my bedroom and searched in case I had it in my hand and set it down absent-mindedly when, still angry with Jack, I collected my papers.

But I knew even as I grovelled about with a lighted candle that it was a forlorn hope. The key wasn't there, had never been there.

Downstairs again I groped under the dresser, my efforts rewarded by dust and disagreeable scufflings hinting at very badly frightened mice.

I sat back on my heels.

What next? I was alone in a creaky old Tower with a storm raging and a door I couldn't lock.

I had mislaid – lost – the key. But where? How?

Another thought came unbidden. Had it been stolen? But who would want to steal it? I remembered the children – dismissed the thought as unworthy and had another of my cold shivers.

What if the killer had come to the Tower when I was out, had seen the key and taken it? What if he was lurking about out there – in the garden – waiting to pounce on his next victim?

Me!

This wouldn't do at all. I realised I was scaring myself, being quite silly reallly – or so I would have dismissed such behaviour in the cold light of day.

But there were many dark hours ahead before reassuring dawn returned once more. So again I applied logical thought by going over the day's events from rising until I left the house to visit Nellie Edgley.

Jack had arrived, we had quarreled. But before him I had another visitor.

Desmond Marks, early and quite unexpected.

I had given him tea and remembered talking to him over my shoulder as he watched me take cups down from where they hung in a neat row on the dresser.

Had the key been there on its usual hook? If only I could be certain.

I remembered bending over the peat fire, pouring boiling water from the kettle into the teapot. My back was to Desmond, watching me and offering to help—

And he was standing by the dresser!

Had he noticed the key and taken it?

But for what purpose?

And with cold terror wrenching at my stomach, I knew there could be only one reason.

If Desmond Marks had arranged his wife's murder and believed I was the only witness, then I was in mortal peril.

Chapter Fourteen

I had been in worse situations with wild Apache warriors storming a beseiged fort in Arizona, one of a group of terrified women and children united in danger shared, and with a loaded pistol in my hand.

An experience of scant comfort in my present situation for here I was completely alone, with the strong probability that a killer, whose face I already knew, was somewhere near at hand awaiting his opportunity to creep into the Tower and murder me.

I could sit up all night and watch the door, with my pistol on the table. Except that I was not at all sure it would be any help since it had not been fired since my return to Edinburgh.

'Discreet investigation' of the problems of 'distressed ladies', as Jack called them, had not up to now called for the use of firearms but perhaps flourishing a Derringer at an intruder would have the desired effect.

The alternative was to retire to my bedroom up the spiral stairs. Except that none of the massive interior doors had locks. This necessity had never occurred to their long-ago builders. A chair set under the door handle would have to suffice. That and the firearm should give me initial protection against any intruder.

But for how long and against what odds, I dared think no further.

And so it was with a feeling of utmost dread that I barricaded my bedroom door telling myself that I was reasonably safe. Listening for warning sounds below was an impossibility since the storm had chosen midnight to unleash all its full ferocity on the hill. This was accompanied by heart-stopping claps of thunder of Wagnerian magnitude that shook the old Tower to its very foundations.

Shutters rattled, doors and floorboards creaked. Such conditions would have been more than enough for any female of a nervous disposition without the additional hazard of a killer on the prowl outside.

Alone and vulnerable, I lay shivering, very sorry for myself, my head under the bedclothes, listening to the storm. At last the thunder faded, silence reigned and I fell into an exhausted sleep.

I awoke to a dog barking.

Thane. Unmistakably Thane.

Turning up the lamp I ran downstairs. To my horror the kitchen door hung wide open, a trail of dead leaves scurrying across the floor.

Thane was in the garden. He stood by the far wall, growling deep in his throat. Seizing my cape, I ran outside.

'Who is it, Thane?'

Hackles raised and bristling, he turned and looked at me.

'Woof!' Still growling but feebly wagging his tail as if to reassure me that the danger was over. Then shaking himself, he trotted into the Tower.

'Who was it?' I asked again, my hand on his shoulder.

If he could have answered that question many of my problems might have been solved that night.

Instead I was left to puzzle it out for myself as once again I resumed my frantic search for the missing key as if it might have miraculously reappeared.

Had someone attempted to break in? If that was the question then there was only one answer. The intruder-cum-killer could only be whoever stole the key in the first place.

And the role of 'whoever' fitted Desmond Marks perfectly.

The lovely old clock with its Westminster chime rolled out six o'clock and there seemed little point in going back to bed, so I blew the peat fire into life, put on the kettle and shared with Thane a very early breakfast.

'Was it Desmond Marks?' I asked, stroking his head. 'He didn't like you much. I wonder why.'

In answer Thane looked at me, that maddeningly intelligent intent expression which confirmed absolutely nothing.

I stared out of the window. First light on the hill is quite magical. Particularly, I was discovering, in autumn, when breaking dawn casts clouds aside with a rose red sunrise above Arthur's Seat, in a celestial panorama breathtaking in its beauty.

A flight of birds echoed overhead, a tide of excited noise and we went to the back door to watch the wild geese, the great V formations – one upon another, hundreds of them – winging their way over the Tower on their way to the feeding grounds in east Lothian.

Each November they came, following the primeval pattern established long before man arrived, and took up residence on the site of an extinct volcano. Back from the Arctic Circle, back home to live and breed another year, fulfilling their ritual of survival.

Intrigued by the wonder and majesty of the scene, I took out my sketchbook and watercolours, but my brushes could not work fast enough. The geese were mere dashes of black paint and the sunrise had faded long before I looked at the result of my labours, so drab and lifeless.

Disappointed as usual at another failure, I tore it out and attended more mundane matters in the kitchen, keeping a sharp lookout still for that missing key.

Consoled and made bold again by daylight, however, I determined to put aside the nightmarish hours when I had allowed my overwrought imagination to convince me that someone had tried to break into the Tower and had been scared off by Thane.

And that I might well be marked down by the killer as his next victim.

Punctually at eight, when we normally breakfasted together if he stayed the night, Jack came by wheeling my bicycle.

'I've fixed the wheel for you.'

Thanking him, I realised he was in a foul temper, unusual for him, stiff-lipped and still angry or hurt, perhaps both, by my harsh words and dismissal yesterday. His appetite was unaffected though, and watching him demolish a hearty breakfast I said casually, 'Someone tried to break into the Tower last night.'

He put down his fork, stared at me for a moment as if searching for the proper words to deal with this dramatic statement. That shake of the head and slight smile of disbelief was more than I could take at that moment.

'You think it's a joke!'

'No, I don't think that.' A weary sigh. 'Imagination is more like it.'

'All right. I wake up in the middle of the night. Thane is barking furiously. I find the back door wide open.'

Jack swallowed his last piece of bacon and said, 'That's easy, Rose. Even for a detective. First, the open door. We know that you don't lock it and that Thane can lift the latch by himself. That's your answer!' he added triumphantly. 'He came in, heard a noise outside – for heaven's sake there was a storm raging most of the night – and rushed out, probably after some prowling animal.'

'Or some prowling killer,' I added grimly.

Jack helped himself to bread and jam, poured out a second cup of tea and leaned back in his chair. He stared out of the window pretending to be thoughtful, but I knew he was merely digesting his bacon and egg and considering the possibilities of another slice from the rapidly diminishing loaf.

Sighing, he eyed the clock and said briskly, 'Must be off. I'm late already. See you tonight.' And coming round the table to kiss me he seemed surprised by my averted cheek.

'Now what's wrong?' He sounded exasperated.

'Nothing's wrong. You can leave the back door key, by the way,' I added casually.

'What key?'

I pointed to the dresser. 'The one that lives there.'

'I know that,' he said wearily. 'Why am I supposed to have taken it?'

'Thought you might have put it in your pocket by mistake.'

Silent for a moment, he regarded me frowning. 'I can only presume by that remark that you've mislaid it and haven't a clue to where it's gone.'

Suddenly it wasn't worth the argument. He would never be convinced that someone had tried to break in or that I was in danger.

Until too late.

'It'll turn up somewhere, don't worry,' he said cheerfully. 'You never lock doors anyway.'

Point out Thane's strange behaviour and he would say, 'Well, you taught him to open the back door.'

'I'm off, I'll leave you the newspaper. You can read all about that riot at Leith yesterday.'

I glanced at the headline. 'Protestors Dispersed. Rioter Accidentally Shot Dead.'

The man's name, Peter McHully, meant nothing to me, but I remembered something significant lurking at the back of my mind. Formless, irritating, refusing to be come forward and be recognised.

Until now. Desmond Marks at the *Pirates* rehearsal talking

to another constable while I waited and Nancy tried to attract his attention. It was so vivid—

'Jack, I'm sure I've seen this man, met him somewhere—'

Jack laughed and shook his head. 'Surely not? How on earth did you reach that conclusion?'

I didn't want to bring Desmond Marks into it again. I shrugged. 'His voice, I remember voices.'

Jack said nothing and I went on, 'I know you don't believe me – I have a strange feeling—'

'One of your intuitions, eh? Go on,' he smiled indulgently.

'Fantastic or no, Jack Macmerry, find out more about this man McHully and you'll have a lead to the murdered woman.'

Jack's expression said that he was biting back the words, 'What murdered woman, Rose? You're letting your imagination run away with you again.'

Instead he merely smiled.

I refused to be provoked. Especially as I couldn't put up a defence since Jack insisted that neither PC Smith nor the dead woman had ever existed. He had already reached his own satisfying conclusions about her disappearance from St Anthony's Chapel and was prepared to stick to it.

This put him in a slightly better mood as he left, thinking that because there had been no further argument, all was forgiven and forgotten.

I read the newspapeer report. It was all there, cautiously written and well-biased in favour of the police, and law and order. The villainous dock workers, refusing to accept the generous wage their bosses offered and the advantages of having daily employment and roofs over their heads.

What advantages, I thought bitterly, remembering the sad gloomy tenement where Ben Edgley and his wife Nellie lived. And she was one of the better tenants, I was sure, trying against hopeless odds to turn a hovel into a home.

What less caring folk were like, I dared not think. But the smell of grime and poverty remained with me after that brief visit, refusing to be banished and telling its own story.

The report skirted around McHully, referring to him only as a known agitator, wanted by the police on sundry other charges. His death, unfortunate but accidental, caused by a stray bullet.

A carefully worded, sanitised version of the scene that I had witnessed. Not a mention of General Sir Angus Carthew either, nor of the presence of armed police and the damage they were doing with their truncheons.

No doubt Jack also knew a great deal more about McHully than he was revealing, information classified as highly confidential by the Edinburgh City Police and unavailable to a member of the general public. Particularly to a nosey lady investigator such as Rose McQuinn.

It was Nancy who provided the vital clue.

Chapter Fifteen

The Carthew carriage rolled up to the front door early that morning and Nancy emerged with the two children looking almost too angelic to be real.

Perhaps she hoped that by arriving so early she might meet Jack. I did not mention that she had missed him by ten minutes.

There was still tea in the pot kept warm on the hob. She drank it gratefully after settling Tessa and Torquil at the table with their picture books and instructions to be patient and keep quiet. I supplied reinforcements of bread and jam to brace them for such unnatural requirements while Nancy explained the reason for this morning call.

'The General decided that the children must have winter coats and hats and sturdy new boots. As they are always up and about by eight o'clock, I decided the sooner we set off the better.'

She shook her head. 'Their poor uncle wouldn't know where to begin to make such purchases especially as Lady Carthew is not well enough to undertake such an exhausting shopping expedition. They both felt it was a more appropriate assignment for their nanny. The General was full of apologies for inflicting—'

She laughed. 'That is the very word he used, Rose – inflicting such an imposition on me. Little does he know that in most households this falls to the nanny whether the mother is fit or not. And little does he realise that the chance of shopping in Edinburgh's best shops is a great privilege, whatever the excuse.'

I still didn't know why I was being told all this when she said, 'The real reason I am here, Rose, is that I have a great favour to ask.' Then pausing for a moment, 'Could you possibly come with me?'

'Why, of course I could, Nancy and I'd be delighted. Although I had better warn you I'm not much of an authority about the needs of young children.'

'I can't believe you would be baffled by such a prospect,' she said firmly. 'You have such excellent taste and you will know at once exactly what is right for them,' she added as if I had some second sight in the matter of choosing bargains where children's outfits were concerned.

'Your confidence is touching, but I'm not sure I can live up to your high expectations.'

'Oh yes, you can. And I'm not the only one who has absolute confidence in your capabilities.' Looking round in case the children were listening, she added, 'Desmond is sure you'll find Nora for him. He is so grateful to you for promising to do so.'

I was somewhat taken aback if this was what he had told her. 'I didn't promise him anything, only that I would try my best to find out where she had gone. I didn't say anything about restoring her to him.'

Nancy looked disappointed and I went upstairs with the distinct impression that she felt let down that I did not boast some magic formula for finding lost wives. She would be even more put out, I thought grimly, if she ever guessed my suspicions that Nora Marks was no longer alive. And that her dear friend Desmond who sang like an angel (her words!) was capable of murder.

I had promised not to keep her waiting and suggested that the children might like to work off their high spirits by playing outside. Obviously a merry game was in progress accompanied by much shrill laughter and chasing round the garden.

Thane discreetly remained invisible. Young children were not his strong point. In that respect he was like any other dog.

When I came downstairs Nancy was standing by the dresser watching them through the window. She held up the painting I had discarded.

'Rose, did you do this?' And when I said yes, 'It's absolutely lovely. Sunrise on Arthur's Seat. You are clever, I wish I could paint. Are you ging to put it in a frame?'

I laughed. 'As a matter of fact, no. I was about to put it in the fire. It isn't very good, Nancy. Honestly.'

'Burn it! Oh no!' she gasped, clutching it protectively. 'Please, please – if you are sure you don't want it, may I have it? I would love it for my wall.'

I was flattered by her enthusiasm but more than a little diffident about parting with what I felt was a poor effort. Nancy, however, refused to listen to my protestations. So I reluctantly agreed that she could have it, adding my name in the corner as requested.

Laying it aside, she pointed to the newspaper. 'Have you read it? Wait till I tell you—'

At that moment Tessa appeared screaming shrilly that Torquil had stolen her scarf and wouldn't give it back. I was to discover that those angel curls hid little demon's horns.

'It'll have to wait until later,' Nancy whispered, disentangling the two children, wiping faces, inspecting hands and setting bonnets to rights as they were led to the waiting carriage with stern warnings to behave.

I could feel Nancy's suppressed excitement as she said, 'This is amazing, Rose. Quite amazing – such a coincidence,' leaving me even more frustrated about what important information was forthcoming.

Outside Jenners, she dismissed the coachman with instructions to return within the hour. A newsboy was shouting, 'Further developments in Leith riots,' and she bought a newspaper as we headed for the children's department where the two small but important customers were persuaded into suitable garments with a minimum of fuss. As they pirouetted around in their new coats, Tessa in a fur bonnet and Torquil with a jaunty cap, I, relieved at how easy it had all been and with ample time to spare, allowed my mind to drift longingly towards the tearoom upstairs.

A situation too good to last. Mutiny broke out over the choice of boots. Tessa hated the style and Torquil, not to be outdone, said the ones Nanny selected made his toes ache.

Nancy, exasperated, summoned an elderly shop assistant used to dealing with such situations who immediately applied reason and persuasion by slipping some barley sugar into the argument.

In our roles as bystanders, Nancy indicated the newspaper. 'Read that, Rose. The name of the man who was killed,' she whispered.

There was no possibility of further discussion as the children, now mollified, were anxious to leave. Instructing the shop assistant to parcel up the expensive purchases which, thanks to their uncle's generosity, had cost enough to adequately clothe an entire family for a year, we headed upstairs to the tearoom.

As we waited for our order, with an eye on the children sitting on the opposite side of the table and swinging their feet from the high chairs, Nancy whispered, 'I'm dying to tell you but it'll have to wait until we get back to the Tower. Perhaps we could manage a chat before I leave.'

And to the children who, having consumed their scones, were showing signs of restlessness in an outburst of horseplay, 'Drink up your lemonade. We'll be going soon.'

'Now, Nanny. Now, please,' they chanted.

The bill paid, also by kind courtesy of the General, we led the way downstairs through briefly glimpsed departments where Nancy and I without our impatient small charges would have been sorely tempted to linger.

As we attempted to leave through the swing doors, the children decided this was an unexpected lark and insisted on going round and round several times, much to the consternation and exasperation of customers attempting to make dignified exits.

Apologising for their behaviour as we grasped small hands firmly, Nancy stared up and down Princes Street and said, 'I told him an hour. This is too bad.'

Releasing the children to put on gloves and rearrange the parcels, which I had offered to carry, this was a perfect opportunity for the two little dears to find a convenient lamp-post and chase each other round it.

While I dealt firmly with that situation, my authority as a complete stranger being recognised more efficiently than that of their nanny, Nancy continued to gaze along the street, anxiously awaiting the carriage which – fortunately for all of us and particularly for the less fortunate passers-by – appeared at that moment.

The coachman was full of apologies. A coal cart had been upset, its contents strewn aross the road delaying all traffic.

Nancy bundled the children inside where they gathered up the picture books that had entertained them on the way from Carthew House. But their eyes darted eagerly towards the windows and I wasn't fooled by this apparent good behaviour, certain that while they were containing themselves admirably they were always on the alert for any further opportunities of mischief.

'It's like catching mice at crossroads,' said Nancy with a weary sigh. 'I had no idea that bringing them into town would be so exhausting.'

Once or twice, keeping her voice low, Nancy whispered

close to my ear, but all I got were the words, 'Peter McHully was—' and lost the rest.

I doubted whether, had she shouted at the top of her voice, I could have heard her above the noise of the horses' hoofs as the wheels clattered along the cobbled streets.

As for myself, remembering how often and in what unpleasant weather conditions I had struggled back to Newington on my bicycle, I sat back and relaxed against the comfortable leather uphostery.

In no hurry, I was content to experience to the full this small example of the luxury enjoyed daily by wealthy Edinburgh citizens with carriages and coachmen at their disposal.

And I learned something of importance during that drive. I remembered where I had seen the young man before. After the Royal lunch, outside the Balmoral Hotel. In a scuffle, quickly suppressed, at the General's carriage.

Chapter Sixteen

Outside the Tower the coachman was told to wait by Nancy and the children were let loose, not unwillingly, to play in the garden: 'Don't get dirty and don't make too much noise.'

As they dashed off shouting gleefully at this unexpected bout of freedom, with a sigh Nancy followed me indoors and sat down at the table.

She spread out the newspaper. 'At last, Rose. I've been dying to tell you. This McHully – I wouldn't forget a name like that. Mrs Laing told me about him. He used to work in the stables at the Carthews – and a right bad lot, he was.'

Pictures were filtering through my mind, the scene of a man being shot down that I would never forget and the scene of the two men in constables' uniforms talking earnestly, heads together, at the *Pirates* rehearsal…

I was so excited by this threshold of discovery and revelation that I was losing the thread of Nancy's story.

'…and Yvonne Binns wasn't much better.'

Who was Yvonne?

'Binns was her ladyship's personal maid,'

'The one who left to look after her sick mother.'

Nancy shook her head. 'That's what Mrs Laing was told to say. But she told me in confidence that things had gone missing. She suspected Yvonne was helping herself to her ladyship's jewels and getting McHully to sell them in Edinburgh. They obviously thought they'd get away with it since poor Lady Carthew seldom has cause to open her jewel box these days, or any reason to wear valuable rings and necklaces, much less a tiara.

'Then according to Mrs Laing, one day there was a terrible row. She didn't hear all the details only that there were angry voices raised in the study. Next day, Lady Carthew told her Binns had been sent for to look after her mother in England.'

She paused dramatically. 'What a lie!'

I decided that the cook-housekeeper's ears would be worthy of close inspection when we eventually met, since they must have been specially adapted for applying to keyholes.

'What was this Yvonne like?'

Nancy shrugged. 'I hardly ever saw her. A fleeting glance on the stairs. Mrs Laing said she was a snob, thought herself too grand to mix with servants.'

I fancied I heard a note of unmistakeable disappoint-ment at having missed this turgid domestic drama as Nancy went on: 'Mrs Laing heard from the stable lads that after being sacked by the General, McHully got work at Leith docks. She was prepared to guess that he took Binns to live there with him. Married or not! Mrs Laing was quite shocked.'

Again my mind did another rapid calculation. Even if McHully was also the bogus Constable Smith, it was unlikely that his victim had been Yvonne. Considering his dubious character, it was much more probable that he had been hired by the murderer to get rid of an unwanted wife, namely Nora Marks.

'But the best is yet to come,' Nancy whispered. 'I didn't know the connection with Binns, or any of this scandal, until Mrs Laing read about McHully this morning.'

She paused dramatically. 'You see, I already knew him. Met him regularly at the Opera Society. Worked the stage lights and when one of the policemen in the chorus fell sick, he took over his role. I can hardly wait until the next rehearsal,' she ended excitedly. 'This news will be a sensation. What a small world it is, Rose.'

It was indeed. And again into my mind flashed the picture

of the two constables, the feeling of triumph that I was on the right track at last. For here was a simple explanation for the stolen uniform. How simple for McHully to extract cape and helmet from the company's wardrobe.

I was also certain that I had the grim identity of the dead woman: Nora Marks, murdered by Peter McHully, at her husband's instigation.

No wonder Desmond was so sure of himself with both victim and murderer now safely dead.

Any further speculations were cut short by screams from the garden.

Torquil dashed in, Tessa at his heels.

'I found it!'

'Give it back!'

'Won't – it's mine.' shouted Torquil.

Further screams and flying fists were intercepted by Nancy pulling them apart. 'Torquil, show me what it is you're hiding.'

Torquil thrust his hand behind his back.

'At once, Torquil.' A look of defiance.

'If you don't give it to me this moment, I will be obliged to inform your uncle and there will be no fireworks party for you this week.'

This produced a wail of anguish from Tessa, 'It's isn't fair – it's my birthday. The fireworks are for me,' she sobbed. 'Uncle promised.'

Nancy's dire threat was enough to mollify Torquil who handed Nancy a key.

A key I recognised. The one missing from my back door.

I put out my hand. 'That belongs to me.'

Nancy handed it over, demanding from Torquil. 'Where did you find this? Did you take it out of the door?'

'No, Nancy,' I interrupted. 'I mislaid it – I must have

dropped it in the garden,' I added with a sudden sense of shame for the fuss I had made, for my ridiculous theories...

Except...

'Please show me where you found it, Torquil.'

Tessa sprang forward. 'It was me, Mrs McQuinn. It was lying on top of the garden wall – over there.'

'Then show me please, Tessa.'

Nancy was clearly bewildered by all this as we followed the two children to where an ancient rose bush grew, sheltered by a projecting stone on the far wall which separated the garden from the hill. Stubbornly surviving wind and weather, growing wilder year by year, this supposedly delicate plant was uninhibited by any gardener's attempts at cultivation. It bloomed defiantly late in the year, fat pink roses one associated with cherubs on a Rubens painting.

'The key was there, Mrs McQuinn,' said Tessa, putting out her hand. 'It was lying on that stone.'

'You are sure?' I asked and two heads nodded in reply.

'There now. Just as well you found it, children,' said Nancy, giving me a questioning look.

Thanking them profusely, my mind was on fingerprints, that new science which had helped me solve my first case. I looked at the key, thought of the tiny hands that had wrestled over it and knew the result would be useless.

'You must have dropped it, Rose,' said Nancy with her usual confidence. 'Someone found it on the hill and placed it there for you to find.'

But I had a much more sinister interpretation that I was not prepared to discuss. I observed that a branch had been broken off and a rose hung loose from its stem, a clean break for which no storm had been responsible.

As we walked into the Tower I carried the rose with me and

placed it in a glass of water. It was after all my only evidence of the intruder who had dropped it when he scrambled over the garden wall.

By accident or design…?

At the exact spot where Thane had set up his crescendo of barking.

Chapter Seventeen

Jack and I went to the theatre that evening to see Dan Leno and as I laughed at this great comedian's antics, I realised that I was in danger of forgetting what it was to be light-hearted. To be one of a great throng of well-dressed people on an evening out on the town enjoying themselves.

Merriment, bright lights. On the surface Edinburgh was in party mood, the beggars and poverty in the closes and wynds off the High Street and in Leith, remote as something from a distant planet.

As for me, I was glad to lay aside my social conscience for a few hours. Perhaps Jack was right and I took life too seriously. And – dare I say it – walking over Waverley Bridge with the street lamps glowing along Princes Street, I could have convinced myself that my obsession with the dead woman I had found was a mistake.

She had merely fainted. But that still didn't account for PC Smith. I certainly hadn't imagined him.

Still, I resolved firmly to put such matters behind me on this lovely evening with a sky full of stars and a full moon rising as we headed towards the Pleasance. There was no wind, the air around Arthur's Seat was wine-clear as walking arm-in-arm we discussed the theatre, laughed again at Dan Leno's jokes.

As we approached the hill, groups of people, mainly men and boys, were carrying bundles of sticks and logs, a long line extending from the road to the crested summit.

Jack said they were preparing for the Annual Bonfire Night on 5th November, when effigies of the first Guy Fawkes would be ceremonially burned.

'There'll be fireworks too – and plenty of carousing. In my young days in Peebles, the whole village was expected to add rubbish and any old wood to the blaze. After the guy was burned we roasted chestnuts in the embers of the fire and for days before the bairns went from door to door collecting a penny for the guy.'

I had almost forgotten those childhood memories of Sheridan Place. Not that we ever had a bonfire in our back garden or were permitted to go to one. But I remembered other neighbourhood children and shared excitement for days before.

'We must go!' I said to Jack.

He shrugged. 'You can if you wish, but I'll be there anyway in my official capacity. The police have to put in an appearance, to keep law and order and the rowdy dangerous elements in check. As always with bonfires, they often get out of control and there can be nasty accidents.'

I told him about the Carthew children and how they were having fireworks too and incidentally mentioned, quite casually, that they had found my missing key in the garden.

'There you are!' said Jack triumphantly. 'Didn't I tell you it would turn up? You must have dropped it taking your bicycle out of the barn. And you imagining all sorts of sinister reasons—'

I smiled sweetly and let it go at that. I'd keep my darker thoughts to myself about exactly where it had been found. By no stretch of imagination could I have dropped it at the far end of the garden on a flat stone, thirty yards away from the barn. The answer to that sinister puzzle was to remain with me, unsolved for some time yet.

Jack was going back to his lodging that night as he had to be on duty at five, something to do with a ship smuggling illegal imports. The police had a tip-off that it would be arriving at Leith on the early morning tide.

I thought in the circumstances it would have been better to

have had supper in Edinburgh after the theatre but Jack was quite determined to see me safely home.

I soon discovered the reason for his insistence. Sitting at the table eating the sandwiches I had prepared, he said casually, 'By the way, a woman's body was washed up last night. Down by Granton.'

At last, I thought. The missing corpse.

'Before you get excited, they believe this was a suicide or an accidental drowning. There were no marks of violence.'

'How long had she been in the water?'

Jack shook his head. 'We haven't seen the doctor's report yet.'

'I don't suppose there was any identification either then.'

'Nothing on her clothes and anything else would have been swept away by the sea.' Tapping his fingers on the table he frowned, his face a masterpiece of indecision, an expression I knew.

'Well?' I asked

'Well what?' He looked confused pouring himself another glass of ale.

I smiled gently. 'Isn't there something else you wanted to tell me?'

He laughed. 'Not really, except that we had Desmond Marks in right away.'

'And?' Was this what I had been waiting for?

'He said it definitely was not his missing wife. He was in a bad way, big strong man like that. Never seen a drowned person or apparently even a dead one before. Quite extraordinary. He nearly fainted clean away. We had to bring out the smelling-salts.'

As I listened I also thought privately that such emotions might be the sign of guilt or remorse. And I added a notch to my growing theory that Desmond had paid McHully, who wasn't so squeamish about violence, to kill Nora for him.

'Was Marks the only one you called in?'

'No. We had all the contacts for those on our missing persons list. The drowned woman didn't fit the description of the old lady or the young girl. The two most likely were the young married woman and the missing schoolteacher.'

Pausing he added rather archly. 'As you well know, Rose.'

I blushed. 'What – what do you mean? Why should I—?'

He held up his hand. 'Because a young lady with a bicycle had called on Miss Simms to enquire after church on Sunday. She volunteered the information without being pressed—'

'Pressed by whom?'

He bowed. 'Me, of course. Who else?' And leaning across the table he took my hand. 'Dear Rose, I knew exactly what was in your mind when you slipped out of bed the other night and took that sheet of paper out of my jacket pocket. I heard you go downstairs and when you came back, you replaced it and climbed into bed again.'

I was appalled. Guilty – caught in the shameful act.

'You were pretending to be asleep,' I said accusingly.

'I do it all the time,' he said cheerfully. 'But I should warn you that the springs on that ancient bed creak like the very devil on your side. You should do something about them.'

Speechless, I looked at him. 'And you have never said a word.'

He smiled sadly. 'I like to keep you on a long rein, Rose of my heart,' he said softly. 'Once I tighten it, I know I'll lose you,' he added soberly.

There was nothing I could say, no denial, because it was true and we both knew it.

'I guessed you'd go after the two most likely and I could have saved you a journey. Mr Winton had been in that morning to say his wife had returned, although she's already gone off again back to her mother. A fairly regular occurrence it seems. According to Miss Simms her sister is still missing from the school. She was very upset at having to see the drowned woman but greatly relieved too that it wasn't her sister.'

There was a moment's silence then I said contritely, 'I'm sorry, Jack. I don't usually pick pockets.'

'No harm done, love.' He patted my hand. 'All is forgiven. But don't make a habit of it, will you?' And he came round the table to give weight to forgiveness with a hug and a kiss.

As he released me, I asked, 'Incidentally, did she look like the drawing I made?' He frowned and I added, 'Remember, the one I did of the dead woman at St Anthony's Chapel?'

He shrugged. 'Well – yes, I suppose, near enough. But in case you're new to this aspect of mortality, bodies who have been immersed in the sea for twenty-four hours undergo quite a rapid transformation.'

After he left I sat down with my logbook and reading it over did not give me any satisfaction. If the drowned woman wasn't Nora Marks nor Miss Simms, as far as I was concerned the case was closed.

Or I had better resume my search further afield. Of one thing I was certain, I would never rest until I had solved the mystery of Nora's disappearance and proved to Jack that I had not imagined the dead woman. And until I had proved beyond all doubt the identity of the bogus PC Smith.

A mysterious hired carriage had been in the vicinity. But what of Charlie, the supposed coachman. Did he exist at all?

There was only one way to find out.

While bicycling along the Pleasance, I had noticed a sign in St Mary's Street advertising 'Coaches for Hire, Vehicles Repaired'. Perhaps they could provide the necessary repairs for that buckled wheel, still rather unsteady, despite Jack's efforts.

Expecting a seedy-looking establishement I was surprised to find a neat room with counter, a potted plant of generous proportions and a glass door bearing the words: Felix Micklan. Prop.

The bell summoned a well-groomed gentleman of thirty-five whose smooth appearance exuded an air of prosperity. It suggested reliability and that the business, like the potted plant, was flourishing.

He looked me over very shrewdly before bowing, obviously at a quick guess estimating the stratum of Edinburgh society I represented.

Satisfied, he said, 'Good day, madam. You wish to hire a carriage?'

I decided not to shatter his illusions by mention of the bicycle outside. 'I should like to hire a brougham for the day. It is my fiancé's birthday and we are to celebrate with a drive to East Lothian.'

His expression took on a barely concealed smirk, his mind racing well ahead. He knew exactly what engaged couples got up to in the country in their hired carriages.

I gave him a date a month ahead. Noting it, he quoted a price which would have cut nicely into my savings had my enquiry been genuine. As he politely escorted me to the door I was frantically considering some means of obtaining the vital information this visit had prompted.

'One more thing, sir. I presume that you are able to provide a coachman if required.'

He bowed. 'Indeed. We have a modest team available for that purpose.'

'How interesting. My fiancé was recommended that we should ask for Charlie.'

'I fear the gentleman was mistaken. We have no employee

by that name.' He shrugged. 'Some other establishment, perhaps.'

'I was sure this was the one he named in the Pleasance.'

Micklan shook his head. 'Definitely not in this area. We do all the private hirings here. That is why it is more expensive having a cab without a coachman – we have to know that our clients are competent and reliable.'

I wondered what were his feelings about this particular client who he watched riding off on a bicycle. I hadn't the heart to mention repairs to the wheel and I was more than a little depressed.

No body, no hired gig and no Charlie.

Should I pursue the subject? Return to Mr Micklan, reveal my identity and ask for a recent list of his clients?

My nerve failed me. I doubted that he would be sympathetic to my quest, especially as gentlemen who hired carriages for more genial and less sinister purposes than murder, doubtless had their own reasons for preferring to remain incognito.

Chapter Eighteen

Nancy was becoming a constant visitor. She arrived over the hill, breathless, clutching her bonnet firmly against the wind.

'Rose – I have an invitation for you. If you're free this afternoon – about four – the General and Lady Carthew would like you to come to Tessa's fireworks party.'

Pausing, she added proudly, 'Isn't that delightful?'

Delightful perhaps, although I had little taste for fireworks that were a series of loud bangs, since loud bangs and smells of gunpowder aroused unhappier memories of Arizona, less innocent and bloodier than childhood's peaceful days in Sheridan Place.

'You have made a great impression on Tessa – and Torquil too. Apparently they asked their uncle if that nice lady from the Tower might come to the party.'

Later I went upstairs to dress, feeling flattered by the invitation, especially as I had not gone out of my way to appear like a 'nice lady' to the children. All I seemed to recall was being rather stern with them, I thought, searching for what might be appropriate presents.

There was a small turquoise bracelet, a present from Olivia which I had never worn. That for Tessa. But what for Torquil? Then I had it. In the bookcase two model soldiers from the Napoleonic wars, perfect for a small boy. So I went downstairs again looking forward to the visit, curious to see inside Carthew House, and to meet the children's invalid aunt.

Thane appeared at the kitchen door as I was about to leave. I told him where I was going. All it meant to him was yet another walk so we set off together. A divine autumn day, perfect for such a leisurely pastime. Here and there the heath on the hill was garnished with bracken's gold and red while below us, by the roadside, the splash of scarlet elderberries.

When we reached the lane leading off the hill to Carthew House, Thane lingered cautiously. Then with what in a human would have been a regretful shake of the head, he darted back the way we had come.

Dusk was fast approaching and already a trail of bonfires blazed across the landscape. I crossed the stile, walked along the lane and reached the iron gate Nancy had informed me led through the stables to the front door.

There were lights in the stables and as I walked across the cobbles a man emerged. Raising his hat gallantly, he greeted me.

I recognised Felix Micklan. Surprise was out of all proportion to meeting him there, for what was more likely than that he had business at the Carthew stables? They could well afford his prices, I decided, walking around the side of the darkened house to the front door, its elegant flight of stone steps, guarded by a pair of bronze lions, whose ferocity had seen more compelling days.

On the circular drive, at a safe distance from the house but visible from the vantage point of the upstairs windows, a space for the bonfire had been cleared and two of the stable boys were busily setting up the fireworks display.

Nancy was expecting me. As I crunched across the gravel she appeared at the door followed by Torquil and Tessa who ran down the steps and seized my hands eagerly as I was ushered into the hall.

A handsome marble floor led across to a fine oak staircase and the upper regions. The walls were hung with obscure family portraits, the famous grandfather and a more recent painting of the General uniformed in full military splendour.

The children, still holding my hands, led me into a small sitting-room where he stood before the fire smoking a cigar.

'Here she is, Uncle!' they exclaimed.

The General smiled. bowed over my hand. 'Welcome, Mrs McQuinn.' And to the children. 'This nice lady and I have met before.' And turning to me, 'Lady Carthew and I are so glad you were able to join us at such short notice. It is a rare treat for the children to have visitors, especially for Tessa on such an important occasion as her sixth birthday.'

And touching the bell-pull. 'Now we are ready to proceed. The fireworks should all be in place. Lead the way, if you please, Nanny.'

'Are you well wrapped up, children?' Nancy asked. 'Yes, Tessa, I am afraid you must wear your scarf and bonnet, even if it is your birthday. You cannot go outside into the cold in a velvet dress.'

The small mutiny quelled by the General's presence, we trooped after her into the garden.

The General, walking at my side, said, 'Unfortunately Lady Carthew won't be able to to be with us. It is too cold for her outside and we have to watch her health most carefully at present. However, we had the bonfire arranged so that she can see the fireworks from her window. Ah, there she is!'

Turning he pointed to a large bow window on the upper floor. I could see Lady Carthew, a shawl around her shoulders, her luxurious fair hair reflected against the lamplight.

The General saluted her, smiling fondly in her direction and returning the kiss she blew to the children, who yelled a greeting as we settled, or rather huddled, close to the wall to protect the children from the sudden chill wind.

At my side, Nancy looked round and said, 'Everyone has been invited.'

Everyone, by which I gathered she meant the staff, was represented by Mrs Laing, the coachman Wilson and the two stable lads.

The bonfire was now well alight but without the traditional

guy. Did the General's finer feelings suggest that this was too bloodthirsty for those of tender years? We all applauded. The last sparks flew off into the dark, then it was the turn of the fireworks: Catherine wheels, Roman candles and finally a batch of rockets.

For the children, all too soon, it was over and darkness descended again. Told by their uncle it was now time for bed, but first there would be a glass of milk and a piece of birthday cake baked specially by Mrs Laing.

I was eager to make the acquaintance of the voluble and knowledgeable cook-housekeeper but, after a brief nod, she scurried back to the kitchen, presumably to prepare supper for the General and his lady.

There were few presents for Tessa. Practical knitted gloves from Nancy, homemade sweets from Mrs Laing and a handsome embroidered workbox from her uncle and aunt.

The General smiled, watching Tessa's delight at the turquoise bracelet and Torquil playing solemnly with his Napoleonic soldiers.

'Thank you for your generous gifts, Mrs McQuinn and for remembering my nephew too. Torquil's birthday is next week and he can never quite forgive his sister for being entitled to the Bonfire Night celebrations.'

And regarding the boy fondly, 'We have to watch him closely as he is not above stealing one or two of the fire-crackers to have an independent birthday bonfire of his own. His father warned me that we have a young arsonist in the making.'

I wondered why there were no presents for the motherless children until the General said, 'The geological expedition is on the move and my brother would be unable to buy presents for his little ones. But as soon as he returns, he will make up for it, lavish as always with exciting gifts from distant places.'

It was time to cut the cake and blow out the candles.

As the General called, 'Wishes, everyone!' I was sure his was for better health for his absent wife, disappointed that she was not yet strong enough to come downstairs and take part in this little ceremony.

We all applauded as the candles were extinguished by Tessa in one triumphant breath. The General produced the sherry decanter and poured out three small glasses. For the grown-ups, he said, to keep out the cold. We talked trivialities and as soon as the cake was consumed, bedtime was indicated for the children.

It was also time for me to leave and about to do so, the General drew me aside. 'I have a matter of some importance I wish to discuss with you, Mrs McQuinn.'

He glanced at the clock and continued, 'Unfortunately there is no time now as I am expecting a visitor, a business acquaintance, at any moment. However, would you be so good as to call again tomorrow afternoon – if that is convenient.'

I couldn't think of any reason why it wouldn't be, and the General replied, 'Excellent. Shall we say three o'clock then?'

And leading me back to Nancy and the children he kissed my hand gallantly and again thanked me profusely for coming, gesturing towards Torquil who bowed and Tessa who curtseyed nicely.

'Lady Carthew has asked me to give you her special thanks and good wishes. She hopes to be well enough to welcome you to our home on some future occasion. And now Nanny will see you to the gate.'

Nancy added her thanks and hoped I thought it had been worthwhile. Apologising for having to rush back to her small charges, she said, 'I will be seeing you again, very soon, Rose. Now that the children have found the way to the Tower and they like you so much, I fear I will never be able to keep them away.'

It was very dark now, a few stars visible among fast moving clouds and the embers of the bonfire on the crown of the hill as I made my way homewards.

No Thane tonight, I feared. All this noisy human activity would keep him well out of sight. Rockets exploding and fireworks shooting up into the sky, destroying the peace of Arrthur's Seat, would signal caution to a shy deerhound.

Lighting the lamp, I conscientiously wrote up my logbook for the day including my visit to Felix Micklan.

Laying the book aside, I had decided to have an early night when a scraping at the back door announced Thane. I was so glad to see him, feeling that he had braved the noisy activity on the hill to visit me.

As he settled down by the peat fire I took up *Dr Jekyll and Mr Hyde*, sometimes pausing to talk to Thane and stroke his head. I felt so warm and comfortable and safe when he was in the kitchen beside me, an unlikely guardian angel come to my hearth.

At last, yawning, I turned down the lamp and said goodnight. As I went up to bed, my last thoughts were of the General and tomorrow's visit.

What was it he wanted to talk to me about that was of such importance? Could this be of a professional nature? I decided it was highly unlikely that a man so elevated in Edinburgh society might require the services of a discreet lady investigator.

Chapter Nineteen

Something wakened me.

The sound of a carriage moving fast along the road. I had no idea what time it was. Still dark beyond the windows, it felt like the early hours of the morning.

Unusual. Some emergency from Duddingston heading to Edinburgh Infirmary by the fastest road.

I was about to close my eyes again and drift back into sleep.

Sounds from downstairs. From outside the Tower.

I sat up in bed.

Thane? He could have got out through the back door.

A loud baying bark penetrated up the spiral staircase to my bedroom. That was Thane!

And something was seriously wrong. Seizing my robe, I dashed downstairs. The kitchen was empty, the back door wide open. An icy wind blew across the floor.

Where was Thane? I could hear him baying and I knew that sound of distress. It came from the front of the Tower and I ran through, opened the door and stared out on to the road.

A flickering light – sunrise?

No, too early. A fire!

A fire. From the ditch where Rory sheltered.

'Thane!'

I ran down the road. The light from the ditch was now a fierce blaze. But Thane was already there. As I ran I saw the huge shape of him dragging a lighted bundle on to the road.

A guy from one of the bonfires—

No! 'Rory!' I screamed.

Within yards of the ditch two flaming shapes, a torch unrecognisable as a man and a dog.

At that moment, as I ran towards them, a clap of thunder and above our heads the heavens opened. Never have I been so glad of torrential rain. Where there had been flames an instant earlier, there were now two bedraggled blackened shapes shrouded in smoke.

Rory was still alive. He staggered forward, face blackened, his old army cape still smouldering.

I ran to him. Thane shivered by his side. Eyebrows singed, silky coat blackened, he managed one 'Woof', and a pathetic tail-wagging.

'Thank God,' I said, 'thank God,' as I took Rory's arm. He looked dazed, bewildered, shaking his head.

'I was asleep. I thought it was a nightmare.'

'Are you hurt?'

He stared at me. 'I dinna ken.'

'Can you walk to the Tower?'

'Aye, I can manage that,' he nodded and attempted to straighten his shoulders.

'Wait, lass.' He walked back to the ditch, his hand on Thane like a blind man being led. Unsteadily, he raked among the smouldering ashes. His few possessions were blackened beyond recognition and he stood very still, looking shrunken, lost. Lifting his head, he sniffed the air.

'D'ye smell onything, lass?'

'Spirits – whisky, I think?'

'Aye, it is that,' he said grimly.

I looked at him, shocked. 'But you don't drink. What happened?'

He seemed too numbed to find words, standing there shaking his head from side to side over the ruins of his shelter.

'You could have burnt to death,' I said, still horrified by that vision of the man and the dog wreathed in flames and the implication of what I now knew without a shadow of doubt.

'Someone tried to kill you.'

Again he shook his head. 'But someone didn't succeed, lass.'

And patting the capacious pocket of his army cape, he took out his Bible and kissed it, a solemn gesture. 'This saved me, lass, and your dog.' And turning his palm outward, he looked heavenward. 'And God's rain.'

Conscious for the first time that I was soaking, wet hair streaming down my neck, feet bare and icy cold, I saw that the torrential downpour had ceased as suddenly as it began. Shivering, I looked towards the blackened ditch.

'Is there anything we can save for you?'

'Nothing, lass. Your dog saved all I had – my life, for what it's worth.'

I took his arm. 'Let's get indoors. I'll get us a hot drink, warm us up. It's freezing out here.'

We made a slow progress the short distance and once inside, Rory cast aside his army cape, rescuing his old clay pipe from the pocket. A controlled gesture, but his hands were shaking. Looking at him closely, I was relieved that apart from most of his hair on head and face being singed off, he seemed otherwise to have escaped serious burns.

At his side, Thane was shivering and before blowing life into the peat fire and putting on the kettle to boil, I towel-dried his coat, examining his head, mouth and ears, making sure he hadn't been burned. He accepted my ministrations yawning, opening his mouth, as if to say, 'It's only on the surface, it'll grow out.'

Satisfied that they had both had a miraculous escape, I ran upstairs, removed my soaking robe and threw on a dry nightdress and my one outdoor cloak.

Downstairs, Rory shook his head and said solemnly, 'Someone wants rid of me, lass. That was no accident. They gave themselves away with the whisky.'

That it was deliberate I had guessed. 'Someone who didn't know you were teetotal. They wanted it to look as if you'd got drunk and set yourself alight, was that it?'

'Aye, that's the way of it. An old trick we used in the army when we wanted to smoke rebel tribesmen out. Straw and kerosene in a bundle set alight. If there was nowt else we used whisky, rum – spirits of any kind.'

He made a gesture with his arm. 'Throw it over the wall, it explodes – and whoosh!'

I made the tea, gave him a cup. 'Someone tried to kill you, Rory. But why? Who are your enemies here in Edinburgh? This isn't India and rebel tribesmen.'

Pausing for a moment deep in thought, he said, 'Everyone has enemies, lass.' But his shrug didn't convince me as he clutched the cup in both hands, as if gaining comfort from its warmth. He wasn't a good liar and I suspected he knew who his enemies were, or could have made a pretty accurate guess.

'I've brought some blankets down for you,' I said, 'A good night's rest then we can think what to do. We'll all feel better in the morning,' I added, falsely cheerful.

He began to cough and looked terrible. I could see he was shaking, suffering from delayed shock. As for that good night's rest, there was precious little night left.

Through the window dawn was glowing over Arthur's Seat as Rory looked around the kitchen with a sigh of disapproval. 'Many a bonny year since I slept wi' a roof over my head.'

'It's never too late to start,' I said brightly. 'Will you be all right on the sofa here? It's very comfortable.'

He nodded absently, and I realised he was exhausted almost beyond speech.

'Thane will keep you company.'

A tail wagged in agreement and although I had suffered only emotional shock, I left them and trailed back upstairs like an old woman. Shivering with wet hair that would take hours to dry, I dropped into bed and slept, to open my eyes when it was fully daylight and felt surprised and a little guilty that I had slept at all.

Nine o'clock chimed in the kitchen and Rory was still fast asleep, Thane on guard, in his favourite place, stretched out in front of the fire.

The room was warm and smelt not unpleasantly of wet dog, so trying not to disturb Rory, I put on the kettle and by the time it was boiling I heard a carriage outside. Next moment, Jack was at the kitchen door, ready for his breakfast.

I was so glad to see him.

'We got our smugglers,' he explained. 'So I thought I'd look in…'

'I have a visitor,' I interrupted loudly but Rory never moved. Thane bounced to Jack's side, he was glad to see him too.

With a finger to my lips I pointed to Rory's sleeping figure and Jack asked. 'What's all this then? When did he move in?'

'He nearly burnt to death in his ditch last night. Thane saved his life.'

Jack whistled. 'Set himself alight with that clay pipe, did he?'

'No, he didn't. But he'll tell you himself. Rory!' I said gently, touching his shoulder, but he never stirred, muttering in his sleep.

'Let me see him, Rose,' Jack demanded sharply and moving me aside, he leaned over the old man, taking his pulse. Touching his face, he raised his eyelids. Then looking at me, he said, 'I think he's had a seizure of some kind. We'd better get him to the infirmary – quick! I was on my way to Leith. The police carriage is outside. I'll drop him off.'

Jack is a big strong man. He picked up Rory gently in his arms as if he had been no heavier than a small, light-boned woman, like me.

'See you later, Rose. You can tell me all about it then.'
With Thane at my side, I watched him carefully place his
burden in the police carriage, tuck a blanket around him.

'Try not to worry.' He might as well have said to me, 'Try
not to breathe.'

Thane went back indoors with me. I took scissors and a brush to his silky coat and managed to remove most of the singed hair from his face. He accepted my ministrations patiently as if he was used to this sort of thing as his daily toilette. Occasionally he licked my face – perhaps indicating that he was grateful – no difficult task, for at less than five feet I wasn't much taller than him.

This was followed by a sigh of long-suffering resignation as much as to ask, what's all the fuss about. His coat would soon grow again. And as I brushed and trimmed, I talked to him in the absence of anyone else in whom to confide my fears.

Certain Rory was going to die, if he wasn't dead already, I had not the least doubt that this was another murder attempt, the opportunity provided by Bonfire Night, to be written off as an accidental firework. Very natural in the circumstances except that the killer had given himself away by including the whisky.

Which meant that he was a hired killer, someone unaware that Rory was a life-long abstainer. Who then was this enemy? And most worrying of all, was there a link with the dead woman at St Anthony's Chapel?

And suddenly a very valid reason flashed into my mind. Had Rory been a witness to the events of that night without realising the significance of what he had seen? Had his curiosity sealed his fate?

I remembered how eagerly he stood on the road intently scanning passing carriages and the more I thought about it, the more convinced I became that I had hit on the truth.

But how on earth to prove it?

I had just given Thane a final brush when Jack arrived.

Anxiously I searched his face. 'Any news?'

He was smiling. 'Can't stay – but I thought you'd want to know that he's still alive and they think he'll recover. A hardy specimen – all that living out of doors!'

'What about his burns?'

'Just superficial…'

And I was remembering the sight of the two figures aflame, a picture I would never forget as Jack went on, 'Amazingly enough, nothing desperate.'

Thane had leaped to his side as usual, his tail-wagging welcome demanding acknowledgement.

Jack patted his head. 'You should have a medal for life-saving, dog, do you know that? Let's have a look at you,' he added stroking his coat and carefully examining his head and ears.

When Jack warmed to Thane, I warmed to him. Turning to me, he laughed. 'This dog really looks as if he's smiling sometimes.' And pointing to the scissors and brush, 'Seems pretty well back to normal too. It's a miracle that they both survived.'

'A miracle indeed – a torrential shower of rain and hail that doused the fire…'

Jack shrugged. 'A blessing all right, we don't usually get rain to order, mostly when it's least wanted.'

'Where is Rory now?'

'I took him into the hospital at Leith. It's run by the Church Council and I know some of the doctors there. They give their sevices free and they're sympathetic to vagrants. I think they aim to save their souls as well as their bodies. Rory created the right impression since he had his bible with him.'

'When can I visit him?'

'Any time. I imagine he'll be glad of a visitor. Look, I must go.'

I kissed him. 'Thanks – and for all you've done for Rory.'

At the door I said, 'Before you go – you think it was deliberate?'

Jack looked thoughtful. 'My first inclination was the obvious one, an accident – a stray firework, a rocket lying about smouldering near the roadside in the dark – that sort of thing.'

He shook his head. 'But the whisky – that changed my mind. I guess it was the work of mindless drunks up at the bonfire on Arthur's Seat carried away and full of booze and devilment. With the fun over, my guess is some cruel brute decided they should set fire to a real life guy. A harmless old tramp.'

Clenching his fists he swore. 'I'd like to lay hands on whoever they were – I hope I get the chance…'

I looked at him. 'You realise, of course, that is exactly what we were meant to think.'

'What d'you mean, "meant to think"?' He sounded exasperated.

'I think we're missing the point – there could be a deeper reason. I'm fairly sure about that.'

'A deeper reason for frightening the life out of an old man and nearly killing him in the process?' He was trying not to sound cynical.

'Perhaps there was something Rory knew – or saw – that was dangerous to whoever got the idea. Don't ask me what, for I haven't the slightest idea – but I'm working on it.'

I waited for the usual accusation that I was imagining things, but for once Jack didn't argue. 'Let's hope you're right and he'll tell us,' he said grimly, 'then we can put the bastards behind bars.'

He wrote down the hospital address and accompanied our goodbye kiss with an affectionate hug for Thane and final instructions that he was to take good care of me.

I found that rather touching, interested to observe that the attack on Rory might have changed Jack's mind and set him thinking about a bogus constable and a dead woman whose body had disappeared: events that he had happily scoffed at as 'imagination'.

I fed Thane and was about to set off for the hospital when his deep bark announced a visitor.

I opened the front door to Desmond Marks.

He was almost the last person I wanted to see at that moment but as I could hardly keep him standing on the step, somewhat reluctantly, I invited him in.

Hesitating, he demanded suspiciously, 'Is that dog about? I heard him barking.'

Ignoring that, I indicated my cape. 'I was just leaving,' I said in tones which to a person of any sensitivity would have indicated that his arrival was ill-timed.

He didn't take the hint, lingering on the doorstep for a moment, peering over my shoulder into the hall. 'I wanted a word with you – urgently.'

'Very well. I'll put Thane into the garden. He won't touch you – but wait here, if you must.' And so saying I said goodbye to Thane who gave me a despairing look as he trotted off across the garden.

Marks was at my heels looking around suspiciously as if the deerhound might be lurking behind the chair I indicated, ready to snap at his ankles.

Watching him sit down cautiously, knees close together, I could hardly contain my anger. This wretched man arrives univited, ignores the fact that I'm about to leave and complains about my dog.

He leaned forward. 'Well, Mrs McQuinn, and what news have you for me?'

'None, I'm afraid. It's early days, You will have to be patient, Mr Marks.'

He gave me a sarcastic glance. 'You haven't abandoned my missing wife, I hope. I have not forgotten our financial arrangement – if that is a problem.' So saying, he made a movement towards his pocket.

I said sharply, 'If you please, Mr Marks, I do not accept payment until I see evidence of some promising results.' I felt even angrier than before. This unexpected interview was not going at all well.

'I am relieved to hear that you are an honest business woman, Mrs McQuinn,' he said in tones clearly indicating he had had servious doubts about that as he added, 'and that this is not just some fanciful little spare-time hobby.'

Before I could frame an indignant reply, he went on, 'Did you perhaps manage to fit in a visit to my sister-in-law Mrs Edgley?'

Longing to slap that smug countenance, I said calmly, 'I called on her immediately after your instructions at our last interview. She had no further information to add to what she had already told you concerning Mrs Marks' whereabouts. And she certainly was not concealing your wife in the house, or would have had any inclination, or considering its limited accommodation, or any ability to do so.'

He looked disappointed, gnawing at his moustache. 'Where do you intend going next?'

I hadn't the slightest idea, unless he was not telling the truth concerning recognition of the woman's body washed up at Granton.

'Perhaps you can give me some other ideas where to pursue my enquiries? Such as other contacts, however trivial and unimportant they might seem to you, so that I can continue my search further afield.'

He cocked an eyebrow at me. 'I was given to understand that searching was your speciality, Mrs McQuinn.'

Under my breath, I cursed Nancy for her part in all this, for giving Desmond Marks a false interpretation of my powers as an investigator. I didn't like the man any better than at our first meeting – less so, in fact, and I had a feeling that he was unlikely to grow on me.

Sadly, I was completely out of sympathy with him, obviously a serious disadvantage for sustaining a cordial and satisfactory working relationship between investigator and client.

'If you wish me to continue then I must warn you that this is a very different case from the ones I normally encounter. The solitary, flimsy piece of information I received from you had a completely negative result.' Pausing, I added slowly, 'I am presuming that you did in fact tell me everything you knew, Mr Marks.'

'Of course I did,' was the indignant reply. 'What on earth would I have to gain by concealing any vital information?'

I shrugged. 'I am merely pointing out that it is essential if I am to succeed that I have all the facts and I must emphasise again – no matter how unimportant or trivial they appear to you.'

A gesture of despair, an expression so glum and crestfallen almost convinced me that he was indeed the distraught husband he pretended to be. Almost but not quite, as I added, 'As you suspect that your wife is no longer in Edinburgh, my best advice would be for you to leave the matter entirely in the hands of the police. They have other resources than those at my disposal.'

'I have already listed Nora as missing,' he said stiffly.

But I observed how at the mention of the police, his face took on, just for an instant, a hunted look. With good reason, if my suspicions were right and Nora Marks was dead. And he knew it, having arranged for her murder. Now that her killer Peter McHully was also dead, had Marks been feeling safe and secure?

I glanced at the clock. 'I am going to Leith. I could look in and see Mrs Edgley again if you think that would help, see if she has had any word from Mrs Marks.'

He brightened at that. 'If you would, I'd be grateful.' And with a curious look. 'What takes you to Leith again?'

It was no business of his, but I told him I was visiting a friend in hospital and he looked politely concerned.

'Nothing serious, I trust.'

'An old gentleman who lives nearby – he got rather badly burned last night.'

He tut-tutted at that. 'It happens every year, these Bonfire Nights. Very dangerous, all those fireworks ought to be forbidden by law. I trust your friend recovers soon.'

As he rose to leave, I said, 'I was sorry to hear about your friend from the Opera Society.'

A puzzled look. 'What friend would that be.'

'Peter McHully.'

A gesture. 'Oh – Peter.' And an apologetic laugh. 'He wasn't a particular friend, Mrs McQuinn, a mere acquaintance. Hardly knew him at all. The company's handyman, he possessed a good voice. Like so many of the Irish, a gift they seem to be born with.'

Pausing he added, 'I didn't realise his real passion, nor did any of us. Didn't flaunt his political opinions in our society fortunately.'

'A sad business,' I said.

'Indeed yes. I understand his funeral is today.'

I followed him to the door. 'Will you be going?'

His face registered genuine astonishment. 'In my business

we are only allowed time off for family funerals.' And poking his head out, he stared across the garden nervously as if expecting Thane to bear down on him. Then turning, he said the conventional thing about a future meeting and his fervent hopes for more news.

I watched him walk down the road past Rory's burnt-out ditch. As he stopped and stared down into it, I wondered if that was just idle curiosity or if there was a deeper, more sinister interpretation.

Closing the door, I collected my bicycle from the barn with another reason for this visit to Leith.

I was curious to see Peter McHully's lady friend, Yvonne, lately Lady Carthew's light-fingered personal maid.

Chapter Twenty-One

It wasn't a bad day for a funeral, if mild winter sunshine could lessen the ache of loss and make bereavement easier to bear.

And it would have been difficult to miss this funeral as the dock workers – the rioters, according to the police description – were out in force with banners and wreaths, with McHully's body carried in a fine hearse with four black-plumed horses.

I followed at a discreet distance to the church with its dusty kirkyard where I parked my bicycle at the railings and stood aside respectfully to let the cortege pass.

'Hello – back again? What are you doing here?'

Turning I saw Nellie Edgley, surprised to see me, so I said I was heading to the hospital to visit a friend.

'It's just down the road there, you can't miss it' she said helpfully. And looking towards the crowd in the kirkyard, she sighed. 'Aye, Peter's got a good send-off, right enough. The lad's heart was in the right place, whatever they say. My Ben's one of the pall-bearers,' she added proudly.

'Sad day for all of you.'

'Aye, and for his wife and a couple of wee bairns.'

That didn't fit Mrs Laing's theory. 'I thought he was unmarried.'

She gave me a puzzled look. 'What gave you that idea?'

'I must have read it in the papers.'

'They got it wrong then. I can't read – never learned. But Ben tells me all I need to know. Says I'm not missing much and the papers are all lies anyways.'

'Did you know the McHullys?'

She shrugged. 'Just moved here – from East Lothian way.'

I glanced through the railings. All I could see were men and the occasional shawled women, onlookers who weren't part of the cortege.

'Is Mrs McHully there?'

Nellie looked astonished. 'Wives dinna go to funerals, hen,' she said as if I'd just arrived from another planet.

I'd forgotten that widows don't in Scotland. Funerals are regarded as men's work, grim, strong and stiff in the upper lips. The widow is expected to stay at home, cry her eyes out and make the ham sandwiches.

Nellie adjusted the pin on her shawl. 'Ah well, I suppose helping hands'll be needed,' she said significantly.

'Any word of your sister?'

'Not as much as a whisper.' Staring at me, she laughed. 'Got Desmond real worried, hasn't she. Serve him bloody well right.'

There wasn't much point in remaining unless I could inveigle an invitation to the McHully house, which wasn't very likely. And gate-crashing a funeral wake with some questions for the widow about her late husband and his fancy woman were beyond the pale of delicacy and decorum.

There are some tricky situations that not even murder can change, and heading to the hospital Nellie had indicated, I realised that it would take more than bright sunshine and a few birds singing in a kirkyard to cheer up my flagging spirits.

Confused now by McHully's matrimonial status, I wondered if Mrs Laing's suppositions about Miss Binns were also all wrong. As for keeping her in Leith where he already had a wife and two bairns – that sounded like a recipe for disaster. If it was true, at that moment I would have opted for Mrs McHully's hand on the pistol that had killed him.

Wheeling my bicycle up the hospital drive, I saw that it was one of the 'cottage' variety, much less forbidding and institutional than those in Edinburgh. This good impression only lasted as far as the entrance hall, alas, where I was met by the traditional hospital smell of disinfectant fighting for supremacy over urine and worse.

It touched a chord of another smell which I had encountered recently, but as I rang the bell and waited, I couldn't think where.

At last I spotted a cleaner with bucket and mop marching purposefully across the floor. Asking for directions, I was told, 'Upstairs. Down the corridor to the right. Far end.'

Climbing the stairs, I found the notice 'Wards' just as a man emerged in front of me, walking fast away.

'Excuse me. Can you help…' I called

He turned quickly, startled. A young man, well dressed. 'Are you the doctor?' I asked.

His face registered terror and confusion as he scuttled off through a door marked 'Staff Only'. In his haste he collided with a nurse pushing a trolley laden with medicine bottles and boxes of pills.

As I helped her set the bottles to rights I asked where I might find an old man just admitted with burns whom I knew only as Rory. Flustered and angry she pointed to the ward from which the young man had so hastily emerged.

I thanked her and said, 'Was that one of your doctors off to an emergency?'

She grunted. 'Never seen him before and if I see him again I'll give him a piece of my mind for his bad manners, that I will.'

At the door I paused. 'This is the room that fellow came tearing out of. I presumed he was a doctor. I wanted to ask him—'

But the nurse wasn't interested. She nodded absently and head down, pushed her trolley rapidly along the corridor. As she was in such an obvious hurry, I didn't detain her.

After all, it might well be life or death, I thought, entering the little room. And there was Rory, lying with his eyes closed.

At first glance I thought I'd got it wrong since the man in the bed didn't look in the least like the Rory I knew. His face was grey where there weren't any red marks of burns, and his beard had been shaved off, his grizzled hair tied back.

They'd also shorn off fifteen years of his age. Nevertheless, he looked very ill, as if he was dying – or already dead, lying there so still, hardly breathing at all.

'Rory.' I whispered.

There was no response.

A sound behind me and another nurse bustled in. This one exuded authority.

'This is not a visiting hour, madam.'

And with sudden compassion pointing to the inert figure, 'Your father, is he?'

'No, just a friend. Is – is he going to be all right?' I asked watching her face anxiously as she took his pulse.

But she seemed satisfied, nodded and tucked his bandaged hand back under the covers. 'We'll know better in a day or two, if his fever doesn't turn into pneumonia. Next time you come,' she added not ungently, 'you should leave your name at the desk. We admit relatives only to our very sick patients.'

'He did have a visitor – before me. A young man, he was leaving the ward here just as I arrived.'

She shrugged. 'That would be one of the doctors.' Then she giggled. 'Young, did you say, Well I never, they will be flattered. Neither of them will see fifty-five again.' She chortled and peered at me as if she thought I was in dire need of spectacles.

I wasn't going to argue but as I was leaving I saw there was now a nurse at the hitherto empty reception desk. This time I might get some information as, presumably, Rory's young visitor had asked for directions too before walking upstairs.

To my question the young nurse flushed scarlet and

whispered guiltily: 'I was – called away – only absent for a minute or two – and visitors are supposed to ring the bell, you know,' she added severely.

I didn't mention that I had done so, twice, without effect.

Walking down the front steps very thoughtfully, I considered the young man who wasn't a doctor yet had known where to find Rory.

There were two possibilities. First, he had read the account in this morning's paper. "Old Vagrant's Narrow Escape from Death. Another Bonfire Night Mishap." Or second, realising Rory was still alive, he had come to the hospital to finish the job he had mismanaged last night but had been disturbed. In all probability by the sound of my footsteps outside coming down the corridor.

I thought again of that brief glimpse of a rather nice face. He didn't look like a killer, but then killers seldom do. I had mistaken him for a doctor. I hadn't seen him before and Auld Rory had never mentioned to me any acquaintance in Edinburgh who might have been his visitor.

And then I had a flash of inspiration. The only person he had ever spoken of, and that so bitterly, was the son he had come to search for. Could the early visitor have been the same alienated son who, no doubt smote with pangs of conscience, had read the newspaper report and come in to see his father.

If that was so, it still didn't explain why he had fled in such terror when he saw me, a stranger, approaching.

Heading back to the Tower, I had reached the road leading to Duddingston from St Anthony's Chapel when the prickling sensation at the back of my neck, with me since I left Leith was unmistakeable.

I was being followed.

I had noticed a closed hackney cab standing outside the

hospital and casually dismissed it. But each time I stopped at the roadends and turned to see what, if any, traffic was to be negotiated, there was the cab again.

The driver with a scarf up to his nose, his face half hidden and a bonnet down over his eyes became a sinister figure anxious not to be recognised.

The road to Duddingston was fairly isolated and not greatly popular with vehicles. Inconveniently narrow, there was little room to turn a carriage without heading well past the Tower where the road widened.

I looked over my shoulder. The cab was behind me, the road ahead deserted. Suddenly within sight of the Tower, the driver whipped up his horse and as the vehicle thundered towards me I had to leap smartly aside.

My bicycle and I almost landed in the ditch and scrambling up, considerably shaken, I watched the cab disappear. Scared, but most of all, furious.

Was I marked down as the next victim? Another accident just yards away from where Rory had been set on fire?

Instead of rushing into the Tower and bolting the door like any sensible young woman, alone and vulnerable, would have done, disregarding my fast-beating heart I remounted my bicycle and pedalled as fast as I could down the road after the cab.

It was about thirty yards ahead of me and turning the corner into Duddingston Village, I lost sight of it. When I reached the church it had gone. The road through the village was quite empty of traffic.

I was baffled and annoyed too since there was no way the cab could have vanished so completely.

A postman emerged from one of the houses, whistling, inspecting his letters. Wheeling quickly towards him I asked, 'Excuse me, I'm looking for a hackney cab.'

Eyeing the bicycle with a puzzled expression, he said, 'A cab, miss?

'Yes, I'm looking for one.'

He shook his head. 'You'll never get one here, miss.'

'It's not for myself. But I thought I saw one on the road heading in this direction.'

Again he stared first at the bicycle and then at me, as if I had gone mad. 'I never noticed it, miss, never even heard it and I've been in and out of gates all along the street. Well, I never.' Pausing, he pushed back his bonnet to scratch his forehead. 'Must be heading for Musselburgh by now, miss.'

And that was true. The driver hadn't turned on the road, or he would have passed me. And this was the fastest route back to Edinburgh. The more frequented and accessible but longer road took in Craigmillar Village.

Thanking him for his help, I returned the way I'd come, certain that I was no longer in any danger.

I wouldn't be followed this time. The second attempt at murder near Solomon's Tower had failed.

I'd live to find the killer another day.

And although that put me on my mettle, it was not a great consolation to my state of nerves. I had plenty to think about as I changed into a skirt and jacket, a more decorous outfit for my visit to Carthew House and an interview with the General.

Shaken by my recent encounter, I could have well done without such an expedition but I was more than a little flattered and decidedly curious to find out what assignment Sir Angus Carthew had in mind for a lady investigator.

Chapter Twenty-Two

As I walked across the hill to keep my appointment with the General I thought how inappropriately mild the weather was. Childhood memories of Edinburgh dictated snow and high winds, frost-burned cheeks by November. Arizona with summer all the year round had added to that illusion.

Today the sun sparkled on the River Forth. Fishing boats like children's paper toys drifted leisurely back to harbour. The landscape down to East Lothian a series of green indentations, the shoreline dotted with a froth of white lace.

And on the horizon, glowering over all, the Lammermuir Hills, a dark and menacing reminder suggesting, even after three hundred years, the threat of, and constant vigilance for, Border raiders streaming forth from its steep slopes and deep valleys.

Nearer at hand, a blackbird seriously misled by the mild weather followed my progress from bush to branch with a song of rapturous passion and joy. Every female blackbird within twenty miles was no doubt marking him down on her card as a future mate.

As the lane came into view I said, 'Well done, Mr B. Keep it up and you'll be in fine voice for the carol season.'

Opening the gate, I heard the children with Nancy in the stable yard, patting one of a pair of fine black horses being groomed. The other stalled horse regarded this activity with moody disdain from over the half-door. At his slight neigh of displeasure Torquil rushed over to pet him too.

When she saw me, Tessa ran to my side, seized my hand, clinging to my arm in her usual affectionate manner.

'Can Mrs McQuinn come with us, Nanny? Oh, please!'

I shook my head. 'Alas no, Tessa. Another time but today I am here to see your uncle.'

As I spoke Nancy hid a smile, looking secretive, she avoided my eyes. 'And we are just off for our afternoon walk. Come along, Torquil.'

Surprised that she did not display her normal curiosity about my meeting with the General, I watched her gather up Torquil who, deaf to all commands, continued to pet the horse.

While she tried to wrest him away, beyond the stall I had a glimpse of the dark interior of the coach house. The General's handsome family carriage and alongside, a smaller more practical vehicle of the hackney cab variety, built for speed rather than elegance.

Jim, the stable boy, polishing its interior looked up and said proudly, 'The General is a keen sportsman, goes in for racing too…' He began a detailed and elaborate explanation of how carriages were adapted, of which I understood only some vague facts relating to wheel balance, betting and courses.

'There are special courses?' I said.

'Aye, miss, there are. Way out on the outskirts of the town.'

Behind me, Nancy said, 'They're very popular with the wealthy young blades of Edinburgh.' She shook her head. 'A very dangerous hobby it can be, isn't that so, Jim?'

Jim grinned. 'Arms and legs – and necks – get broken regular, miss. And it don't do the horses no good either.'

As we left him, Nancy sighed. 'The things men will do for thrills, Rose. According to Lady Carthew, the General fancies himself in the role of an ancient Roman charioteer.'

There was something I meant to ask her then, something that seemed important at the time, but as we had reached the front door where our ways divided, she said, 'I mustn't delay you or you'll be late. That would never do, would it?' she added mysteriously and, seizing the children's hands, she headed towards the drive with my promise that of course they might all come and visit me at the Tower very soon.

Waiting at the front door, I realised that what I imagined as gardens could be more aptly described as grounds of a large estate. None of this had been evident on the short cut across the hill on my first visit in the gathering dusk of the Bonfire Night afternoon.

Mrs Laing opened the door, looking flustered and wiping her hands on her apron, somehow inappropriate to the fine mansion which deserved a bewigged footman or at least a uniformed maid to attend such lowly chores.

There was no need to introduce myself. 'You are expected, Mrs McQuinn. Sir Angus is attending to Lady Carthew at the moment, but he will be with you presently. Would you care to take a seat in the library?'

I followed the large homely lady whose countenance looked as if those scarlet cheeks had been acquired through being poised perpetually over the heat of a blazing stove. No doubt thanks to secondhand reports from Nancy, she was as curious about me as I was about her and less subtle at hiding the fact.

When she made no move to leave and continued to wipe her hands on her apron, I decided it might not be curiosity after all that detained her but perhaps fears for the welfare and safety of the silver.

A rather lengthy silence was broken by, 'The children are out with Nanny Brook.'

It seemed odd to hear her so described. Jack had known her as Nancy Craig, Brook came through the wishes of a parent's second marriage.

I was reminded that nannies belong to the upper rank of domestic servants and are called by their surnames. This I had learned when I returned to Edinburgh and visited our housekeeper from Sheridan Place days, Mrs Brook, Nancy's relative, who was not the sad widow I had thought of since childhood days.

In fact she had never been married at all. 'Mrs' was merely a courtesy title to gain respect from junior domestics and also to keep the attentions of lascivious male servants at bay.

'She will be sorry to have missed you, Mrs McQuinn. She thinks very highly of you,' said Mrs Laing valiantly making conversation and I smiled at this recommendation.

'We met briefly as I came through the stable yard.'

'Oh!' she said in tones of astonishment more appropriate to news of a meeting on a distant planet. 'Did you really?'

Another silence and I walked over to the window and looked out across the garden.

'A lovely gracious room, isn't it?' said Mrs Laing. 'This is the only part of the original house that wasn't pulled down by Sir Angus's grandfather. They kept it intact because of the grand view of Arthur's Seat.'

I noticed a small domed building almost hidden by trees which had been invisible in the growing darkness of my first visit. 'What a pretty gazebo.'

She stared at me. Perhaps the word was unfamiliar. I substituted, 'A summer house.'

She made a face. 'No, Mrs McQuinn. That is the Carthew family vault. Sir Hector decided he loved the house he had built so much that if he couldn't take it to heaven with him, then he'd do the next best thing and be buried in his own garden. So he had the ground...' Frowning, she searched for the word.

'Consecrated?' I offered.

'That's it! The family have all been laid to rest there, but Sir Angus and Lady Carthew will be the last,' she said sadly. 'As they have no children to follow, Sir Angus has left orders for it to be sealed up when the time comes—'

A sound of footsteps. As the General entered the room, Mrs Laing bobbed a curtsey and withdrew.

'Do sit down, Mrs McQuinn. I am sorry to be late. My dear wife requires my attention to deal with her toilette. In the temporary absence of a lady's maid, I have become quite adept at such matters,' he added with a rueful smile as he looked down at me. No great difficulty for a man of six foot three and a woman who could only reach five by standing on tiptoe!

Smiling, he regarded me with such warm friendliness that I realised again how devastating he must have been as a young man.

He had charm and power. That produced a fleeting thought of Desmond Marks whose good looks were superficial, his charm a mite insincere in the certainty that every woman he met was ready to be his willing slave.

Not so the General. There was no hint of flirtation in his manner. I doubted if the soldier in him would have known where to begin as he took a seat opposite.

'And now to business, the reason for this visit, Mrs McQuinn. I suppose you are wondering why I brought you here,' he added gently.

I wasn't prepared to guess, so smiling politely, I waited.

'Nanny Brook was showing the children a remarkable painting of sunrise on Arthur's Seat when I happened to be passing by the nursery.' He paused and looked at me. 'She informed me that you were the artist. Is that so?'

I agreed modestly. 'Miss Brook asked me if she could have the painting. I was somewhat reluctant to let her have it.'

His eyebrows shot up at that, his expression suddenly shrewd. 'I am sure your reluctance was advisable. The painting would sell in an Edinburgh art gallery for a considerable sum of money. Such landscapes I know do very well—'

'Sir,' I interrupted. 'You are mistaken. I had no intention of selling it. I simply did not consider it good enough. A poor effort and that was my only reason for not wishing to part with it – as a present. Painting is a hobby that gives me great pleasure but I do not set myself up alongside professional artists.'

The General shook his head. 'You are wrong, Mrs McQuinn, you have my word for that. However, your modesty does you credit.' And sitting back he regarded me narrowly. 'An admirable trait in a young woman,' A vigorous nod. 'As a matter of fact, your expertise is the reason why I asked you to come here today.'

Ignoring my gesture of protest, he went on, 'My little niece Tessa is showing signs of having exhibited some of her late mother's talent. Dear Ellen was a most talented artist.' He sighed deeply, remembering. 'Tessa was very taken with your painting. Indeed she has persuaded Nanny Brook to allow her to hang it on the nursery wall during their visit with us.'

Again that shrewd glance. 'I am certain that her father would be prepared to buy it for her.' He watched my expression. 'For a not inconsiderable sum.'

'It is no longer mine to sell, sir. A gift to Miss Brook. It now belongs to her.'

'Perhaps she could be persuaded to return it to you ?'

'That is her business.' I tried not to sound indignant at this proposal with a gesture of dismissal I hoped was not too impolite. The interview was a disappointment but it had convinced me that here was a man used to getting his own way, and paying for it if necessary.

I picked up my gloves. I suppose I should have felt flattered but instead I was disappointed that this had been his sole reason for inviting me to call at Carthew House.

No secret assignment. My 'discretion guaranteed' was not being called into action.

'One more moment of your time, Mrs McQuinn, if you please. Tessa has expressed a keen desire to learn to paint. She is so enthusiastic, she feels this would also bring her closer to her mother who recognised her talent and had just begun to give her lessons. I will be candid with you, Mrs McQuinn, the child misses her dreadfully. She is quite heart-broken.'

As he paused to let that unhappy fact sink in I remembered the loving manner in which she greeted me, her craving for affection.

'I wonder if I could call upon your time and your good nature to take her on as a pupil, say, two afternoons a week for the duration of her stay with us.'

I was taken aback by his request but the thought of sad, motherless Tessa succeeded where nothing else would have done.

'Of course, sir, I am willing to help. Although I am not at all sure of my capabilities, but if you think my services will benefit Tessa at this present unhappy time.'

He looked at me, nodded. 'Excellent. I am most grateful. But you have not mentioned a fee for these services. May I ask…?'

I must have looked appalled. I raised a hand in protest. 'It would be my pleasure to help Tessa. I certainly don't need paying for that,' I said indignantly.

Still regarding me, he rubbed his chin thoughtfully. 'Nanny Brook was right in her praise of you.'

So I had Nancy to thank. She had been responsible for this interview and the proposed lessons for Tessa. And that explained why she had behaved so mysteriously when we met in the stable yard.

'There is no way I could accept your services without due payment,' the General continued. 'Come, Mrs McQuinn, Nanny Brook tells me that you are a business-woman. You must know then that to succeed, there are strict rules about such matters. That even the humble labourer is worth his hire, or so we are told.'

And the salary he offered for six hours' tuition per week deprived me of speech. I had to ask him to repeat it twice in case I had misheard, for it would have kept many talented young artists from starving to death this winter in their cold draughty Edinburgh garrets.

And I knew I could not afford to turn down such an offer. I had no investigations on hand except the search for Desmond Marks' missing wife which had reached an impasse and I feared would never repay my few enquiries.

So I agreed. Looking very pleased, the General showed me to the door himself with some polite enquiries about Vince and the possibility of a visit from Balmoral. He added again how he had enjoyed our meeting at Princss Beatrice's luncheon. Tactfully there was no mention of our next disastrous encounter at the protestors' march in Leith and McHully's savage killing.

'On the next occasion when your brother is in Edinburgh, we will arrange to have you both to dinner.'

As I made my way back through the stable yard, I presumed from the General's parting remark that 'we' included Lady Carthew.

I was in such a daze of disbelief that the Tower was in sight, before I turned and looked back the way I had come. Something jolted my memory, something important that I should have remembered, that had slipped to the back of my mind while I was talking to Nancy.

I shrugged. It would keep for the moment. And hugging secret joy at this totally unexpected little windfall from General Carthew, I concentrated on the mundane matter of what would be required in my new role as an art teacher.

Chapter Twenty-Three

Jack came by that evening and was surprised – and, I felt – pleased – that I had found a temporary situation unconnected with solving crime. He was particularly impressed by the salary I was being offered for six hours of painting lessons each week.

I could just imagine his thoughts rushing ahead…

Maybe this taste for teaching and dealing with small children would rekindle my early abilities and persuade me to apply for a post in one the newly opened schools in the Newington area.

While we were talking Nancy looked in on her way to rehearsals, very proud and excited since she had known from the outset of the General's intentions. As I suspected, she had planted the idea firmly in his mind by assuring him that before marriage I had been 'an excellent teacher of general subjects' in a Glasgow school.

She particularly wanted me to share her good opinion of Sir Angus and when I mentioned his generosity she clapped her hands delightedly.

'I could have guessed, Rose. Such a lovely man – and a lovely house too. I am so lucky. Oh, is that the time? I must rush!' As she left she looked longingly in Jack's direction but tonight no offer to escort her was forthcoming.

Thane arrived next day as I was leaving for Carthew House. He followed me across the hill but realising my destination, he hesitated, although he had accompanied Nancy and me on other occasions, taking his leave when the lane came into view.

Now as he lay down staring after me with a somewhat woebegone whimper, I had a strange feeling that he did not like that part of the hill, or the lane either. Come to think of it, I had never seen him leave Arthur's Seat. Perhaps there was a reason too subtle for a mere human to comprehend.

As I opened the gate to the stable yard, I looked back and he was still regarding me intently. His attitude was very similar to Nancy's when she anxiously watched the children crossing the road in safety.

Ahead the yard was deserted today, the horses in their stalls. At the front door, Nancy was waiting and she led the way into the library where a desk had been prepared in readiness for Tessa's first painting lesson.

A kindly action, since most parents or relatives would have regarded the fine library as out of bounds to small children. I had imagined we would have been banished to the upstairs nursery with our paints, to sit behind those stern, barred windows installed to restrain small children from leaning out too far and hurling themselves into the gardens below.

I had brought my own colours and paper but that would not be needed. There was a splendid array of materials, paintboxes and brushes, some of which had doubtless belonged to Tessa's mother.

A sound of excited footsteps on the stairs and the door flew open to admit Tessa and Torquil. Tessa hugged me in her usual exuberant manner and rushed to the desk as Nancy said, 'Shall I take Torquil—'

'No, Nanny,' he shrieked, 'I want to stay.'

Nancy shrugged with an apologetic and hopeful glance in my direction. 'If you don't mind, Rose…'

I could hardly refuse.

'Very well, then. There are things I have to do.' Obviously relieved, she turned to Torquil, 'Be good now and do as you are told.'

I wasn't sure how to begin with the little girl sitting opposite, her paint brush already poised over the paper, so I decided perspective would be a good thing. See if my pupil could draw straight lines.

Embarking on a beginner's lesson of simple objects, a box, a book, I demonstrated how to mix the paint and colour for her drawing.

She learned fast. 'Done those! What next, please, Mrs McQuinn,' she asked eagerly.

There was no lack of copyable objects all around us and I saw at once with a feeling of intense relief, that the General's faith in his small niece had been justified. Even at six years old, she displayed a natural talent for drawing and an eye for the correct colours.

The only fly in the ointment, so to speak, a very small but insistent fly, was Torquil. He stood by my side, snatching brushes, darting at colours Tessa was also using and thereby arousing her wrath.

There was but one solution and that was to include him in the lesson. His sister did not make any fuss, restricting her feelings of annoyance to a despairing heavenward sigh. Soon it was obvious that Torquil had inherited little artistic skill, adept at sloshing paint on paper, an activity which kept him quieted and afforded him considerable pleasure.

'Look at me, Mrs McQuinn. Look what I have painted.' Questioned politely, I was told it was a firework.

I was quite content to let my two charges paint to their hearts' content, to get the feeling of colour and shape for this first lesson, while reflecting on my own good fortune in being at leisure to enjoy such delightful surroundings.

The handsome panelled room with bookcases stretching from floor to high ceiling, the great carved fireplace with its log fire, and everywhere Kelim rugs and comfortable leather armchairs.

The feeling of affluence abounded. Beyond the window, I

caught a glimpse of the General and Lady Carthew leisurely strolling arm-in-arm, warmly clad for their afternoon walk, no doubt a routine activity for a mild winter day.

All around them in their lovely garden, trees shed golden leaves across their path, touched by deepening purple shadows enriching the landscape with a texture and richness lacking in bright sunlight.

Glancing towards the window, they saw me and waved as they entered the front door. I was looking forward to my first meeting with Lady Carthew and as the General led her into the library, she smiled through her veiled outdoor bonnet and took my hand.

'I am so glad to meet you, Mrs McQuinn, for I have heard much about you.'

A surprisingly warm handshake, firmer than I had expected, having anticipated an invalid's limp cold-fingered hand.

She looked at Tessa's painting, her arm around the little girl's shoulder. 'That is very good, my dear. You are clever! Your dear mamma in heaven will be so proud of you!'

Turning to me and with a smiling glance in her husband's direction, she said, 'I wonder if I might persuade you to do me a painting of Sir Angus.'

I shook my head. 'I fear that portraits are beyond my skills.'

Her eyes widened as she looked again at her husband. 'I was given to understand that you drew people as well as landscapes.'

'Mere pencil sketches, alas. I have never had the boldness to translate them into colour. A very different matter.'

She smiled again. 'I am sure you are too modest and anyone who can paint such lovely sunsets must have other artistic abilities.' And to Sir Angus, 'We are surrounded by such talented people, my dear. Our niece and nephew here,' she added, kissing Torquil's mop of curls, 'and a nanny who sings. We are so looking forward to the Opera Society's performance.'

'Indeed, yes, *Pirates* is our favourite in their whole repertoire,' said Sir Angus.

As I remembered that Nancy had told me of their enthusiasm and support, listening to Lady Carthew's pleasant resonant voice, I would not have been in the least surprised to learn that she had been, or had secret aspirations to be, a singer.

Her appearance impressed me. Tall and slim but without the invalid's frailty which I had anticipated from her confinement to the house and lack of social activities. And I felt a rush of compassion for whatever ailed her and kept this attractive young woman from leading the active life that her station in life demanded.

I considered her again. There was no apparent physical infirmity, from surface appearance anyway, but perhaps some female affliction. Observing her affection for Torquil and Tessa, her devotion to her handsome husband, and without any knowledge of her medical history, I would have hazarded a guess that she was in continual distress at being unable to produce a child to their marriage, a son to carry on the Carthew dynasty.

Many wives had been cruelly abandoned for this sad omission by more ambitious husbands and I thought with new regard for her husband's obvious tenderness and devotion.

Turning to leave, she said, 'It has been a great pleasure, Mrs McQuinn. Thank you for giving these little ones so much of your precious time.'

Did she not know how much I was being paid for these services, as she continued, 'No doubt we will meet often. I shall look in from time to time to see how Tessa progresses.'

I hoped too that I would see her on my visits and that her

remark was not merely a polite rejoinder. At that moment I entertained hopes that we might even become friends for there was something very appealing and sincere about Harriet Carthew.

Anyone who met the Carthews, or was five minutes in their company, must be immediately aware of the bond between this older man and his young second wife. Doubtless there had never been and never would be a breath of scandal to rock this happy household.

I felt confident that the General would never stray like the obnoxious Desmond Marks. Here was a man who having given his love would remain true for ever. For better or for worse, till death did them part and they were laid to rest together for all eternity in the peaceful vault waiting in the garden.

And as I left longing to remain in their company, I felt bitterly lonely. Envious too, wistful that the love of my life, Danny McQuinn, and I never had the chance to grow old together.

Chapter Twenty-Four

Back in the Tower, the more I considered my stroke of fortune in becoming acquainted with the Carthews, the more it seemed that fate had opened this door of opportunity when all other doors were apparently closing. With no offers of new cases for several weeks now, I was in growing despair.

And as if to confirm my fears, Desmond Marks arrived late that evening. He seemed a little reluctant to accept my invitation to cross the threshold, staring around suspiciously for signs of Thane in the vicinity.

Persuaded to take a seat, looking uncomfortable and remaining vigilant, he said, 'I have to tell you, I am here to terminate your investigation into my wife's disappearance.'

I was immediately on the alert. Were my suspicions correct that she was dead already and this was a cunning move to prove his innocence?

'You will be glad to know,' he continued, 'and I am happy to report, that I have just received a letter from her posted in Glasgow. When her sister was unable to – er, offer her hospitality—'

I thought the word ill chosen and would have called it 'refuge'.

'—Nora decided to visit an old friend she had worked with long ago. Someone I thought had dropped out of her life when we married. They had met again in Edinburgh by chance and Nora had failed to inform me.'

He sighed. 'You know what women are like, Mrs McQuinn. She remembered this old friend and hoped to punish me for, well, my indiscretions, shall we call them? However, this friend, with more intelligence than I would have credited her with, persuaded Nora that I had probably suffered long enough. Kind of her, was it not? And to cut a long story short, my wife has decided to remain in Glasgow on her friend's charity a little longer while considering our future together.'

Pausing he smirked. 'I have not the least doubt that she will shortly come to her senses, decide to mend her ways, return home and resume our life together.'

In his place I would not have been quite so confident. Nora Marks having once tasted freedom from tyranny might not care to resume their cat-and-dog existence, as Nancy described it.

'I am glad your mind is at rest, Mr Marks,' I put out my hand. 'May I see the letter, please?'

The request seemed to surprise him and he shook his head. 'I do not have it with me. Is a gentleman's word not good enough for you, Mrs McQuinn?'

In his case it was not, but I said, 'When closing a case it is usual to see some evidence of the missing person's return.'

Ignoring this statement, he stood up thanked me briefly and in a hurry to leave, thrust an envelope into my hand. 'Your fee, Mrs McQuinn. Two pounds for your trouble. I trust that is adequate.'

I would have liked to refuse since my only expense had been a bicycle ride to Leith. However, I decided to accept, two pounds would be very useful and pride has no place in an investigtor's life.

Showing him out, I said, 'You will, of course, be informing the police so that they may remove Mrs Marks' name from the missing persons list.'

He gave me a mocking smile. 'I have already done so.'

'Then you will find that they will also wish to see the letter you received from her.'

'Indeed yes. As a matter of fact I left it with them,' he said triumphantly.

As I watched him go, I decided I must talk to Jack, confirm that Marks was speaking the truth with the evidence now in police records.

The letter was vital. I imagined it being checked against other examples of Nora Marks' handwriting. For her husband was clever enough to think he could outsmart the police and any woman investigator by telling a pack of lies.

There were several plausible reasons. First, he was in the insurance business and almost inevitably would have a hefty premium on his own wife's life. An important consideration to anyone with even a mildly suspicious mind.

Then there was his association with Peter McHully who might well have been her hired killer and was now conveniently dead.

As for Desmond, feeling safe with his wife's body buried in some unknown and secure place, it followed that when she did not return from Glasgow, it would be assumed that she had vanished once again and in the passage of time, would be presumed dead.

Meanwhile the letter she had supposedly penned was undoubtedly a forgery. It was not unknown for a guilty man to travel to another town and drop such life-saving material in the nearest mailbox, worth the price of a train journey to prove his innocence.

When Jack arrived, most of my theories were proven to be wrong.

'Yes, Rose. We have the letter. He brought it in this morning.'

When I pointed out very solemnly the chance of it being a forgery, Jack laughed.

'Come along, Rose. We are on to all that.' He grinned. 'You can't teach the police anything about forgery. First thing we do is check letters with other examples of the sender's handwriting.'

'Has Marks produced some'

'No. Said he didn't know proof was expected. Sounded quite hurt and belligerent that we should doubt his word. So the lads told me. Anyway, he didn't think it would be a problem, said there must be birthday cards she'd sent him at home—'

'And did he take the letter back?'

'No. But why do you ask that now?'

'Isn't it obvious – he could have copied her signature from these birthday cards or whatever.'

Jack shook his head. 'No chance of that. We kept the letter.'

'When was it posted?'

'Two days ago, in Glasgow, according to the postmark. And before you ask – yes, he was there—'

'A remarkable coincidence, don't you think?' I said triumphantly.

'Yes, but it happens to be true. We had a plain-clothes lad make a few enquiries at the Edinburgh office on a supposed personal matter. Told Mr Marks was away to their Glasgow office that day.'

'I'm amazed at you knowing all this, that you didn't arrest him on the spot.'

'Wait a moment, Rose. We have nothing to charge him with. All I'm telling you is the normal elementary police procedure in such cases. Where missing persons are concerned, we check every detail.'

And at the mention of insurance policies, he said, 'That isn't new, either. Your father would have told you that false claims are a perpetual menace. Men who would never think of pocketing a silver spoon from a friend's table will happily defraud the insurance companies.'

'I was thinking about something much more serious than fraud,' I said grimly.

'Such as?'

'Murder.'

Jack stared at me and laughed. 'You surely don't think he murdered his wife? Rose, partners go missing every day of the week – a violent row and they take off, swearing never to return. But mostly like Mrs Winton, when tempers cool, they are back home within the week. Husbands and wives don't go round murdering each other, except if there is a very good reason—'

Pausing, he looked at me intently. 'So you thought it might be Nora Marks you – thought – you found in the old chapel.'

'It still might be,' I said obstinately.

'Not unless Desmond Marks is a superb actor. Remember, he said he didn't recognise her, looked ready to faint away.'

'You've said the words, Jack – a superb actor. He might just get away with it.'

'Hold on, Rose. To have a murder we have to have a body. Where is it?'

'I suspect he has found some place on the hill where no one will ever find her. You have told me often, there are plenty of deep fissures and caves miles long under Arthur's Seat.'

'True enough, they are rumoured to go right into the very core of what remains of our once-active volcano.'

He thought for a moment, then shrugged wearily. 'But I'm not prepared to go into all that St Anthony's Chapel business again, Rose. And you might as well know that the woman washed up at Granton has now been formally identified.'

'Who was she?'

'A woman from Fife out walking her little dog. He rushed into the sea, got into difficulties. She panicked, went after him, couldn't swim and drowned. Her father came and identified her. Heart-broken, his daughter was a middle-aged spinster who had devoted her life to taking care of her elderly invalid father and had ironically died first. That's life.' Pausing, he sighed sadly. 'No more cases to solve, Rose?'

I still wasn't convinced about Desmond Marks. 'There will be, given time,' I said firmly.

'And if not, you've found a pleasant occupation – and a very well-paid one – with the Carthews,' he said cheerfully. 'How did the lesson go?'

I told him about Tessa's progress and the meeting with Lady Carthew and how I was going to enjoy it all.

'You liked her ladyship, didn't you. That was a lucky break. And you have Nancy to thank for it all,' he added complacently.

And as he spoke, at the back of my mind, an uneasy shadow lurked. Something I had seen, a picture I couldn't quite put together. Like a jigsaw where I had been interrupted at a vital link.

Was it something to do with Desmond Marks that still plagued me?

If only I could remember what it was…

Before it was too late.

Chapter Twenty-Five

I rode out to Leith that morning to see Rory in hospital. As the nurse at the reception desk was involved with a woman holding a screaming infant, I made my own way unheralded to the ward.

Rory was asleep and he still looked grey and frail, a stranger without all the hair that had once concealed his features.

As if conscious of my presence, his eyes flickered open and I took his bandaged hand. 'Feeling better?'

'Dinna – like – this place. No' for the likes o' me.'

He looked towards the white ceiling and his eyes closed again as if the effort of speaking had exhausted him.

I waited for a few minutes hoping that he night talk to me again but he seemed to have drifted back to sleep, breathing heavily.

A nurse I hadn't seen before bustled in and wished me good day.

To my question about Rory, she looked anxiously at his still figure. 'We must remember that he's an old man and he's had a terrible shock. But his burns were minor and they are making satisfactory progress so we certainly aren't giving up hope that he will make a complete recovery.'

And ushering me towards the door. 'Try not to worry, my dear, these things take time. And your father is in excellent hands here.'

I didn't bother to explain but asked, 'Has he had any other visitors?'

She nodded. 'A young man has been in to see him – twice, I think.'

When I asked his name, she seemed surprised. 'I just saw him as I was on my rounds.' And eyeing me curiously. 'I presumed he was a relative, but they'll be able to tell you at the desk downstairs.'

Following her instructions, I asked the nurse at reception about Rory's visitor.

'There's a book there,' she pointed, 'for folks to sign their name, who they are visiting, the time and so forth.'

Obviously the hotel reception was not run on the most efficient lines for when I looked through the last two days there was no entry for Rory.

When I pointed this out, she said defensively. 'Well, they are supposed to sign in and out as a courtesy. We don't make a strict rule. We haven't time for that, miss. But Mr Rory definitely had a visitor. A young man, a couple of times – I pointed out the book to him and told him to sign but there were other folks. He seemed to be in a great rush.'

'What was he like?'

She seemed taken aback at the question. 'As a matter of fact, I do remember him. Tall and slim, fair hair, good-looking chap. Very polite.' she added, smiling at the memory and obviously impressed, she blushed slightly.

I rode back to the Tower, excited by my latest discovery and when Jack arrived, I told him about Rory and his young visitor.

'Don't you see, this must be the same one I thought was a doctor. Remember how he bolted through the staff door when I spoke to him.'

'Why on earth should he do that?' he laughed. 'And you wearing only one of your two heads!'

I ignored that. Jack inclines towards the facetious on occasion. I forgive him these little lapses, presuming it is the stress of his work.

I said severely, 'He obviously didn't want to be seen. However, since he's been in twice to see Rory, there must be some connection. He didn't leave his name at the desk which is a pity. I'd like to meet him.'

'Did this nurse say what he looked like?'

'Oh yes. Tall, slim, fair, good-looking. She seemed very impressed.' I paused. 'Don't you see, Jack, he's got to be Rory's estranged son. If only we knew how to contact him.'

Jack smiled. 'Well, I can help you there. I know exactly where this mysterious fellow is at this moment.'

'You do!'

'Yes, Rose. Come with me.' Instead of hurrying towards the door, he pushed me in front of the big mirror over the fireplace.

'Behold! Tall, fair and slim – we'll leave the good-looking out of it.' And pointing at our reflections he smiled. 'There you are, Rose. That's Rory's visitor.'

'You, Jack!'

'Aye, Rose, the very same. I've been in Leith on a case and looked in a couple of times. Like the nurse said I was in a great rush and hadn't time to stop and sign the visitors' books.'

I could hardly suppress my disappointment when he asked, 'How did you think Rory was? Did you see any improvement?'

'Not a great deal.'

'Nor did I.' He sighed. 'But I was also there on official business. Hoping he might have recovered sufficiently to tell us something about that fire,' he added angrily. 'That doesn't seem likely at the moment. We'll just have to be patient.'

'As the nurse told me. From the only words he muttered when I was there, I gathered he hates being in hospital.'

Jack sighed. 'And that's another problem we have to sort out. We must make some future plans for him. He can't go back to living in a ditch again.'

'I agree. Didn't you tell me the hospital is run by the Church Council?'

'Yes. I'm hoping they might find a place for him.'

'If he'll accept,' I said doubtfully. 'How do you think he'll take to living under a roof after half a lifetime in the open?'

And there we had to leave it. On a cheerier subject, Jack returned to my painting lessons with Tessa. Pleased that I was to be so occupied for the immediate future, he added, 'You've finally given up on that other business?'

I knew exactly what business he meant.

In the face of no body ever being found, I had no alternative but to accept that I had made a grievous mistake. The woman I had seen at St Anthony's Chapel, as Jack had insisted right from the start, had merely fainted, perhaps she had fallen, as he maintained, had been momentarily stunned, recovered and walked away.

I could have accepted that, but the bogus constable was another matter.

And then Jack produced a rather shocking suggestion which he put to me with a certain male reluctance. As if this wasn't quite the ticket to discuss with a lady.

I guessed from my days of rougher living in Arizona that there were certain matters that even the toughest and crudest of men talked freely about to each other, but regarded as grossly indecent for even a saloon girl's ears. Strictly male territory, from which wives and sweethearts must be protected and excluded. And I knew I was being privileged to enter that forbidden world when Jack said he suspected the two had maybe been playing some erotic love game.

'A game – like charades?' I asked.

'Sort of.' He looked uncomfortable. 'Some couples find it very stimulating to their love-making, if they – er, well dress up.'

Without going into details, Jack said these activities were usually quite harmless. Harmless, I thought, not unaware of rumours concerning gentlemen's clubs in Edinburgh catering for the more grotesque tastes of the wealthy. For those who could afford them – children, boys... My mind shuddered away from further imaginings on which, I suspected, the police might be well paid to turn a discreetly blind eye.

'Let's suppose,' Jack was saying, 'that this particular couple found making love in the open more exciting, dangerous even. And from a practical angle, if they were both married to other partners, out of doors was the only safe place where they were unlikely to be discovered...'

Surely they could have found a sanctuary a little more comfortable than a ruined chapel on a cold night was my contribution.

'A hotel bedroom, perhaps. Is that what you're thinking?' Jack shook his head. 'Dangerous places for illicit lovers. Walls have ears and waiters have eyes. There's another problem – I can tell you of cases where the only time men can – er, perform – is with the thought of the irate husband walking in the door at any moment. Anyway, back to our illicit lovers.'

His eyes narrowed as he continued, 'Let's suppose the woman's fantasy was being made love to by a policeman in uniform.' Pausing he grinned at me. 'And that is by no means far-fetched, I assure you. Ask any handsome young, or even not so young, bobby on the beat. Suppose these two had been drinking, had over-indulged, perhaps the woman had taken some stimulants. She lost consciousness and at that moment, a nosey women arrived on the scene with an inquisitive dog.'

He regarded me thoughtfully. 'You believed that your bogus PC Smith was McHully, didn't you – before he was killed that day at Leith?'

The memory was still painful. 'I had only a glimpse of him, but yes, I felt sure that we had met before.'

'If you are right, then McHully, who had a wife and two

bairns in Leith, was a bit of a womaniser—'

'That fits. According to Nancy via Mrs Laing he was carrying on with Lady Carthew's maid and when she was dismissed, she had gone away with him.'

Jack considered that for a moment. 'We could take that a step further. Perhaps he had also discovered a lucrative sideline indulging rich Edinburgh ladies in their fantasies.'

I was doubtful about that, remembering the dead woman's neat but shabby clothes, the darned petticoat. 'She wasn't dressed like a rich Edinburgh lady.'

'Well, she wouldn't be, would she, if she didn't want to be recognised, she'd want to look as anonymous as possible – and to be practical – wear something suitable for the heather on Arthur's Seat. Her maid's clothes would be perfect for the occasion.'

He frowned. 'You know, I think we're getting somewhere with this, Rose, solving your mystery. Let's think back, you met the constable on the road, remember. He had gone for the carriage—'

'What about Charlie, the driver?'

He shrugged. 'That's easy. They'd hired it and invented him for your benefit.'

'As a matter of fact I looked in at the Pleasance hiring establishment and was informed by Mr Micklan that he did not have a driver called Charlie in his employ.'

Jack's eyebrows raised at that. 'Well, well, you have been busy. What led you down that particular road?'

'I noticed that they did vehicle repairs and I was concerned about my buckled wheel.'

'The one I mended,' Jack said heavily. When I murmured that it felt rather insecure, he said acidly, 'Thanks for your cofidence. I thought I had done rather well. And what else did you find out?'

'Nothing useful. However, I met Mr Micklan coming out of the stables at Carthew House.'

'A guarantee of good workmanship and reliability. The General would only deal with the best. Now where were we?'

'The bogus PC Smith,' I reminded him. 'And the uncomfortable dalliance of illicit lovers.'

He looked thoughtful. 'Supposing our constable was merely bringing the cab closer to the chapel. They wouldn't have parked it nearby in case it attracted the curious and for the same reason, he didn't want to carry his lady friend fifty yards back along the road.'

I could see that would be difficult to explain as I remembered something else. 'Jack, wait a minute – what you just said about stimulants, being drunk. When I bent over her, I thought it was some sort of strong perfume, a distinctive smell.'

'Go on.'

'Now I know exactly what it was,' I said excitedly. 'Because I encountered it again very recently. The same faint smell was in the hospital corridor when I visited Rory.'

Jack whistled. 'Chloroform. They could have been experimenting with chloroform. That's very interesting, Rose, very interesting indeed. And there was no way the man could explain to a nice respectable young woman what you had interrupted. So he kept to his role of a police constable – to get rid of you as quickly as possible.'

I remembered how nervous he had been, but it still seemed too fantastic a solution. When I shook my head in disbelief, Jack said, 'I know, Rose, but I assure you people like this exist in your nice respectable Edinburgh. Quiet, well-behaved citizens who never put a foot wrong in their business and family lives by day and then – at night – the whole scene changes.'

'Like Dr Jekyll and Mr Hyde.'

'Exactly. Our Mr Stevenson knew a thing or two about this city he lived in. His student carousings down Leith Walk must have revealed goings-on that even he dare only hint at in print. You have to be a policeman to be aware of Edinburgh's seamy side. Doctors know too. Your stepbrother Vince must have had to deal discreetly with cases of excessive drug-taking and of venereal diseases among rich patients, as well as child prostitution.'

He paused. 'Your father was aware of it too, Rose, make no mistake about that. But he would have kept the knowledge of such corruption well away from his little daughters. He must have felt you were safe from such things in Orkney.'

Jack's theory was still difficult to believe, but somewhere there lurked a grain of truth. And I knew he was being kind, giving me the benefit of the doubt, as it were. For the only other explanation, which he must have toyed with, however reluctantly, was that I had dreamed up the whole thing. That would not have suited his purpose – or his love for me – at all.

So fantastic it might be, but the perversions of the rich were a fact of life. In the society in which I lived. I thought I had witnessed a murder. But in the absence of a body, or an identity for the bogus constable, Jack's explanation was remotely plausible and one I might as well accept.

Accept, too, that this was one mystery I was never going to solve.

Or so I thought…

But once again events were to prove me wrong.

Chapter Twenty-Six

That night I brought my logbook up to date with new revelations about the scene I had encountered at St Anthony's Chapel and how it might be interpreted, remembering that faint perfume which I now believed could be chloroform.

As far as I was concerned, the woman might still be dead, of course, not from strangulation but from an overdose of a substance used for operations in hospitals and in recent years more widely in alleviating the pains of childbirth. Her Majesty the Queen had been quick to seize upon its advantages.

Next morning there was a letter from my sister Emily in Orkney. I opened it with some heart-fluttering, so often hoping for an invitation that never came. But this time my expectations were to be fulfilled.

Emily suggested that I should consider a visit next year, when the weather turned warmer, in the spring perhaps. I reread this affectionate letter, more encouraging than any I had received so far since my return to Edinburgh.

When I mentioned it that evening, Jack added his enthusiasm.

'What a splendid idea, Rose. We could go together for a holiday. I've always wanted to see Orkney…'

I listened, careful to conceal my expresssion since I was not at all sure about this proposal, recognising the need for caution and feeling the same diffidence that suggestions of visiting his parents continued to arouse in me. Our present arrangement suited me very well. Until I had – if ever – accepted as certainty that I was truly a widow and allowed myself to be persuaded into marrying Jack Macmerry, I intended to avoid encounters with his close kin and the possiblity of embarrassing explanations.

Nevertheless it was with a cheerful heart, bearing the good

news that my sister Emily had not abandoned me entirely, that I prepared to resume my duties at Carthew House.

Approaching the front door, I often glimpsed Lady Carthew sitting at her upstairs window and later during Tessa's painting lesson when the weather was mild, we observed the General and his lady enjoying an afternoon stroll in the gardens.

'There's Aunt Harriet!' Tessa would shout, tapping on the window and waving wildly.

In return she received a greeting, a cordial smile, but I was disappointed that Lady Carthew did not come to the library to inspect Tessa's progress as she had promised, especially as that deeper acquaintance I had hoped for seemed unlikely to materialise.

The Carthews had few visitors. One day I met the family doctor Hamilton Pierce taking his departure. His stout frame, white hair, distinguished countenance and soothing manner must have inspired confidence in the most fainthearted of his patients as well as making a considerable dent in their bank balances.

Introducing us, the General said, 'Torquil has a sore throat, but there is no cause for alarm.'

Dr Pierce smiled and picked up his bag. 'None at all. But we will continue to keep an eye on Tessa for a day or two.'

'And of course on Lady Carthew,' the General added anxiously.

The doctor smiled rather sadly I thought. 'Naturally we must keep her ladyship free from any possible infections.'

He wished us 'Good day' and left. As the General followed me into the library, he said, 'Dr Pierce has served this family for many years. He is a fine man, a trusted friend as well as our adviser. You will no doubt have heard of his contributions to medical science in Edinburgh.'

I hadn't heard of him but Jack reinforced the General's opinion that Pierce was well known as a physician of high repute who had, on occasion, been called in by the police to help them investigate circustances where death by poison was suspected.

When I arrived at Carthew House, Nancy was throwing a ball to Torquil in the garden.

'Why, hello, Rose!' She seemed surprised to see me and indicating the boy, 'He is much better. Tessa has escaped the sore throat but seems rather listless. She was sick after you left yesterday and made a great fuss about missing her lesson today, but her uncle was quite insistent.'

Nancy shrugged and gave me a puzzled glance. 'He intended sending you a note this morning.'

'There has been no word from him. But as I am here anyway I had better see Tessa.'

Leaving her I went inside across the hall to the library and, hearing the General's voice, I tapped on the door and opened it.

Tessa wasn't in evidence but the General had a visitor. A young man was at his side, both of them looking out of the window. Already the afternoon sun was falling low in the sky, its blinding light shining into the room and I couldn't see his face clearly.

'I beg pardon, sir,' I said to the General who swung round to face me. 'I thought Tessa would be here.'

'As you can see, Mrs McQuinn, she is not,' he repied stiffly. 'Did you not receive my message this morning that I wished her afternoon lesson to be cancelled?'

'I received no message, sir.'

He gave a sigh of annoyance. 'The stable boy had strict instructions to deliver it to you immediately. This is too bad, a wasted journey for you.'

Not wishing him to feel badly about that, I said, 'It is just a short step back across the hill.'

He made a gesture of dismissal and nodded towards his visitor. 'Mr Appleton and I have important business matters to discuss, so if you will excuse us…'

The young man continued to display apparent indifference to the General's urgency, staring out of the window, his hands on the sill, as if something in the garden below was of vital importance.

As familiar voices drifted up from outside I realised he was watching Nancy and Torquil so apologising once again, I withdrew and as the front door opened the children rushed across the hall to greet me.

'Tessa saw you arrive from the nursery window,' said Nancy as Tessa seized my hand.

'Can I have my lesson now, please?'

'Not today, dear,' said Nancy firmly.

'But I am quite well again,' Tessa wailed. 'I promise not to be sick again.' She began to sob, clinging to my arm. 'I love painting and – and just being with you.'

Nancy looked at her, sighed and said, 'She was inconsolable when her uncle said she was not well enough. She has her heart set on her painting, the highlight of her day.' And putting an arm around the little girl's shoulder. 'There, there, now, dear, don't cry. There's tomorrow—'

But Tessa refused to be consoled.

'Tell you what,' said Nancy, 'Why don't we see Mrs McQuinn home?'

'Yes! Yes, please!' And as Tessa brightened at the prospect, her brother joined in the chorus.

Nancy led the way through the stable yard. 'The fresh air will do her good.'

'Catch!' shouted Torquil throwing the ball to Tessa who

immediately released my hand and raced after him across the lane and on to the hill.

As we proceeded more sedately in their wake, I told Nancy of my embarrassing moment of upsetting the General by interrupting an urgent business meeting in the library.

'A young man was with him—'

'Oh, that would be Mr Appleton – his stepson.' And I remembered Nancy telling me of a smiliar occasion when Torquil had burst in with a cut knee and disturbed his uncle.

Lowering her voice in case the children were listening, she said, 'Mr Appleton's visits are not very regular, thank goodness. And Mrs Laing believes – told me in confidence of course – that he only comes to borrow money. To get the General to pay his gambling debts. As you can imagine, the General would do everything in his power to avert that kind of scandal.'

That was the day I heard from Bertha Simms. Back at the Tower there was a letter waiting for me.

'Dear Mrs McQuinn,

Further to your investigation regarding my sister, would you please come and see me at your earliest, tomorrow if possible.

This is very important.'

The last sentence was heavily underlined.

Chapter Twenty-Seven

I set off immediately. With a feeling of excitement and renewed hope that perhaps the case was not closed after all, I took the sketch I had made of the dead woman.

Bertha greeted me with a sigh of relief and led the way into the little parlour.

'I take it you have heard from your sister,' I said.

She bit her lip, a moment's hesitation. 'I know that she is well,' was the guarded reply.

'Then I gather she is no longer a missing person. That is such a relief for you.'

Bertha nodded. 'It is – thank God.' She looked at me frowning, undecided, before taking a deep breath and continuing. 'She has met – someone – an artist, and has gone to Italy with him.'

I did not immediately understand her tone of reluctance. 'But that is splendid news,' I said, somewhat taken aback at her solemn expression. 'A great relief,' I repeated.

She regarded me me doubtfully. 'I don't know about relief, Mrs McQuinn. Actually I am a bit shocked by such news. Of course, I'm happy for her if that's what she wants. But it is really quite terrible.'

'Terrible?' I asked.

She leaned forward, her manner confidential. 'This artist fellow is quite well known in London…' She mentioned a name that wasn't well known to me. 'But he has a wife and four children. There will be a fearful scandal if – and when – this comes to light. She begs me not to tell anyone but I don't know what to do.'

I thought that her sister going away with a married man should have been a lot preferable to receiving news that Mabel was dead, as she went on, 'I have no idea how I will be able to face anyone at our church. We've always been such a good-living, respectable family, never had any call to hide our heads. And now this – it is awful, don't you agree?'

And with a sigh. 'The police will have to be told the true circumstances, of course. I can only hope that we will be able to rely on their discretion.'

As I listened I considered how her opinion of me would have plummeted earthwards had she know that her trusted lady investigator was living in sin with a detective sergeant of the Edinburgh Police.

Now I wondered why she had summoned me with such urgency. Perhaps aware of my puzzled expression, she said, 'It is on another matter that I wished to consult you, Mrs McQuinn. Remember when the police called me in to identify the drowned woman, just in case—' she shuddered, 'in case it was Mabel. Dreadful, dreadful, such a thought!'

I nodded agreement.

'Of course, at the time I was so relieved that everything else went out of my mind.' she paused. 'But now I think I know who the poor creaure was.'

'You do!' Here was success at last, and from the most unlikely quarter.

'I have been thinking about it ever since and I am sure that I have seen her before. At the time, I wasn't sure, it was days later and I racked my brains to think where and when. You know the sort of thing, the more you puzzle over something like that, the harder it gets to remember. Then in a flash, one day when you least expect it, it all comes back.'

Again she paused. 'Yesterday when I was looking through a box of letters for an address, I found this—' Stretching her hand out to the sideboard she picked up a photograph of two girls, smiling, arm-in-arm. 'That's her, I'm sure, that girl with Mabel.'

Here was triumph, success at last. 'What was her name? Do you remember?'

Bewildered, Bertha shook her head. 'That I can't tell you…Ivy, Ida – something like that, but I can't for the life of me recall her surname. I'm not even sure that I ever heard it.'

Success followed by instant failure. Defeated once more I was back at the beginning again. 'Why did you send for me, Miss Simms?' I reminded her gently. 'Wouldn't it have been more appropriate to tell the police?'

She looked away. 'You must understand why I'm not telling them. They would have to know all the circumstances, all about her.' She pushed the photograph aside. 'And that includes where Mabel met her. In a mental asylum,' she added in hushed tones.

'It was a few years ago when Mabel started having fits, convulsions, and it was diagnosed as epilepsy. But Mabel was so ashamed, she didn't want anyone to know that she had ever set foot in – in – the loony bin, because that's what she called it. She said people would make their own minds up about it, say she was going mad!'

She shuddered. 'Poor lass, she would die of shame if any of this ever came to light.'

'Miss Simms, illness is a disease, not a crime,' I reminded her gently.

'You tell her that. She bore it nobly. She tried hard to keep it from her devoted pupils at the school. It was so degrading, she said, like being marked with insanity.'

What would her artist lover think about epilepsy? Was he more enlightened or had she been too ashamed to tell him? I wondered, as I studied the photograph again, trying to see a likeness to Mabel's companion, to recognise features that might belong to the older, dead face on my drawing.

'She was a bit older than Mabel,' said Bertha. 'Not nearly so bonny.'

In reply to my question, she continued, 'Alas, Mabel gave me no address. They are travelling around Italy. It may be some time before they return to London.'

Time was not on my side in this investigation so I asked, 'Where is this hospital?'

'In Dean Village.' She scribbled down the address. 'I used to visit Mabel twice a week. When she came out she was not much better and, I feared, made a thousand times worse by her experiences there. However, she'd become great friends with this Ivy or Ida, and they kept in touch.'

I asked for details and there was some confusion over the right dates which I wrote alongside the address. But at last I rode off having promised Bertha to be the soul of discretion and thanking heaven that I cared not a jot for the thin skin of conventional respectable Edinburgh society which I had long since abandoned.

The exterior of the Asylum for Diseases of the Mind, however, was enough to strike terror into the heart of anyone with a nervous disposition. A large grey, gloomy establishment with high, barred windows struck an unhappy resemblance to a prison rather than a place dedicated to the care and cure of unhappy people who were sick in mind.

First impressions were not improved over the threshold where the atmosphere was hardly calculated to inspire patients with feelings of hope and confidence in their future prospects.

I made my way across the dark hall to a tiny desk occupied by a tight-lipped woman whose forbidding countenance suggested a stern and unyielding approach to life's problems. She eyed my approach with caution and suspicion, her expression indicating that frivolity would be instantly punishable by incarceration in one of their cell-like wards.

Under that eagle eye I presented my business card and

showed her my drawing. Hardly glancing at it, she demanded, 'Name, please.'

'I believe it to be Ida or Ivy.'

She threw down her pencil and regarded me contemptuously. Then seizing the drawing between finger and thumb, she handed it back. 'I am afraid I cannot assist you. You must understand that people who come here are treated with the utmost confidence and respect. That is the earnest wish and command of their relatives who sign for them to be cared for within this establishment.'

And once signed in I felt doubtful if they ever came out again. 'It would be of tremendous help if you could possibly consider your records for the dates I have written down and see if there was a woman by the name of Ida or Ivy.'

Opening a drawer with a deep sigh of resigned toleration, she withdrew a ledger and thumbed quickly through it. Snapping it shut again, she said in tones of some satisfaction, 'You have my assurance that there was no one by either of those names resident here at the times you are enquiring about.'

As that statement indicated plainly, I had neither excuse nor desire to linger. Outside the rain fell steadily as I rode away, a fitting end to a frustrating interview. But at least I was one of the fortunates of this world. I could walk out freely and escape from those forbidding surroundings.

And I thought with compassion of the plight of those whose relatives wished for many purposes, not always kindly and regrettably often quite nefarious, to shut away some member of their family in such an asylum for the remains of their days.

In the Tower I removed my wet garments, feeling that I had reached an all-time low. I had now encountered and abandoned the last remaining straw, frail as it was, of my investigation. Unless Mabel could be contacted when she returned from her travels and provide more useful information than had been forthcoming from her sister, this would remain one of my unsolved cases.

As for Bertha, I guessed that she could be wrong, that I could put no vote of confidence in her vague description and feeling of recognition for Mabel's companion at the asylum.

I wrote up my logbook and wondered whether I should include a line drawn across making the end.

But instead I closed the book. That note of finality could wait until tomorrow.

Tomorrow, I remembered, was the opening of *The Pirates of Penzance*, bogus constables and all.

Chapter Twenty-Eight

Quite suddenly we were into the dead time of the year. I had forgotten in the ten years since I left Edinburgh that as winter progressed there were days when all colours faded, Arthur's Seat turned hostile, cold, forbidding and oddly lifeless, as became an extinct volcano.

The days were short, so bitterly cold that I was careful never to let the peat fire go out, for the Tower with its stone walls and many draughts was highly uncomfortable and many times I needed to wear my cape and scarf indoors, my hands freezing on the simplest household tasks.

My sole companion through the day was Thane, who spent long hours stretched out before the fire. Then suddenly sitting up, alert as if hearing a command, he would lift the latch on the kitchen door with his nose and trot away across the garden.

This procedure was always slightly unnerving, to observe him race up the hill, always with the thought at the back of my mind of the inevitable day when my faithful deerhound, about whom I knew so little, might no longer return.

One bright note on an otherwise gloomy horizon had been the opening night of *The Pirates of Penzance* at the Pleasance Theatre. The Opera Society had worked hard on their production as had their accomplished orchestra and chorus, recruited from a talented piano teacher and the local church choirs.

Desmond Marks sang 'A policeman's lot is not a happy one' in splendid voice, so well received that an encore was called for. Even though I did not like the man, I realised that there should have been a better future than an insurance office for his talents.

Jack was very impressed. At the interval I looked round for the Carthews, remembering that Lady Carthew had said when we first met that she was looking forward to the performance. As Gilbert and Sullivan enthusiasts, Nancy told me that weeks ago she had purchased front row tickets.

In vain I craned my neck through the performance, but the two best seats in the house remained empty.

As we gathered in the Green Room afterwards to drink coffee and mingle with the cast, Nancy came over carrying a large bouquet. Interrupting a congratulatory kiss on her cheek from Jack, I asked about the Carthews.

'We're all disappointed, Rose. I can't understand why they haven't come. They are so supportive and it does help to boost our sales having the General's name associated with the company as patron.'

Then with a shrug and by way of apology, 'Perhaps Lady Carthew had a chill. I've heard her coughing during the last day or two, and she's so delicate. But they might have let us know,' she added reproachfully. 'We could have sold those two front seats. We had a full house for the first night and we've had to turn people away.'

I looked across from the table where we were seated and to where Desmond Marks was surrounded by admirers, mostly female.

He saw us and Nancy smiled and acknowledged his greeting. Holding her flowers to her cheek in a carressing gesture which was also I thought a coy challenge to Jack, she whispered, 'These were from him. Such a nice kind man. So thoughtful. Nora should have been here to see him on stage tonight. Any wife would have been proud of such a husband,' she added, from which I gathered she had been given some plausible and uplifting version of Nora's sojourn in Glasgow.

It was soon evident that Nancy was a popular member of the chorus. Couples drifted past and gave her a hug. Coffee and cakes were served, the room very crowded and noisy.

As there was a spare seat at our table Nancy invited one of the constable players to join us. Introduced as Alec, he sat down politely but continued to look over his shoulder.

'Have you seen Mr Robson, Nancy?' he asked anxiously. She hadn't. 'He was coming tonight. Wanted to see the show.'

Nancy smiled. 'It was you he really wanted to see, Alec.'

Alec shrugged modestly. 'He's the manager of one of the big Glasgow theatres. They are casting for the Christmas pantomime.'

'And Alec's been offered a part,' Nancy said proudly.

As we murmured congratulations she giggled, 'It's *Cinderella* and you'll never guess what part Alec's to be playing.'

I hazarded a guess. 'Buttons?'

'No!' Nancy laughed. 'One of the Ugly Sisters.'

I looked at him again. Pleasant-mannered, slim, slightly built, nice-looking but in no way outstanding. They were chuckling about the transformation scene, wigs, costumes and so forth. At that moment, for me, something slipped into place, although my brain wasn't yet quite ready to absorb what had been staring me in the face, my thoughts interrupted by Nancy.

'There he is, Alec. Over there. Your Mr Robson, talking to Desmond.'

At that, Alec bounded from his seat and began to weave his way hastily through the throng.

When we left the theatre all the hiring cabs were taken so we had to walk the short distance back to the Tower while Nancy regaled us with the exciting prospect of a friend's wedding in Queensferry on Saturday. The General had given her time off and Mrs Laing would put the children to bed.

Jack showed little interest in our women's talk of what to wear. However, as Nancy prepared to leave us at the Tower, he gallantly offered to see her and her bouquet safely back to Carthew House.

It was a fine evening, no wind and a rising moon on the hill, a romantic setting indeed, so I decided for once that we should both escort Nancy home while I hardly listened to Jack's talk about Peebles, trying to sort out what nagged me about what I had seen that evening.

There was a lot I wanted to consult Jack about when we left Nancy. Instead, we quarrelled. It began with Jack saying, 'You were very quiet back there, Rose.'

I started to explain, but knew I hadn't his full attention. He wasn't even interested and cut in with, 'You know I'm away home this weekend. It's Ma's sixtieth birthday. She's expecting you.'

'I didn't know I had been invited,' I replied, fully aware that once again I would refuse, although I remembered Jack looking hard at Nancy when she said, 'Your parents are lucky to live in Eildon. The Borders are so lovely. I've only been there once – long ago – and I loved it. I've always intended to go there again,' she had ended with a wistful sigh.

Perhaps that was intended to wring Jack's heart and even wring an invitation out of him, I thought uncharitably as he said, 'You don't have to be formally invited, Rose. Ma expects you – she wants you to be at her birthday party.'

'I can't come with you, Jack. I'm sorry.'

He was angry. 'Why on earth not?' he demanded. 'This is a very special family occasion and the folks are dying to meet you.'

I knew what was in his mind and he might as well have added, at sixty Ma is getting desperate for grandchildren and the best present I can give her is for us to announce our engagment and get married as soon as possible.

So it all ended by Jack going off in a huff and leaving me

with a lot of entries on the day's events for my logbook.

I didn't sleep well that night with Jack's anger adding to those other images of the evening which refused to be banished.

Nancy arrived next day. As the children were sent out to play in the garden to give us a bit of peace together, she said, 'You'll be going away with Jack this weekend?'

'Not this time,' I said firmly.

But Nancy wasn't prepared to let it go at that. 'But why not – such a lovely place, I do envy you. And I'm sure his parents are very nice people,' she added reproachfully.

Realising I wouldn't get off without an explanation, I said, 'If Jack took me there, it might be misunderstood by them.'

'Misunderstood? I don't see—'

'They will presume that Jack and I are engaged,' I said patiently.

'But aren't you – secretly, I mean?' She wasn't the least dismayed by this information. 'Well now…' She sounded surprised and, a less charitable person might have said, rather pleased.

Further explanation seemed necessary. 'Don't you understand, Nancy. I can't get engaged or married to Jack until I am absolutely certain that I don't already have a husband.'

She frowned. 'But you're a widow, Rose.'

'On paper, yes. But I have no definite proof that a husband reported missing is dead. And until that reaches me – if ever – I am not free to marry anyone.'

I thought I had acquitted myself quite well although I feared that all this confession might have accomplished was to give Nancy renewed hopes where Jack was concerned.

After she left, I got on my bicycle and rode out to Leith to see Rory.

There was no one in reception and I made my way to the ward upstairs.

The bed was empty.

What had happened. Had Rory died in the night?

Before I could give full rein to panic, a nurse bustled in bearing a pile of bed linen.

She greeted me cheerfully and to my question, she smiled. 'He is making a steady improvement. And as there wasn't much more we could do for him and he hated lying in bed, we decided he should be moved somewhere more comfortable.'

My further enquiry was directed once more to the reception desk.

The nurse had returned. 'Mr Rory has been moved into one of our houses.'

'One run by the church charity organisation?'

'Yes, but residents pay a nominal rent for their room and food.'

I looked at her, ready to ask how a penniless vagrant was going to pay for accommodation, when one of the senior nurses I had met on my earlier visit came across the hall.

Recognising me, she smiled. 'You've come about Mr Rory.'

I said I'd just been told he had been moved into a rented room.

'That is so. We felt he will be much happier—'

'But he has no money,' I interrupted.

She smiled enigmatically. 'Don't worry, my dear. All that is being taken care of.'

'By whom?'

She shook her head. 'I'm sorry, I'm not at liberty to give you that information. Financial matters, you must understand, are confidential.'

'But I must know—' I began.

She held up her hand. 'I can only tell you that Mr Rory has

a benefactor who is providing the room for him, new clothes and anything that he needs.'

When Jack looked in that evening, I was glad to see him. As always when we had disagreements, we said we were sorry for being cross with each other and made up our quarrel. There was no more mention of the visit to his parents and as we had supper together, I told him about my visit to the hospital and the news about Rory.

'You know what this means,' I said excitedly.

'He'll be a lot happier—'

'Not that, Jack. This mysterious benefactor – you must be able to guess who he is.'

He shook his head. 'I have no idea.' And hastily, 'It certainly isn't me.'

'Of course not. It can only be one person – his estranged son. The lad he came to Edinburgh to find.'

'The one who disgraced him, he told you,' Jack said slowly. 'If that was so, then I think paying for him in a home is highly improbable.'

'Then who else could it be?' I asked, as I kept seeing, over and over, the young man who I had mistaken for a doctor on the day after Rory's attempted murder.

'Whoever it is,' said Jack. 'I'm glad someone is taking care of him. It's a great relief. I'll try and find out more about it when the inspector and I are in Leith tomorrow. We have had a tip off that the smugglers in that neck of the woods are extra busy just now. Hope to catch them red handed.'

Waving goodbye to him next morning, the best of friends and lovers again, I decided that whatever Jack's thoughts about Auld Rory's benefactor, I was certain I knew his identity and that it was his estranged son.

I just wished I could meet him face to face.

Chapter Twenty-Nine

My lessons with Tessa continued. Her brother had been bribed to stay out of sight with Nancy while the little girl and I sat alone in the huge library in the afternoon.

Tessa was making good progress but I was beginning to feel trapped. I had lost my first fine feelings about Carthew House. This was not what I wanted, to teach painting. If Gerald Carthew did not return until spring, then I felt that I was under a moral obligation to continue this pleasant, undemanding activity until he did so, while at the back of my mind, I remained involved in a mystery I had little hope of solving.

Unless by a miracle there was some contact from Bertha Simms or her sister regarding Ivy or Ida, who just might provide a clue to the dead woman at St Anthony's Chapel.

As for the General and Lady Carthew, after that promising start they ignored my existence. As the weather threatened to close in and Arthur's Seat settled down for a long winter of fog and mist, with rain beating in from the east, they no longer strolled in the afternoons in the cold mist-shrouded gardens and remained upstairs in what had been indicated as her ladyship's private sitting-room.

I had no reason to feel ungrateful or to be dissatisfied with my situation. My fees arrived regularly each week, waiting in an envelope on the library table. But I must confess to disappointment, having had such high hopes of getting better acquainted with Lady Carthew, that I now found myself in the same position as Nancy, Mrs Laing, the laundry maid and the outdoor staff – one of their paid servants. I presumed Mr Kennock, the factor who lived at the lodge, qualified for a higher echelon.

Then one day, as well as my fees, there was an informal card, would I come to dinner with them on Saturday evening. It was signed 'Harriet Carthew'.

The weather had turned bitterly cold, the roads were icy and we were precipitated into wintry sleet with flurries of snow. It was no longer feasible to use the short cut across the hill without having my skirts sodden wet and my boots soaked, so I took the longer road through Duddingston village to the front gates, seizing the opportunity to buy some much-needed provisions.

I bicycled off along the road through the village past the old kirk, on my left a narrow lane bore a notice: 'Strictly Private Property'. Its significance had gone unnoticed until now, since most of my daily activities lay eastwards in the direction of Newington and Edinburgh and I rarely had reason to set foot in Duddingston.

Dismounting briefly, I decided this lane must lead to the Carthew's stable yard. It was evidently in constant use, the ground churned up by horses' hoofs and wheel marks.

My immediate goal however was a group of shops. Having made my purchases, I followed the road leading past the fourteenth-century Sheep's Head Inn, where high stone walls terminated in handsome gates and the drive to Carthew House wound its way through rhodedendron hedges to emerge at the distant prospect of the front entrance.

On my right, a narrow path from the drive led to the barely visible Carthew family mausoleum. Curiosity has always been my weakness not readily overcome, so I decided to have a closer look at the imposing circular building, influenced by many and varied styles of archiecture, including classical Greek pillars and a cupola.

The windows were tiny slits between narrow ornamental

stones, and by wedging my bicycle firmly against the wall, I
managed to stand up on it rather precariously and see inside.
Alas for my trouble, it was too dim to reveal more than the
shapes of what were presumably coffins and grave covers.
Remembering the melancholy information that the vault was
to be permanently sealed after the General and his lady were
laid to rest therein, a grim but interesting thought came
almost unbidden.

The perfect place to conceal a dead body!

As I stared through the window my mind flew back to the
mysterious disappearance of Charlie and the hackney cab. Of
equal importance, I saw one answer as to how the closed and
sinister hackney cab which had stalked me after that first visit
to Auld Rory in the Leith hospital had apparently vanished on
the road past the Tower. Not into thin air but by using the
'strictly private' lane at the entrance to Duddingston village.

Certain I had hit on the solution to the dead woman's
disappearance, I still had to prove it. There was a little
consolation in knowing how the deed had been done, but by
whom and why? I was as much in the dark as ever regarding
motive or identities for victim and killer.

It was very aggravating. Had I stumbled on convincing
proof at last? I knew that when I discussed this theory with
Jack his response would be, 'Imagination!'

But who was likely to be brave enough to invade the
General's territory armed with a search warrant and such a
monstrous supposition, without one shred of evidence?

Oddly enough it was the gossipy Mrs Laing who shed some
light on the case.

Nancy was waiting to take Tessa and Torquil for a promised
visit to see the new kittens at the stables. As we spoke, Mrs
Laing rushed into the hall. Would I mind posting some letters
for her on my way back through the village?

'I wouldn't trouble you, Mrs McQuinn, but seeing you have your bicycle, I'd be greatly obliged to you. It'll spare me that long walk on such a bitter day. I have a bit of a cold and I don't want to get my feet wet again.' An illustrative sneeze made her face even more scarlet than ever, her nose beacon red.

Assuring her it was no trouble, with a last hug from Tessa, I followed her into the kitchen. As she handed over the letters with more remarks about the trial of walking down that long drive, I remarked quite casually that I had never had a chance to look at the mausoleum before.

'What is it like inside? Is it used as a private chapel?'

'Not at all. Purely a burial place,' she said in rather shocked tones. 'And the door is kept locked at all times. That's my responsibility,' she added proudly, nodding towards a pantry door. 'The keys are kept in there, along with those to the other locked outbuildings.'

Interrupted by a vigorous clanging of a bell on the wall opposite, she rose sharply to her feet and straightened her apron.

'Gracious me, that's Lady Carthew. She's waiting for her afternoon tea. And me here gossiping. I'll pour you a cup, warm you up, before you go,' she said generously. 'No hurry, the post doesn't go until five.'

After she left, I cautiously opened the door she had indicated and there on the rack with labels tagged to them were various keys.

But none readily identifiable as that for the mausoleum.

Here was a quandary indeed. It was growing dark outside and I could hardly take a bunch of unlabelled keys on the off-chance of finding the right one. And that achieved, how could I return it without encountering Mrs Laing and offering a more credible explanation than idle curiosity?

And there was an even greater chance of being observed, perhaps by the General himself, as I bicycled down the seldom-used path. And how could such an action be explained or justified to him?

Suddenly I had a better, more daring plan. During our days in Arizona, Danny and I lodged briefly in Phoenix with a bank robber's widow. He had died, shot down on the job, she'd tell us proudly. Such a tragedy.

We had our suspicions that Delia must have assisted him on some of his nefarious activities since she was an authority on safe-breaking and, what was now important for me to remember, picking locks.

'It's dead simple,' she'd say, 'Any woman can do it. All you need is a nail file, or if you don't have that, a hairpin will do – and all women have hairpins.'

I never expected such knowledge to be of any use but now I had both the instruments required.

Glad that I hadn't been persuaded to accompany Nancy and the children, I set off down the drive and, looking round to make sure there was no one about, I rode down the path to the mausoleum.

There, with a heart beating somewhat faster than usual, I put Delia's method to the test. After some frustrating moments in which two of my hairpins would never see better days, success! The lock turned and I opened the door.

The smell that rushed out at me was terrible. Decay, strong and horrible. And it wasn't from the sealed coffins neatly stacked on the shelves, either.

That dreadful stench was familiar. It hurled me straight back to Arizona and a besieged fort where the dead – both Indians and whites – lay unburied under the blazing sun.

Then I saw it. On the middle of the floor a large travelling trunk, the kind most often fitted to the back of hackney cabs.

With mouth and nose somewhat inadequately protected, I lifted the lid. A blanket shrouded what was certainly a body, since the thin white fingers of one hand protruded.

A woman's hand.

Triumph at the success of my ingenuity wrestled with horror and an overwhelming need for fresh air. Closing the door which automatically locked behind me, in the shrubbery I was very sick indeed.

Recovering, I realised that one part of my mystery was solved but that I had not the faintest idea how to proceed. I was certain only about one thing.

To reveal what I knew was to put myself in deadly peril from the still unknown murderer.

Chapter Thirty

The urgent sense of imminent danger persisted and, certain that every rhododendron bush might hide a lurking assassin, I rode swiftly back to the village.

Emerging at the ornate gates unscathed, I was reminded at the sight of a pillar box of Mrs Laing's letters. Taking them from my pocket, I flicked through them.

One caught my eye. 'Miss Yvonne Binns, Carthew House.'

The significance of the name leapt out as I said it loud. Across the envelope Mrs Laing had scribbled, 'Gone Away. Address Unknown.' The postmark was a week earlier, the town indecipherable. But I regarded this new evidence with a feeling of triumph.

'Got it!' I said and instead of returning to the Tower, I rode across Edinburgh to the Asylum for Diseases of the Mind where the dour lady once again sniffed at my request that she might oblige me by consulting her ledger.

As I suspected. There was an Yvonne Binns.

And this was the woman Bertha Simms had identified in the mortuary as her sister's long ago friend.

'Ivy or Ida was the name you gave me,' said the dour one reproachfully. 'Could have saved yourself a journey had you given me the correct name in the first instance.'

With so much of my evidence at hand to complete the puzzle I guessed that the killer must have forced the lock of the Carthew vault and put the murdered servant inside.

Now I knew I was on the right road and the search had narrowed down considerably.

To someone with knowledge of Carthew House.

At this stage evidence pointed to the late Peter McHully, former Carthew coachman, alleged lover of the disgraced maid who had followed him to Leith.

The obvious answer, simple and not at all unusual, was that she had been blackmailing him with threats to tell his wife. In a panic he had killed her and, with his knowledge of Carthew House, had deposited her in the mausoleum. A temporary measure until he found a more permanent place. But he had himself been killed before this could be accomplished.

It seemed crucial to pass my information on to someone – but who? How I wished Jack was around. I dismissed rushing to the City Police, trying to get someone to take seriously that I had discovered the body of a murdered woman, without some very exhaustive and, I was sure from their point of view, some very pertinent questions regarding my sanity.

Meanwhile the General's dinner party was imminent and I could hardly burst in with such a sensational story: Did he know that there was a dead body in the family vault? His wife's personal maid hadn't gone to England to take care of her sick mother after all but instead had got herself murdered just a mile away.

That would prove embarrassing when the General asked me how I had made such a remarkable and gruesome discovery.

'By breaking into the mausoleum with the use of two hairpins and a nail file to pick the lock,' would certainly put an end to any hopes of furthering my amiable acquaintance with the General and his wife.

To say nothing of my being henceforth considered a very unfit person to continue painting lessons for their little niece.

I envisaged us all trooping out across the gardens, Mrs Laing with mounting hysteria and the delicate Lady Carthew in imminent danger of a heart attack at such a dire revelation.

Murders in the Carthews' society happened only to other lesser persons. The idea was monstrous that such a fate should befall her personal maid or anyone who had ever been received over their hallowed threshold.

I decided Dr Pierce would be the obvious person in whom to confide, if I could manage to get him aside. Otherwise I'd await Jack's return and, with a great sense of relief, put the matter in the hands of the police, used as they were to dealing with embarrassing situations.

I devoted a considerable time to my logbook writing up all I had discovered so far, my observations, deductions and conclusions. As an extra precaution I made a careful copy addressed to myself, care of my Edinburgh solicitor Mr Blackadder with the melancholy instruction: 'to be opened in the event of my death'.

I should have enjoyed the walk across the hill. Arthur's Seat looked divinely beautiful, something out of a fairy tale. Snow had been falling steadily all day and lay two inches deep as I set off for Carthew House. Taking the long way round by Duddingston village where I posted my letter, any fleeting anxiety about how I was to get home that evening was consoled by thoughts of the Carthew carriage or of other guests whose vehicles might be diverted to include the Tower.

The walk down the drive was enchanting but as I glimpsed the mausoleum and recalled the horror within, I gave some thought to the General's high standing in the community. How terrible this revelation would be for him and his family. Sensational murder, however remote, casts its gloomy shadow, its indelible stain.

Or was I concerning myself unnecessarily. Perhaps he had influence enough with the city fathers to have the grisly discovery and its aftermath concealed from the press. And I spared a thought for his poor sick wife as we trooped in to dinner, the table with its silver and sparkling crystal glasses magnificent in candlelight.

I was seated on the General's right. 'Our invited guests included your brother, Dr Laurie,' he whispered.

'We invited him specially should he be in Edinburgh,' said Lady Carthew with a smile in my direction.

The General explained that the expected large dinner party had been whittled down by the sudden snowstorm. Two couples who lived at some distance from Edinburgh had telegraphed their apologies since the treacherous weather made travelling too hazardous.

Looking out of the window, relieved that Nancy was staying at Queensferry overnight, I hoped that her friend's wedding had not been similarly blighted.

Around the table were Dr Pierce and his wife Molly, and next to me the Factor, Kennock whom I had not met before. An elderly widower of dour aspect he had, like Mrs Laing, served the family for two generations.

Kennock lived at the lodge gates and it soon became apparent by the quality of his conversation that he was also general factotum and handyman, inside and outside the house, and that he performed his duties with a considerable amount of grumbling and resentment. No doubt the Carthews kept him on either through kindness of heart or because they were disinclined to look for a replacement since Kennock was keen to whisper proudly, 'They'll never find anyone else to do all the work I do for them for what they pay me. A mere pittance.'

Obviously he was not in awe of the General whom he addressed by his first name, having known him as he said, 'since he was a wee bairn'.

The dinner promised to be extremely pleasant. Mrs Laing had prepared the food and also served at table. Having deputised for Nancy and put the children to bed, she now appeared almost unrecognisable in a pristine starched white apron and cap. Compliments were heaped upon her by the assembled company as one excellent course followed another: soup, salmon, roast beef and a Scotch trifle.

'Her Masjesty will be dining on just such a meal as this, which was served the last time I was honoured to be invited to dinner at Balmoral Castle,' the General told me.

I was not used to wine in any excess, but each course had its special serving and I allowed him to top up my glass rather too regularly.

In a lull in the conversation Lady Carthew leaned over and looked in my direction. 'Perhaps we could prevail upon Mrs McQuinn to tell us what it is like in the Wild West of America.'

I recalled saying, 'Do please call me Rose,' before launching into some of the more respectable and amusing incidents I had witnessed in a world whose culture was romantic and exciting, if also constantly endangered by outlaws and savage tribes.

Lady Carthew watched me, smiling. A good listener, she occasionally raised her glass to her husband, an affectionate tribute. In candlelight, a beautiful woman with her heavy golden hair and well-defined features, the wide mouth remote from the rosebud demanded by fashion.

But I fancied these looks which depended on good bone structure would endure into old age long after her contemporaries' fragile roses and cream had faded and withered away.

At my side Kennock asked Sir Angus, 'Have you heard from young Appleton lately?'

I pricked up my ears as the General replied, 'Not very recently, thank God.'

I regarded him sternly. That was a lie since Appleton had been in the library with him only a couple of days ago.

Kennock was shaking his head sadly. 'We had such hopes of

that young man, did we not, Angus? When my Maggie was alive, as you know he was a particular favourite of hers, having no bairns of our own.' He sighed. 'She always said the lad would go a long way.'

The General nodded somewhat absently and flourished the wine bottle in my direction. 'May I offer you a sip more, my dear.'

Not wishing to disappoint him I held out my glass.

'We were hoping Detective Sergeant Macmerry would be accompanying you this evening. We sent him an invitation – is he to be absent from Edinburgh for long?'

As I explained Kennock was leaning forward impatiently, looking frustrated, obviously with a great deal more to say that his employer had no desire to hear. Clearly eager to change the subject, the General switched over to Solomon's Tower and its ancient history.

Listening politely, I was disappointed too; my preference was for more gossip about the stepson who was the black sheep of the family. As the evening progressed I was already turning over in my mind schemes for calling in at the lodge and striking up a better acquaintance with the dour factor.

Somewhat preoccupied with my own thoughts, and a growing wine haze, I heard little of the conversation which concerned local politics and names still unknown to me.

My American experiences no longer in demand, I seized the opportunity of eating a great deal more than usual. This was food of a quality and variety unlikely to come my way very often. With great enthusiasm I had accepted second helpings of everything, especially the delicious Scotch trifle, heavily laced with excellent sherry.

Beyond the windows, the gardens presented a romantic picture with the snow now falling steadily, lying heavily on trees and bushes. Beyond a mild flutter of apprehension, quickly quelled, regarding my homeward journey, I had no complaints. Twirling my wine glass, prepared to call the world my friend, I had no desire to be anywhere else than at this splendid dinner party surrounded by charming people in a warm candlelit room.

Mellowed by good food and wine I had reached the stage where my mind no longer observed with its usual clarity, totally ignoring common sense's whispered warning that I must resist the General's 'just another sip.'

At last a clock struck eleven. Caution and sobriety restored in a manner that would have done credit to Cinderella, I remembered that I must go home – without further delay.

Rising somewhat unsteadily I announced my departure, the signal for others to leave the table. The doctor and his wife were staying the night as always, while in the hall Mrs Laing held out my cloak.

As Kennock opened the front door we were all thrown backwards by a fierce blast of wind as several inches of snow piled against the front step now hurled itself across the floor.

Kennock shouted, 'I'm away, Angus. Thanks, yer ladyship. Goodnight, all,' and he plunged off down the steps while I stared after him in dismay.

The General took my arm. 'My dear young lady, you must not even consider venturing back to the Tower in such weather. And, alas, I cannot provide a carriage since the stable lads have alternate Saturday nights off to go into Edinburgh. Had I known that we were in for such a storm…'

Suddenly I felt very scared. The fairy tale romance of the white world out yonder had vanished into a nightmare straight from the Brothers Grimm. But determined to put on a brave face, I said, 'I shall manage very well, sir, thank you. It isn't far—' and stepping boldly forward I promptly collapsed into the snow.

The General raised me to my feet, dusted the snow off my cloak.

'We cannot allow you to leave in this.' And turning to Lady Carthew who stood well back in the hall, a shawl about her shoulders. 'What say you, Harriet?'

'Of course you must stay, Rose. I'll instruct Mrs Laing to prepare a room.'

And even as I protested at being too much trouble, the General closed the door firmly on the snow. Following him inside, I realised that I had no alternative.

Dismissing ingratitude with the merest flicker of unease, I decided to regard this as an unexpected opportunity which might offer interesting possibilities.

Chapter Thirty-One

Mrs Laing, apologising profusely, led the way to the nursery quarters at the top of the house, explaining that Sir Angus's grandfather had intended them for his vast family as well as spare rooms for visiting children and their nannies.

'It is the best we can do for you at short notice, Mrs McQuinn. No more than a cot bed in Nanny Brook's sitting-room, I'm afraid,' she said, opening the door and frowning as she looked me over. 'But then you're just a wee lass. I've put in a warming pan.'

She went on breathlessly, 'You won't be lonely with the children next door. They have been asleep for hours but it'll be a pleasant surprise for Tessa to see you in the morning.'

And surveying the room anxiously she put down the candle. 'I'm sure you'll be comfortable enough. It's just for one night – that's the bathroom and WC across the corridor.'

I look around, seeing the room Nancy was so proud of as bleak and scantily furnished. High, barred windows beyond the reach of curious children made it impossible for anyone under six feet tall to admire the view. The result, despite some of Nancy's possessions added for a homely touch, was still depressingly like a prison cell.

I like to know where I am before I go to sleep in a strange bed and I remembered that Nancy had pointed out the nursery wing from the stable yard. By standing on tiptoe on the solitary wooden chair I looked through the barred window directly on to Arthur's Seat and the short cut we took from the Tower.

I shivered. Alas, all the warming effects of the wine had now vanished. Longing for my own bed, I stared from my high perch across a vast white wilderness rising to meet a full moon peering from behind fleeting clouds.

Suddenly a tiny shadow moved near the stile.

It was Thane.

I could recognise his shape outlined against the snow. Running back and forth, staring across as if – for I knew it was impossible – as if he could actually see me up at the high window.

Taken by surprise, I spoke his name.

'Thane!'

He could not possibly hear me either from that distance but again he seemed to be waiting, alert and listening, running backwards, forwards, the way he did when he wanted me to follow him.

'Thane!' I called again.

At that moment, the moon was obliterated by fast-moving angry clouds and white flakes of snow beat against the glass, blotting out all else.

Too chilly to remove more than my dress, still shivering, I crept into bed. Certain that I would never sleep, presumably the wine took effect and I drifted away.

I was woken from a confused and frightening dream by a dog barking outside. The low eerie howl of an animal in distress. Thane!

I got up, pushed the chair over to the window, stood on it and I could see him, not racing back and forward but standing still, his forepaws on the stile, staring directly across at the house.

A moment later and he had disappeared.

How weird. Perhaps it was part of my dream, I thought, snuggling back into the warm bed and falling asleep again almost immediately.

Suddenly I was back in Arizona, sitting by a camp fire and Danny was there by my side. How rarely I dreamed of the man who still filled so much of my waking thoughts – and now for an instant from paradise the present had merged into the past. Deliriously happy to be with him again, laughing as he was telling me to be careful as I warmed my hands at the fire...

Closer – hearing its roaring, its crackling flames.

I sat up in bed, Danny and the dream were gone.

I smelt smoke, through the base of the door, I saw flickering light. The pungent smell of burning wood was real.

Raised voices, a faint sound of footsteps outside... I ran across the room, seized the door to open it.

Nothing happened. It was jammed, or I was locked in. Coughing, choking, I had to get air. Back to the chair at the window, looking for something to break the glass, calling for help.

'Help, help!'

The room behind me was full of acrid smoke, the chair wobbled and I was falling, falling...

My head struck something hard – it hurt.

Then above me a shadowy figure outlined by flames from the now open door.

The Angel of Death.

But this angel had strong arms, human arms seized me, gathered me from the floor. A familiar voice whispered, 'It's all right – you're safe now.'

I was being carried through the smoke by a man in a nightshirt. A young man I had met before.

Young Appleton.

A distant clang of bells. The fire engine...

I opened my eyes in Lady Carthew's sitting-room, presumably still unscathed by the fire.

Someone – the young man in the nightshirt – was stroking my forehead with gentle fingers.

'That's a nasty bruise, Rose. But you're all right – the fire's
out.'

I sat up. 'What about the others, the children…'

'Everyone escaped. You're not to worry. Here, drink this.'

I did as I was told and watching me, he said, 'Dr Pierce is
with Angus – he took the worst of it.'

'What happened? Are the children safe?'

'Yes, they're fine,' he said bleakly. 'Whatever happens,
Angus has to remain the brave soldier, the gallant gentleman
to the end.' His voice was bitter. 'The children – that was his
first – and naturally – his only thought.'

He paused and I asked, 'What caused the fire?'

'Young Torquil, I'm afraid, has all the makings of a fireraiser.
As far as we can gather from the story Tessa sobbed out, Torquil
stole fireworks from her birthday bonfire and matches from the
kitchen. He decided while Nanny was away to have a nice little
display of his own. And he set the bed on fire.'

I looked at him again. The black sheep of the family, the
wayward stepson, the scoundrel who only appeared at
Carthew House with a begging bowl for his gambling debts
had saved my life.

'And Lady Carthew, what of her?'

He gave me a mocking glance and laughed softly. 'What
indeed, Rose? What indeed?'

And suddenly it was all there staring me in the face. The
smile, the laugh, those fine eyes, delicate bones, large mouth.
All the things that did not add up to the frail invalid now
made sense. Nancy's suspicions about a wig, the day I had
interrupted the General and 'Mr Appleton', who had
remained at the window his back turned to us…

'You aren't young Appleton, are you?'

He shook his head and smiled gently as I said, 'You're
Harriet Carthew.'

He bowed. 'One and the same, I'm afraid.' And with a grin. 'A bow or a curtsey – I wonder which is appropriate?'

I was putting the facts together. 'And Rory is your father. You're his estranged son.'

He nodded. 'Correct! Harold Frederick, known as Harry, at your service. But no longer estranged.' And regarding me gravely. 'So what are we to do with you now, Rose McQuinn? How are we going to fit our discreet lady investigator into this tangled scheme of things?'

Aware for the first time of my own peril, I said, 'You might make a start by telling me the truth.'

'And throw yourself on our mercy, is that it?' Although he said the words softly I was in no doubt how dangerous he could be as, narrow-eyed, he studied my face. 'Angus was right. You're a clever young woman and he suspects that you already know too much for your own good.'

Still in a state of shock and disbelief, I guessed what he was going to tell me.

'We must never forget that Angus is very fearful for his reputation. He would kill to defend it. God knows he has killed often before on the battlefield. The legitimate business of a soldier's career defending Queen and Empire.'

He paused, regarding me dubiously and went on, 'That's where Lady Carthew comes in. I don't know how much you know of life beyond the conventions of our present society, or how tolerant you might be of the many odd trappings that make up the human condition.'

Letting that sink in for a moment, he added with a sigh of resignation.

'Perhaps you know that men do not only love women, they often love other men.'

'As in ancient Greece,' I said helpfully.

He ignored that. 'What I am going to say may disgust you.

It began in the Indian Army with two men who fell in love, a forbidden passion to be concealed at all costs, for this was as bad as it could be. One was a General and the other, his seventeen year-old batman. They managed the relationship discreetly enough since blind eyes were conveniently turned on the behaviour of a brave but formidable General.'

He shrugged. 'Besides, a lot of what might scandalise more civilised society goes on secretly among men denied their natural needs of sweethearts and wives.

'At the beginning, my terror was in case my father ever found out. It would break his heart. A milksop son who hated violence and should have been a lass was bad enough for him to cope with. Better have him believe that I had died a brave soldier's death. He could live with that, bask in proud memory, so I went missing on patrol, let Angus spread the story that I had been captured by tribesmen and was to be presumed dead.

'A very convenient arrangement since he was about to retire to Britain, with his title and the family home. But it had never occurred to him how difficult living in Edinburgh society might be. Difficult and dangerous for two men to carry on a relationship where he was well known and his neighbours might be curious.'

He sighed. 'I was all for putting an end to it, painful as that would be, rather than endanger his reputation and be landed in jail accused of sodomy. But he wouldn't hear of that.'

Pausing, he smiled. 'Clever Angus had an ingenious solution. Even as a little lad I had loved dressing up in Ma's clothes and Pa beat the hide off me, when I cried and said I wanted to be a girl. What a blow for the frontier army man, wanting his only son to be a fighter like himself. It wasn't until Ma died that he realised I didn't have the makings of a tough soldier ready to die for Queen and Empire. But I had taken her shilling and honour had to be obeyed.'

He shook his head sadly. 'I knew I had broken his heart then—'

'No, you didn't. If it's any comfort to you, he once told me how wrong he had been about you. His one regret was that he had forced you into a life that your gentle nature abhorred. That you hated violence—'

His face brightened, eyes widened in delight. 'Did he really tell you that?'

'Yes, he did. But that he knew you were a brave young lad who would step in between snarling dogs and that you'd once rescued children from drowning in a raging torrent.'

For the first time he laughed. It was as if a load, an intolerable burden, had been suddenly lifted from his shoulders.

'Please go on,' I said.

'You want to hear the rest? Angus decided that when we came to Edinburgh I should be his new wife, Lady Harriet. Oh, it would be a great lark fooling everyone for a while. But I had doubts, I warned him that we'd never get away with it and that he was crazy to even consider such an idea, but he assured me it was purely temporary, give him time to settle things at Carthew House before we quit Britain for good.

'So I agreed – reluctantly. But when Angus decides something – well, he's used to being obeyed and as I learned long ago, others meekly follow. And when I lost my nerve he said be patient, a few weeks only and we'd disappear abroad again, settle down in Italy.

'The one thing he hadn't bargained for was being hailed as a returning hero in his home town. Edinburgh's pride, with all the publicity, the limelight, the brave son she would not relinquish. There were even invitations to Balmoral.' And with a rueful laugh, 'That was the one thing I regretted, having to miss a meeting with our dear Queen. But we were safe enough, she never invites the wives along.'

His brow darkened. 'One thing Angus hadn't bargained for was finding out that my father was living in a ditch half a mile away from Carthew House. Do you know that Pa has the second sight?'

Without waiting for any comment, he went on, 'He was sure I was still alive, that he would have known if I were dead. And that was why he came to Edinburgh. As a child I was always asking Ma about Scotland, about the Castle and when Pa read about Angus coming home, he thought he'd know if anything more had ever been heard of me. Then one day he saw us driving towards Duddingston in Angus's racing gig.'

Pausing he took a deep breath. 'He recognised Lady Carthew, on one of her rare outings, as his one and only son. And I made the mistake of telling Angus I'd seen Pa and I was sure that he'd recognised me. You know what happened next,' he added grimly.

'The fire. That was dreadful. Unforgivable. I accused Angus and he swore it was vandals but I heard his gig come back that night. He knew that if he admitted he had been behind that, it would be the end of us. I don't hold with murder and I'd never forgive him – never – for killing my own father to protect his reputation. Not even to keep us both out of prison.'

He gave me an apologetic look. 'Sorry I scared you that afternoon in the hospital when you came in to see Pa. I wasn't intending to run you down either when I followed you back from Leith. I had to get back into Lady Carthew and it was very important that you didn't follow me on your bicycle down the lane to the stable yard.'

As he spoke he poured a glass of water for us both. 'Sorry I haven't anything stronger to offer. Sure you want to hear the rest?'

I said of course and he continued, 'Good, because it's easier coming from me than from Dr Pierce. If anything happens to Angus – which God forbid…'

Again he paused, staring mutely out of the window, a prisoner with a vision too awful to contemplate. 'Quite frankly, I'm growing weary of the role of the seldom seen, delicate invalid wife Lady Carthew.'

He shrugged gloomily. 'I'm bored. I'm still young and I want some action in my life, the idea of living like this indefinitely – until death do us part – fills me with horror.'

There was silence for a moment then he added, 'Don't mistake me. I love the old man. I'm grateful to him – for everything. But I can't bear all this play-acting indefinitely. Sometimes I feel as if I'm trapped in a nightmare from which I'll never escape. Despite all his promises, his reassurances about finding us a place in some less conventional tolerant society – if such exists!'

He sighed wearily. 'I suspect it's all a pipe dream – for us to start again where an old man and his young lover won't raise an eyebrow.' And brushing a hand across his eyes… 'One hell of a business. God only knows how it will all end.'

In the silence that promiused to be lengthy I said, 'Did you know that there's a dead woman in the mausoleum?'

'A dead woman, eh. Is there really? Well, well, I'd like to bet there are quite a few of them.' And although his glance was mocking, he looked alarmed. 'Any idea who she is?'

'I can make a guess, but I thought you might know. Yvonne Binns, lately your – I mean Lady Carthew's – personal maid.'

He jumped to his feet, swore. 'So that's what – where…'

Recovering, he gulped more water but his hand shook. 'Anyone else know about this?'

For my own safety I said, 'Yes. Detective Sergeant Macmerry – my friend Jack, he knows.'

Harry groaned. 'So that's it. Couldn't be much worse. All I know is that Binns was blackmailing Angus. She knew about us, like Mrs Laing, who must know, or at least have strong suspicions, but prefers to pretend that such things don't exist. Old Kennock hasn't any idea, but Pierce has. Angus trusts him, they've been life long friends and he told me Pierce knew about episodes in his university days before he went to India.'

Again he groaned. 'About Yvonne. She came to help Mrs Laing. Had worked in an institution making uniforms so she was invaluable as a dressmaker – very useful – as Angus didn't know a thing about women's clothes, so she had to be let into the secret. She would have soon found out anyway, but it was always a potentially dangerous situation and although Binns was paid well to keep her mouth shut, she got greedy.

'Well, she didn't know what she had taken on. Angus wasn't the one to stand for that – public exposure, the newspapers. He refused to discuss it with me, said he'd paid her off, sent her away and that was the end of it.'

Pausing he shuddered. 'You know I had an awful feeling that he wasn't telling the truth. I always knew somehow. Blackmailers don't vanish all that easily and I couldn't shake

off the thought that maybe he'd paid someone to get rid of her
– permanently.'

Looking at me, he said grimly, 'And now I think you have
given me the answer. I have to say that wasn't a wise move,
Rose. If Angus finds out what you know, you might find
yourself joining the other dead ladies in the vault.'

And letting that sink in, 'You're safe with me – for the time
being. You were Pa's friend, I owe you that – it makes you
special—'

The door was flung open and Dr Pierce rushed in. I knew
by his expression even before he uttered the words, 'Harry –
I'm so sorry – Angus – Angus – is – is…'

Harry make a choking sound. Then he screamed, 'No! Oh
God, no!'

With that terrible cry of anguish, he staggered to the door,
turned and sobbed. 'It can't be true – tell me that it isn't true.'

Pierce shook his head sadly. 'It is true. Not the fire, Harry.
Sit down and listen. Angus has been ill, seriously ill, for a long
time now. This exertion was just the final straw.'

Harry clenched his fists. His expression furious, he looked
as if he'd like to hit Pierce.

Putting his hands over his face, he sobbed. 'I never knew.
And I wasn't with him. Dear God, I wasn't even with him.'

Then turning, he ran out of the door and the doctor turned
his attention to me. Assuring him that I had suffered no injury
beyond a bruise on my forehead, while he examined it, I asked
for the children.

'They are very well considering, and already fast asleep
again. Mercifully it will all seem like a bad dream to them in
the morning. Torquil will be reprimanded but he is only a
little boy. A dreadful lesson, and I doubt he will ever play with
matches again. Their father will be contacted and in the face
of such a family tragedy, I imagine he will wish to abandon his

expedition and return immediately. Meanwhile Mrs Laing will take care of them until their nanny gets back later today.'

And with a sigh. 'It's a miracle that it wasn't a lot worse.'

Following him downstairs, I thought of Nancy for the first time and how dismayed she would be at missing this sensational piece of drama.

In the library we were followed by only the faintest whiff of smoke, more akin to autumn fires than the deadly blaze that had engulfed the nursery wing.

'I'm sorry about Sir Angus,' I said.

Dr Piece shook his head. 'It was not totally unexpected. This is the way Sir Angus would have wished to go. Seeing himself as a soldier still, facing danger, dying bravely in action – saving the lives of two small children.'

He shook his head. 'A sad business, the real reason for his retirement and return to Edinburgh, knowing that he hadn't long. And all my visits supposedly to see Lady Carthew, when he was in truth the invalid. But I was sworn to secrecy. Harry was not to know, he was not to be made unhappy by carrying such a burden. He wished their last months together to be happy memories only.'

Pausing, he looked at me intently. 'Harry has told you.' It was a statement not a question.

'Yes, everything about Lady Carthew, that is.' I stopped and added what was beginning to sound suspiciously like melodrama, if murder had not been involved.

'Did you know that there is a dead body in the vault?'

There was no surprise or shock this time, he merely nodded and said, 'So Sir Angus has just informed me. His dying words were to tell me that Harry was in no way involved and he made me promise that I'd protect him at all costs – a young man with his whole life before him,' he added bitterly. 'When the Binns woman found out about Lady Carthew, she had to go.'

He paused and looked round, then with a shrug continued, 'She was blackmailing Angus. Wanted five hundred pounds to keep quiet. So Angus said he didn't have that much in the house but he'd meet her at St Anthony's Chapel and hand it over. When she arrived there was no Angus, instead there was a police constable in the hackney. She panicked, saw prison ahead for herself so she took to her heels and ran up the hill. He followed her, they struggled, he used the chloroform he'd stolen from my bag – I always carry it for difficult childbirth cases – and she was unconscious instantly. His instructions were to drive her to the shore, put her in the sea, so that it looked like suicide. Unfortunately in his panic, he overdid the dose. He saw that she was dead and realised he had to get her into the cab along the road. Scared to carry her in case anyone saw them and rushed over to offer assistance, he went down to bring the cab closer.'

He stopped and regarded me grimly. 'And that's where you came in, the nosy lady with a deerhound.'

'The constable played his part very well,' I said. 'Am I right in guessing he was Peter McHully?'

'Indeed you are. A petty villain who had once been employed in the stables and would do anything for money.'

'Were he and the woman lovers?'

'Who on earth told you that? McHully had a wife and children in Leith and as far as I can gather he'd hardly known Binns.'

'Did Sir Angus know that he was a member of the Opera Society?'

'Yes, indeed. And as he was familiar with Gilbert and Sullivan, he must have guessed that the constable's uniform from *Pirates* would come in very useful. I suspect McHully was well ahead of him – a spate of local burglaries in which a bogus constable was involved.

'After your untimely arrival, McHully lost his nerve, put Binns in the hackney trunk and deposited her in the mausoleum. There was method behind this – Angus told me that McHully had already decided that the five hundred pounds should now be his to keep his mouth shut.

'You know the rest. McHully also had to go. Not too difficult for a man in the General's position to whisper in the ear of an ambitious armed policeman at the Leith riots that this was a troublemaker. Just a stray bullet, that was all that was needed. No doubt assured of promotion and that he was doing society a service – there are corrupt policemen too, you know,' he added gently.

'You look tired and shocked, Mrs McQuinn. It's a long time until dawn and we'll see you home. The snow is still deep but presumably we'll be able to get my carriage out of the stables. Molly had a shock, I gave her a sedative, but she'll be keen to go home and I have a lot to do here.'

'Thank you for your offer, but I'll walk. I'll go across the hill. Yes, I'm quite sure,' I added firmly, cutting short his protests.

Truth was, I was nervous. I knew too much and I wanted to put as much distance as I could between Carthew House and safety.

I gathered my cloak in the hall and opening the front door I saw that even in the midst of crisis and sudden death Mrs Laing had cleared the snow from the steps.

The doctor had followed me. He put a hand on my arm. 'Mrs McQuinn, one thing before you leave us. I must ask this of you. A lot depends on how you answer.'

I didn't say what I was thinking. Even my own life.

'I can keep a secret, if that's what you mean.'

'That's good.' He gave a deep sigh of relief. 'Discretion is the word.'

'And mine too, doctor, I assure you. I'm used to keeping people's secrets. That's my professional standing – discretion guaranteed.'

He seemed satisfied and when I looked back I saw that the blinds were already drawn in the main part of the house. Past the still smouldering, blackened rafters of the nursery quarters, I spared a thought for the bereaved Harry as I walked out of the stable yard.

Wearily I crossed the stile on the hill. A joyous bark greeted me. Thane bounded forward, leaping through the snow. I put my arms around his neck, hugged him, knowing I was safe at last and that it was no dream that he had tried to warn me of danger last night.

He was wild with delight as he led the way, carefully making a track for me to follow across the hill to the Tower. There I removed my sodden boots, hung up my skirt wet to the knees. Thankfully the neglected peat fire had not gone out. I blew it into life and with Thane lying before it, feeling secure and guarded, I locked the door, climbed the stairs to my bed and slept until darkness fell again late that afternoon.

I was awakened by Thane barking and a ring at the front door bell.

Jack, I thought, pulling on a shawl.

Not Jack. A visitor.

Harry Roderick.

'May I come in?'

I was scared but he looked so grief-stricken, so lost, I hadn't the heart to turn him away, to threaten to set Thane on him.

Wordlessly I led the way into the kitchen where Thane accepted this stranger as a friend who patted his head and spoke kindly to him, while I made tea from the kettle kept hot on the hob.

I said I was sorry about Sir Angus. 'What will you do now?

'That's all been worked out, cut and dried, without my knowledge,' he said bitterly. 'Pierce tells me that when Angus – knew – he hadn't long he drew up a will leaving me in my real name enough money to live comfortably for the rest of my life. I'll take it and with Pa we'll begin a new life together, I fancy the Highlands, as soon as he is fit enough to travel.'

'What about Lady Carthew?'

He gave me a mocking smile. 'Oh, didn't you know, she died in the fire, poor lady. Trying to help her husband save the children, her poor heart gave out. Just as well, she wouldn't have wanted to go on living without him. Everyone will understand and sympathise.'

'That's quite ingenious.'

'Isn't it just! We have it all planned, Mr Appleton and the good faithful family doctor. The Fiscal will accept their death certificates without question. Then after the military funeral at Edinburgh Castle, both coffins will be carried to the vault – Lady Carthew's duly weighted down – and as Sir Angus ordered, the vault will be sealed for all eternity with past members of the family and one extra, Lady Carthew's personal maid, decently but anonymously coffined.'

I shuddered. 'What about the real Mr Appleton? Was he left anything in the will?'

'He hasn't been heard of for years, last sighting in Australia.' With an earnest glance. 'Do you think it'll work, Rose?'

When I frowned, he added, 'It all depends on you, you know. My future and the General's fine reputation lie in your hands. We can't force you to keep silent and we can't kill you because there's no one left to order any more killings.'

'So what do you want me to do?'

'I want you to forget all this, pretend it never happened and believe every word you read in the newspapers about the tragic death of the gallant soldier and his lady rescuing their small nephew and neice from a fire.'

As he was leaving I asked after the children. 'Fine really. Incidentally Torquil thought the flames meant that the devil had come for him for his wickedness, so he asked for another offence to be taken into consideration. Something about stealing a key from your house to play robbers and jailers. Lost his nerve and put it on the garden wall for you to find next day. Did you ever get it? You did! Excellent!'

Harry laughed. 'He's not a bad wee chap, really. A bit wild but I expect he'll grow out of it.'

Another mystery solved I thought as I waved him goodbye. 'Take good care of Auld Rory.'

'You bet I will!'

When Jack arrived back from Eildon, he was appalled to hear of my misadventures after the Carthew's dinner party, the disastrous fire and my rescue more or less unscathed, by the ne'er-do-well stepson.

And that was all I told him and everyone else, including Nancy, fending off questions with the promised discretion guaranteed. Which wasn't difficult since the guilty, both humble and proud, had met their fate, meted out by a greater justice than that of trial in our earthly law courts.

To this day, if ever it is mentioned, Jack believed that my grim discovery in St Anthony's Chapel was no more than disturbing a pair of illicit lovers who had been experimenting with a dangerous drug, such as chloroform.

I let him think he was right. That's good for a man. Besides, there are some secrets meant to be kept for ever.

And this was one of them.

Other titles available from Allison and Busby
by Alanna Knight

In the Rose McQuinn series:

The Inspector's Daughter
1894. In a desperate attempt to recover from the loss of her
husband and her baby son, Rose McQuinn returns home to
Edinburgh from the American Wild West. Before long she
unwittingly steps into the shoes of her father, the legendary
Detective Inspector Faro, by agreeing to investigate the strange
behaviour of Matthew Bolton, husband to Rose's childhood
friend Alice. Alice is convinced Matthew is having an affair
but Rose suspects he may have been involved in something
much more sinister – the brutal and still unsolved murder of
a servant girl. From her isolated home at the foot of Arthur's
Seat and aided by a wild deerhound who has befriended her,
Rose starts to piece things together, until she gets too near the
truth and puts her own life in danger.

An Orkney Murder
On a long-anticipated family visit to Orkney to see her sister
Emily, Rose is unprepared for the sinister and unexpected
events that occur following the discovery of a body by an
archaeological team excavating a nearby peat bog. But the find
is not that of the legendary thirteenth-century Maid of
Norway, as they had expected, but that of a local woman, long
presumed to have drowned. In this the most personal of all her
investigations, Rose realises that revealing the killer's identity
can destroy for ever the happiness of those closest to her.

Ghost Walk
Since the disappearance and presumed death of her husband,
Danny, three years ago, Rose McQuinn has managed to
overcome her grief and begin her life afresh. She has fulfilled

her ambition of becoming a 'Lady Investigator, Discretion Guaranteed' and is on the threshold of marrying her lover, Detective Inspector Jack Macmerry of the Edinburgh Police. But pre-wedding jitters become the least of her worries when a nun from the local convent claims to have received a letter from Danny. Is the elderly nun simply confused, or could Danny really still be alive? Unnerved and determined to find out the truth before her wedding, Rose begins to investigate. However, after two suspicious deaths, all the signs suggest that a ghost is about to walk back into her life…

In the Tam Eildor series:

The Gowrie Conspiracy
July 1600. After rescuing King James from a runaway horse, the enigmatic Tam Eildor finds himself in the monarch's favour, and the royal benevolence is furthered when Tam agrees to investigate the murder of Margaret Agnew, the Queen's midwife. As Tam and his good friend Tansy Scott set about discovering who could have attacked her and why, they come across rumours of a buried secret from the King's past – a secret that could put the King and members of the court in danger. With treacherous forces at work, the King is led away from the palace to Gowrie House in Perth, and into the heart of a mystery that still puzzles historians today…

The Stuart Sapphire
August 1811. George, Prince of Wales, has his own reasons for welcoming Tam Eildor to the Royal Pavilion. His latest mistress, Sarah, Marchioness of Creeve, has been murdered in the royal bed; strangled with her own string of pearls. Newly created Prince Regent, George realises that a sordid scandal must be avoided at all costs, and enlists Tam's services to quickly and – more importantly – quietly find the killer. But

murder isn't the only crime Tam has to solve: on the same night as the Marchioness's death a priceless gemstone, the Stuart Sapphire, was stolen. With a double investigation on his hands and his own life in constant danger, Tam struggles to outwit the sinister forces that seem determined to prevent him from discovering the truth.